The
LOVELY
DAY

The
LOVELY
DAY

%

BY DOROTHY EVELYN SMITH

E. P. DUTTON & COMPANY, INC.

New York

For

MY HUSBAND

1

SHE was early awake: much too early.

The window was dark behind its flowered curtains. The skylight framed a pale star. The mirror, the blue-and-white china jug on the washstand, the round face of the alarm clock were blurred points of light in the dimness.

Her mind, groping from sleep, saw the room as a well of dark water in which she drowned; floating slowly, reluctantly to the remote star-pricked surface along with the drowned clock, the mirror, the jug. . . .

The clock's tick threaded the silence with a shallow diligence, and presently she became aware of it.

The clock. . . . It always meant something in the busy routine of her life, but today, surely, it had a special significance. The tick of the clock beat in her body, so that the sluggish blood ran swifter and she battled against the returning tide of sleep.

A cock crowed.

As if the sound had manipulated a switch the skylight paled, the star vanished and a tiny wind stirred the flowered curtains with an impatient hand. A damp smell of earth came in. And suddenly she was wide awake, filled with a growing excitement.

This was the day. It was here. It was now. . . .

She stretched her strong little body in the warm cave of the bed and happiness leaped through her limbs. She rose and padded across to the window and pulled the curtains back, leaning out into the damp freshness of the dawn.

There was mist, but the wind was in the right quarter. There was the *feeling* of sun behind the grayness. It was going to be a lovely day. Almost she could sense the invisible trees stirring, stretching limbs as she had stretched a moment ago; taking deep breaths of damp, exciting air and rustling dew-wet clusters of leaves in morning toilet.

The cock crowed again and another answered it, far over to the east. That would be one of Clough's roosters. . . .

She wondered if Bob were awake. More than likely he was up and about already; moving about the farm with the quiet, deceptive deliberation that accomplished so much more than all the loud stampings and scurryings of his younger brothers or the hired man. Bob would get through the best part of a day's work before he arrived at Platt's Corner scrubbed and brushed and dressed in his good blue pin-stripe suit. The willing horse—that was Bob. . . .

She got back into bed, shivering pleasurably from the damp freshness of the morning. It was barely a quarter to five.

She felt wide awake, quite ready to get up. She would have been glad to get up and move about the quiet house feeling that she and Bob were awake together in a sleeping world. But she might wake Dad, and that would make him even more awkward than usual for the whole day. Bad enough for Mum as it was, having to cope with Dad alone, and the housework, and the shop to see to. Better stay put until six, anyhow; then she'd get them a cup of tea and light the fire and get breakfast.

I'll do the potatoes, too, she thought, and shake the mats. That'll give Mum a bit of a start. Young Les can do the shoes and the dishes.

She wondered if Les were awake, and hoped not. They hadn't got him to sleep until all hours last night, and he'd a long day before him; an exciting day, what with his solo and all. She worried about that for a little. She hoped he hadn't caught a cold, tearing about the house last night in nothing but his underpants, silly cuckoo, too excited to sleep. Showing off to make Mum laugh. And of course Mum had encouraged him as she always did. Les was the only one who could make Mum laugh like that, tears running down her face.

"Look, Mum, I'm Caruso . . . I'm Nelson Eddy, Mum. Now I'm Webster Booth. . . ." Singing bits of *Parted* and *The Indian Love Call*. Bowing and smirking and laughing, sticking his skinny little bottom out till Dad had fetched it a swipe with his slipper and made him laugh t'other side of his face.

He'd just got to sing his best today. You never knew who might be listening. Some famous singer on holiday who'd take a fancy to young Les and have his voice properly trained, or send him to a good school or something. . . .

Wish I didn't feel so guilty leaving Mum for the whole day!

It's only once a year, anyhow. One day out of the whole blessed year. She doesn't get even the one day, poor old Mum. Still, she's old. She had good times when she was my age. She's often told me about them. Guy Fawkes and Christmas socials and a week at Blackpool every summer. Golly!

She tried to imagine what it would be like to spend a whole week of idleness by the sea. With Bob. . . .

Just Bob, and blue sky, and a fresh, salty wind whipping over jolly little dancing waves. The band framed in a glitter of lights against a night sky. Swooping, screaming switchbacks and tiny motorcars bumping the breath out of you. Ices and swimming pools. Dancing on the Pier with the black water slapping far below. Pushing about in crowds. Getting away from crowds to lie full-length on high green cliffs sewn with rosy clusters of sea pinks, and gulls serenely sailing overhead. . . .

Some day, she thought, wriggling contentedly. No hurry, I'm only twenty.

All life lay before her. All eternity. . . .

And in the meantime, here was today stretching out rich with promise, glittering with happiness, endless as eternity itself.

She fell asleep as suddenly as she had waked.

The mist drifted past the window; drifted and thinned and vanished. Light seeped into the room, strengthening and brightening; showing up the shabby rug, the patched blue quilt, the crack across the face of the alarm clock, the cheap little treasures on the dressing table. It picked out a gold thread in the brown hair so carefully clamped with bobby pins about the round head. A finger of sun pointed at the bland white brow, the absurd little nose, the firmly folded lips, the fresh, sweet cheeks on which brown lashes lay; so young, so touchingly helpless in the quiet oblivion of sleep.

Young Les waked and grunted, turned over, and curled himself into a stuffy little ball. Only the top of his head appeared above the bedclothes.

He nearly fell asleep again, but something kept tugging him back from sleep. Something nice, but he couldn't remember what. His eyes were unfocused, slack with dreams.

Then suddenly he did remember, and was wide awake on the instant.

[9]

The puppy!

Joy poured through him; joy so swift and powerful that it was almost pain.

He seized the pillow in his arms and buried his face in it until he gasped for breath and sat up, breathing quickly.

What would the puppy look like?

Brown, perhaps, with floppy ears; or black and curly; or white with black patches on it and tiny little squashy paws all pink underneath and a fat pink stomach. . . .

He knew just how it would feel. Very warm, and square, and clumsy. . . . His hands curved round the imaginary small body, pressed its tubbiness against his cheek, his chest. He lay down, cuddling it under the warm bedclothes, whispering to it. It smelled stuffy and exciting. It tried to suck his finger, bite his neck. It pushed itself against him with little whimpers and damp snuffles. . . . He rolled on his face in ecstasy; then he remembered that he was lying on the puppy, and turned again, cradling it tenderly in his arms. He experimented with names. "Prince," he whispered. "Spot. Bob. . . ." No, Rose wouldn't like that. "Jock. Scottie. . . ."

Somebody was moving about downstairs. That wasn't Mum's step —too light and quick. Rose must be up. It must be getting late! What if he missed the bus; never sang his solo, never got the puppy. . . .

Rose wouldn't do a thing like that. She was right set up over that solo. For weeks she'd been fetching him cracks over the head about it, and then giving him candy. Rose was right fond of him. She'd never let him miss the bus.

Secure in that knowledge, with his knees drawn up and the thought of the puppy cradled in his arms, Les fell asleep again.

"Your tea, Mr. Collinson."

Brian rolled over watching the maid move plumply about the room, drawing back the curtains, smiling, as all women smiled when they looked at him; as they always had done. Once he had never questioned their admiration. Now, he wondered sourly what other emotions the smiles camouflaged. Pity, perhaps, or an involuntary recoiling. Even amusement. . . .

"It's going to be a lovely day," the maid said, dawdling amiably. "Shall I pour your tea out, sir?"

"Because I've had half my face torn off, that doesn't make me a paralytic," Brian snarled.

"Oh, Mr. *Collinson!*"

"That'll shut you up for a few days!" he muttered viciously, as the girl blundered, tearfully resentful, from the room. How I loathe fat women with cows' eyes, he thought.

He drank scalding tea and lit a cigarette, drawing the smoke deep into his lungs. God, that felt better! He lounged stiffly across the untidy bedroom, avoiding the looking glass, and stared out of the open window.

Beyond a stretch of empty emerald turf the church stood facing the hotel, solid and gray against lightly moving clouds. Graves blossomed with roses, blue spikes of delphinium and pink and white antirrhinums.

A man dressed in blazer and ancient white flannels came out of the church and walked with bent head along the graveled path, between rakish headstones. Brian's eyes followed him out of sight, noting, with an actor's quick and accurate observation, each movement, each gesture of the tall, prematurely stooping figure.

Put him in corduroys, or pierrot costume, you'd still know he was a parson, he thought. It's a sort of aura they get. . . . I wonder what he gets out of it—all this God business. I wonder if there's anything in it for me. Anything that would fill this ghastly emptiness. . . . He doesn't look a bad sort. Not like that chaplain at the hospital! His spirit recoiled from the memory of hearty hands, bright, false smile, the mixture of Army and Air Force slang boomed in a fearful man-to-man voice, that had curled his spine and sent him cowering under the bedclothes in self-defense. Anyway, it's rather a comic idea, me taking to good works as a last resort. . . .

The church clock chimed the half hour. If he were going to grab a bathroom he'd better get going.

He hitched into a black-and-scarlet dressing gown and seized his shaving tackle.

He opened the door of the nearest bathroom and shut it again with a muttered oath as its occupant squeaked in protest. Silly old bitch, he thought, why can't she lock the damn door! What did she think I'd do to her, anyway?

[11]

Grinning morosely, he shut himself into the next bathroom and prepared for the inevitable.

With a little practice you could bath, dress, brush your hair, even manage your tie without looking in a mirror. But not shave. You had to shave at least once a day.

The thing was to get the lather on quickly, plenty of it. Then, by the time you had pulled your face into all the usual grimaces, and ploughed through the lather, the thing came as rather less of a shock.

Rinsing and patting carefully, Brian faced the mirror and the reality, as he was forced to do every morning at this hour.

You'll get used to it, they had told him. In a few months you won't notice a thing.

That was eighteen months ago, and he noticed it more than ever.

It would have been better if they'd left the scar, he thought despairingly. Ugliness wouldn't have mattered. I could have coped with ugliness—commercialized it. It's this fearful tight, surprised look they've given me, with that damn smirk pulling up the corner of my mouth. . . . I look like a porcelain pig. No, more like one of those beastly dolls you used to win at fairs. Chin Up. . . . He posed in front of the mirror, mouth stretched in a mirthless grin, eyebrows arched: deliberately mortifying himself.

Tears smarted behind his eyes. He blinked savagely and turned on the bath taps.

The doorknob rattled.

"Is anyone there?" asked a timid voice.

"No!" Brian roared, splashing and lathering.

"Oh, sorry! I thought there was . . ." the voice quavered.

Feet slapped away down the corridor.

He slipped beneath the water and stared at his navel.

Nobody here. . . .

By God, and that's true! he thought bitterly. I'm nobody. I'm not a real person at all. . . . What's left of Pilot Officer Collinson? Nothing but the hideous travesty of a face, and a permanent limp. . . . What's left of Brian Collinson, the film actor? Nothing but a few images on strips of celluloid, already outdated. . . . What's left of Bunny Collinson, the undergraduate, whose world was his personal oyster, just waiting for him to crack it open and help himself? Dead. Dead as mutton, all three of them. And nothing born in their place.

I wish I'd died when we crashed. . . . Donaldson and Beatty and Kent. And that nice kid with the red head they shoved in as navigator at the last minute. . . . My God, I remember how set up he was, grinning all over his freckled face. . . .

Why didn't I die, too, before they got their claws on me? Sawing and hammering and patching the bits together, and everybody as pleased as Punch with the result. . . .

Suddenly he suffered one of those terrible waking nightmares, mercifully becoming rarer with time, when he went through the whole thing again in a swift, indescribable anguish.

Light, blinding light. Agonizing heat. Intolerable pain. . . . Beatty scrabbling at the ground, trying to pull himself along. He had no legs. His large moon-face was idiotically surprised. . . . The little navigator screaming for his mother. Screaming and screaming. . . . Donaldson lying in a queer-shaped heap—out, lucky devil, before the flames got at him. . . .

He slid beneath the water, rolled over and over, slapping out the flames with water; beating off the nightmare with the sane, clean smell of coal tar. . . .

When the shivering and twitching subsided he got out and toweled briskly, limped back to the bedroom, dressed and went down into the lounge.

There were no letters for him. There never were.

The papers had not yet arrived.

Ted was polishing the door brasses. He smiled and held the swing door open.

"Going out for your morning breather, sir?" he said briskly.

Sometimes Ted was bearable, but not today. Brian passed him with a curt nod and went out into the cool, impersonal brightness of the morning.

Ted went on polishing the brasses, whistling between his teeth. No amount of snubbing could choke Ted off. Got 'em again, he thought understandingly. He thought with satisfaction of the super polish he had put on Mr. Collinson's shoes this morning. He wasn't on duty for the breakfast, but he'd see to it that Mr. Collinson got a good plump piece of the haddock and a double portion of butter, if he had to brain the entire kitchen staff for it. What a lad! thought

Ted. . . . Funny he never gets no letters. You'd think there'd be a girl. Wife, or something. Or his Ma. . . .

Brian crossed the broad strip of sheep-cropped turf and the narrow road and seated himself on the low stone wall of the churchyard, facing the hotel. The building was old, red-brick and creeper-covered. Once it had been a famous inn, a hide-out for highwaymen. The original frontage still remained, but a sizable annex rose behind it, filled with chromium plate and fluorescent lighting and deep seductive chesterfields.

There were roses in the garden. A tennis court lay on one side, and on the other, tables with gay umbrellas dotted a daisied lawn. Behind the hotel the Yorkshire land plunged steeply down and rose again in wave on gray-green wave of bracken broken by patches of woodland. On the topmost wave the moors began. The heather was hardly in bloom yet but gorse was a golden blaze.

A microscopic car, windows winking in the sun, snailed along a hidden road through the heather.

In spite of himself he began to feel better. He took a number of deep breaths, holding the sweet, clean air in his lungs and dispelling it sharply. He flicked open his cigarette case and then decided against smoking. I'm smoking too much, he thought. And the gong would be going any minute now.

People were beginning to dribble out through the swing doors, and stand about in cheerful little groups relishing morning appetites. The two Langley girls and their redheaded mother. Mr. and Mrs. Selby with their spoiled brat. Major Thring. Old Miss Brent smiling and chattering.

I must remember to be polite to the old trout, he thought, to make up for scaring her in the bathroom. Ted, too. I'll have a word with Ted later on. And that woman who brought my tea. I'll turn on the old charm. . . .

Oh, hell! What does it matter if they do hate me! I couldn't care less. I don't matter any more. Neither to myself nor to anybody else. I'm done. Finished. Nobody wants me. Nobody needs me. I haven't got a job. My pension. . . . He laughed sourly. I suppose I can sell vacuum cleaners as well as the next man. Limp and grimace and put on a bright, brave act. . . . It wouldn't work for long, anyway. Too many heroes limping and grimacing and banging at doors. I'd be better dead. Ain't it grand to be bloomin' well dead! . . . But I shan't die. I shall go on limping and grimacing and having doors banged in my face. Years and years of it. And no earthly use to anybody. Oh, God! . . .

What made me come to this place, anyway?

Go on—face it!

Just because we came here together once, a million years ago. I sat on this wall and the swing doors opened and she came out into the sunshine. . . . She was in white. Her legs were bare—lovely, slim legs—and her little toenails were coral pink in the white sandals. Beryl, my darling. . . .

That's why I sit here like a fool every morning, I suppose. I sit here and wait and watch the swing doors, hoping she'll come walking towards me with that pale, smooth head of hers shining in the sun, and that air about her of poise and elegance and perfect balance. . . .

She was balanced all right. She knew what she wanted; and it wasn't a boy with a plastic grin and a permanent limp and a bit of ribbon to pin on his chest. An out-of-work actor with a pension that would just about keep her in nylons. . . .

So what. So I'll get the hell out of here tomorrow and forget her.

What's wrong with today? I'll go today. Where? I don't give a damn where. Anywhere, so I don't have to sit on this wall and watch those swing doors. . . .

The church clock sounded nine sonorous strokes. A split second later the gong boomed and the small groups of hungry chatterers began to drift in through the swing doors again.

Brian gave them five minutes; then he limped over The Green and followed them into the dining room. And he quite forgot, after all, about being polite to old Miss Brent, who fluttered her table napkin at him and told him what a lovely day it was going to be. And the plump portion of haddock was pushed about his plate and taken back half-eaten to the sorrowing eyes of Ted. As for the chambermaid, he never gave her another thought, even when he stumbled profanely over her pail in a dim corner of the corridor, on the way upstairs to pack.

Andrew Stevens shut the door of his beloved church and hurried down the path between sunlit graves, blinking in the strong light.

What a lovely day, he thought gratefully. I thank Thee, Lord, for this beautiful day, and for all Thy manifold blessings.

And although he knew that it was childish and irrational to believe that God had caused the sun to shine so brightly, the air to sparkle, the wind balmily to blow, just because it was the Choir Outing, still, he couldn't quite suppress the notion that his hopes for fine weather had been answered.

Glancing at the hotel across the green he saw a pajama'ed figure at an open window. He felt fairly sure it was that young pilot, the boy who had crashed so badly. He wondered whether to raise a hand in salute, and decided against it. The fellow was so reserved, sensitive to the point of surliness. Understandable, of course, in one whose face, in a sense, had been his fortune. His nerves would be all to pieces, no doubt. He never came to church, made no friends in the village. I want to help him, he thought, and all I do is leave him alone. Am I failing in my duty? . . .

He sighed and hurried up the vicarage path, which was sadly overgrown with weeds. He entered the house by the back door. Auntie Ag had whitened the front step yesterday and she wouldn't be coming again this week.

I wish Audrey could have a maid, he sighed. I wish we could run to a gardener. Why do they saddle us parsons with enormous old-fashioned houses and then pay us so little? We're worse off really than many of the cottagers.

He stood still in the dark, untidy kitchen, suddenly stricken with remorse because already he had forgotten about the lovely day God had sent at his request. . . .

"That you, Andy? For goodness' sake hurry! We've nearly finished breakfast, and the kids have to be dumped at Kathy's." Audrey's voice came from the breakfast room: a little shrill, as it had been for the past few weeks. She had too much to do, of course. He knew he ought to have stayed to help with the children. But somehow the day never seemed to go well unless he started it by a few minutes alone in the church.

He loved to be alone in his church. Alone with the Voice that was implicit in the stillness; the colored light from the windows dropping all around him; the feeling that came to him sometimes of being up-

borne by powerful wings, cradled in them, until his soul fainted in
ecstasy. . . .

He made a humorous entry into the breakfast room. The twins,
Ruth and Peter, applauded loudly, bouncing sturdy blue-linen bot-
toms in their chairs. Allegra, smooth and brown and self-possessed,
watched his antics with tolerant eyes.

Audrey was cross. She snapped at the children, slopped lukewarm
tea in his saucer, glanced frowningly at the clock.

"I suppose it's too much to hope you remembered to fetch your
shoes from Crossland's!"

He looked stricken. Her lips tightened with vexation.

"Andy—you really are the limit! Those you're wearing leak. The
soles are half off. If it rains, you're sunk."

"It won't rain, darling. It's going to be a magnificent day. What
time are the children going to Kathy's?"

"Oh, you know what Kathy is. 'Any old time,' she said. She won't be
up for hours yet, but they'll be all right in the garden. Cook will
keep an eye on them."

For a covetous moment husband and wife visualized the well-kept
gardens, the bottomless luxury, the starched, efficient staff of The
Limes, home of their friend and neighbor, Doctor Cartwright, and of
Kathleen, his amiable and elegant wife. . . .

"I'll take them over right away," Andrew said. "You go primp. We
can do the dishes tonight."

"Just how do I primp?" Audrey demanded bitterly. "Put on the
green-and-white voile with the tear in it? Or my blue spotted cotton that I've worn four years already? *Peter! What* did I tell you
about the honey! Take it from him, Allegra. You *aggravating* child!"
She dealt Peter a smart slap and he set up a piercing howl. His
twin dutifully followed suit. Andrew blew his nose and looked
harassed.

Audrey flung out of the room, tears absurdly making her see double. Two grandfather clocks. Two small blue coats thrown down by
the hall stand. Two holes in the stair carpet. (Somebody would
break their neck—two necks—sooner or later.) Two hateful, dishev-
eled visions of herself in the bedroom mirror. . . .

Later, smoothed and powdered and cool-looking in the green-

and-white voile, with the tear skillfully pinned up, she watched Andrew and the children cross The Green. Andrew was driving an imaginary chariot drawn by the prancing twins. Allegra minced along, beautiful and aloof, riding, as her mother could tell, the milk-white charger that was her latest secret love. Allegra was sufficient unto herself.

Their voices came through the open window, young and carefree. Andrew was young and carefree, too. Only she was old and worldly wise; heavy with knowledge.

At the corner of the lane they turned, waving to the window. Peter, forgiving and forgetting, blew extravagant kisses. Ruth, walking backwards, sat down abruptly and picked herself up, laughing while Andrew flicked at her stout little rear. Allegra's pigtail shone in the sun.

My darlings, she thought. Oh, my darlings . . . I didn't even kiss them good-by. Suppose one of them had an accident while I was away. Was killed. . . . Don't be a fool. What harm can they come to in Kathy's garden? Of course, there's the pond. . . . If Kathy exerts herself enough to take them for a walk, they just *might* go past Clough's field where the bull is. . . . Oh, shut up, you ass!

She looked for a scarf to match her dress, went down into the untidy kitchen and rubbed the shoebrush over her shoes.

Why do I love them so much when they're away from me, when they're asleep, and let myself be such a beast when we're all together? She gazed earnestly into the mirror. I'm a hag. I'm bad-tempered and I look it. It isn't that I don't love them. I adore them. But three children under six, on Andy's salary! And now this other one . . . I must tell him soon. I'll tell him today. Surely we can get away for an hour together, if it is the Choir Outing. Or will it spoil the day for Andy?

As she set off for Platt's Corner he came running across the green and joined her, thrusting his hand beneath her arm.

"Darling," he said breathlessly. "The kids are quite happy. Kathy wasn't up but Cartwright's playing with them in the garden. You look lovely, my dearest. I do like that frock. Oh, well, all right, I always did like it, then!"

"Andy . . ." she began.

"We mustn't forget to bring them back some rock," he said happily.

"No," she agreed.

Auntie Ag piled a stiff mountain of porridge onto a plate, made a golden lake of syrup in the middle and poured a river of milk all around.

"Now then, Jack!" she called.

Her voice was shrill and cracked. She had only two visible teeth. Her back was humped and her hands like birds' claws. But she was kind and clean and hard-working. The whole village respected her, knew her affectionately as "Auntie Ag." All but Mrs. Cope, who lived next door and owned the cottage. She wanted the cottage for her married daughter and was always seeking an excuse to get Auntie Ag out.

Jack loved his Auntie Ag with a doglike devotion. She was the only mother he had ever known, for she had looked after him for twenty-seven years.

He was sawing logs in the garden at the back of the cottage. He sawed logs all day long. Colonel March, who owned more acres of woodland than he could afford to cope with, had given him leave to help himself. The blacksmith had made him a little cart on wheels and Jack would saw the tree trunks into manageable sections and haul them back to the cottage and saw them up into logs. Whatever the time of year, there was always a bright fire at Auntie Ag's and a good supply of logs in the back garden for the neighbors to buy.

Once every month Jack hauled a load of logs up to Colonel March's house and dumped them in the stable yard. It was his way of saying "thank you," and the Colonel knew better than to offer money for them. Once he had done so, and Jack had been very angry. He had roared loudly and beat his hamlike fists together; and for the rest of that day he had sulked in the woods, ashamed for the Colonel's lack of manners.

"Jack!" Auntie Ag called again. "Come at once, unless you want to miss the bus!"

That brought him loping and grinning across the yard into the kitchen, where he washed his hands and face with great thoroughness and sat down before the mountain of porridge.

He sat with folded hands and screwed-up eyes while she said: "Bless this food oh Lord to our use, and us to Thy service, Amen." Then he began shoveling at the mountain; continued to shovel until there was nothing left on the plate but a spoonful of milk. This he poured down the leg of the table.

"Waterfall," he said happily.

Auntie Ag shook her head at him.

He got to his feet.

"Good-by!" he said loudly, waving his hand.

"Here—wait while I put yer new red tie on!" Auntie Ag cried. She fetched the tie and fastened it round his neck. "You want to look smart, don't you, Jack? You'd best put yer other coat on. Let's see yer hanky. Here, tek this clean 'un. You'll not need yer mack, it's goin' to be a lovely day. . . . There, that's my lad. Now you look fine. Be good now, and enjoy yersen."

She watched as he went loping away up the lane. He was tall and wiry and immensely strong. His thin blond hair glinted in the sun. Every ten paces or so he turned to wave at her, grinning delightedly.

Mrs. Cope from next door came out to borrow a pinch of tea. She followed Auntie Ag into the kitchen and clicked her tongue at the milk puddle on the floor.

"Ee, what a mess!"

"I can't seem to cure 'im of that," Auntie Ag admitted. She wiped the leg of the table and the floor quite clean. "Still, yon's soon cleared up. If he never does nowt worse'n that, he'll do."

"If!" Mrs. Cope said ominously.

Auntie Ag pretended not to hear. She wasn't all that set on Mrs. Cope, who had been heard to say more than once that yon lad ought to be put away. . . .

Still, she didn't want to offend her. It was best to keep in with your neighbors; you never knew when you might want them. So she measured out the tea, refraining from reminding Mrs. Cope that she had not yet paid back the last lot, and said it was a grand day for the Outing.

"You're not afraid to let yon lad go off by 'imself?" Mrs. Cope marveled.

"I'm none afraid of 'im goin' anywhere," Auntie Ag said stoutly. "He allus goes along wi' t'Choir. Sunday School, an' all, an' Band of

'Ope. He's as good as gold is our Jack. I can trust 'im anywhere."

"Aye, well. So long as 'e don't pour 'is soup down the table leg," Mrs. Cope sniggered; and then turned the snigger into a sniff as Auntie Ag's face registered offense. "I must say, I could do wi' a bit of an outin' meself, but I never seem to get the time, let alone the money."

When she had taken herself off, Auntie Ag stood at the window and allowed herself to worry a little.

Jack was so good. As good as gold he was, sawing away at his logs all day, and bringing the money home regular as clockwork. What with the log money, and the bit she earned by charring, they just made do.

But fear always hung over Auntie Ag.

What if she ever got queer and couldn't work for a few weeks? . . . What if some interfering old busybody started wanting Jack put away in an Institution or something? . . . What if she couldn't pay her rent? Small though it was, it came hard some weeks. What if they stopped her bit of a pension? . . . Mrs. Cope would be right set up if any of these things happened. She'd have Auntie Ag out of the cottage before you could say knife!

She did hope Jack would behave nicely at table. He was quite a clean feeder really. So long as they didn't set him near a table leg.

Well, worrying wouldn't buy the baby a new bonnet!

Rose would see to him. She'd promised, and she wasn't the sort to forget. She was a good-hearted girl, was Rose. Auntie Ag was making her a piece rug, for when she got married to Bob Clough. They took a rare long time to make, if you made 'em properly, but it didn't seem as if there was any hurry, what with yon father of Rose's and yon stepmother of Bob's. . . .

Mr. Batley lowered his morning paper to glower at Rose.

"What's the idea, getting yourself up like a tart, to go to t'Choir Outing?"

"Now Dad!" pleaded his wife.

Rose smiled determinedly.

"I've yet to see the tart that couldn't get herself up smarter than me!"

"Don't answer me back, miss! An' you"—turning on the anxious

Les—"you can give up grinning like a tomcat! I've had me bellyful of you, just lately! Much more, an' you'll not get to t'Outing, solo or no solo."

"I never grinned, Dad."

"Yes, you did. Now dammit!" Mr. Batley exploded, "will you give up answering back, the two of you! . . . Our Rose, march into t'pantry an' tek off yon muck you've got on your mouth before you leave this house. An' you needn't think you'll put some more on, soon as you're rid of me, because you won't. Give it here!" He leaned from his wheel chair holding out his hand which was large and knotted, pale from long invalidism: the hand of a frustrated man.

Rose hesitated, mutinous. Then she caught her mother's anxious eye, and at once she opened her purse and fumbled for the lipstick, which she silently handed to her father. He threw it in the fire with a contemptuous grimace. Rattling his newspaper ostentatiously he began to read again.

Rose went into the pantry and scrubbed at her mouth.

"Good-by, Mum. Good-by, Dad," she said equably.

"Good-by, luv. Have a good time," said her mother. "Good-by, Les. Mind you sing up!"

Their father merely grunted.

Brother and sister walked sedately out into the brilliant sunshine; walked like Agag, delicately; afraid to hurry, lest they should seem heartless, afraid to linger, lest they should be recalled.

When he reached the crown of the hill Bob turned, as he always turned at this place, to look down on the land he loved.

He loved it with a deep, inarticulate passion that had less to do with ownership than he imagined. He belonged to the land more than the land belonged to him. He was the willing slave of the land. He had served it from the days he had first toiled at his father's heels, hauling a little wheelbarrow, stamping small, stout boots and spitting in imitation of the farmhands.

Clough's. . . .

The land lay below him, colored and fruitful. The forty-acre over on the right. The fallow ten-acre. The ripening wheat rippling in the sun. The orchard, its boughs bent with fruit. The grazing land dotted with red cows. The small triangle they called Hobson's Choice because, for some reason, it would grow nothing well but cabbages. The pond, white-scattered with ducks. The three ancient oaks spreading benevolent arms above the roof of the big barn. The homestead, gray and square and unpretentious, with outbuildings huddled about it and smoke spiraling from a chimney. . . .

His heart warmed with love for the land that owned him. This cool, wind-swept Yorkshire country; this solid gray house with its back to the moors.

His clear gray eyes narrowed as he remembered his first sight of Edie.

Easy and cheap as his mother had been stern and unyielding. Masses of yellow hair growing out dark at the roots, flopping about the narrow, painted face. The dirty nails and broken slippers and the blue satin housecoat with the port stain down the front. . . .

He remembered his father's shamed evasions, his brothers' adolescent sniggerings and bewilderment. He remembered the everlasting scenes, the shouted oaths, the screams; his mother's beautiful Waterford glass shivered in a thousand pieces on the unswept floor. He remembered the ill-cooked meals, the neglected flower garden, the incredible muddle of the house—cheap, dirty finery strewn over chairs, lying on the floor—the waste, the wicked, wanton waste. . . . He remembered the lies, the unpaid bills, the neighbors' curious, pitying glances. . . .

How could Dad have done it? he thought. How *could* he have put her in Mother's place?

He leaned against the stonewall on the crest of the hill and began rolling a cigarette. He saw his youngest brother, Hugh, come out of the house and stroll across the yard, the collie frisking at his heels. He saw him stoop to the wheel of the blue cart that had been brought up this morning for repair. The sound of hammering came, faint but sharp, on the still air.

His body stiffened, the cigarette held tensely between his fingers. Edie had come out of the house. She walked across the yard and stood by Hugh. The lad straightened up, stood there talking to her, swinging his hammer.

Let him alone! Bob thought savagely. Let him alone, you bitch! He had half a mind to go back.

Why was he going to the Outing, anyhow? To see Rose? . . . It was no good seeing Rose, falling deeper in love each time they met. That led nowhere. There was no future in it.

How could he bring a girl like Rose to live in the house with *her!* He couldn't turn her out: she was his father's wife. . . . The only way he could marry Rose was to turn out himself, get a job on someone else's farm.

He couldn't do that, either. He couldn't leave his father, bedridden and helpless from his stroke, to *her* tender mercies.

Hugh was tough. If she tried her tricks on Hugh, she'd get what was coming to her. But Ben was different. Ben was soft like Dad. He'd have to watch out for Ben. The woman was shameless.

He remembered the night she had come knocking at his door. Iodine, she said. She'd cut her finger and she wanted the iodine.

He'd bandaged her finger, got her the brandy. She'd leaned against him, made out she felt faint. . . . He remembered with satisfaction the red mark his fingers had made across the white mask of her face.

She'd get the same from Hugh.

But not Ben. He'd have to watch out for Ben. . . .

They'd never be rid of her while Dad lived. The farm life bored her to tears; but it was a meal ticket, it was a roof and a warm bed; it was a place where she was missus. She'd too much sense to throw that up for a night on the tiles. And nobody in their senses would ever want her for more than that, even if they were blind drunk. . . . If only she'd go right away; leave. . . . But of course, she never would. They were struck with her. . . . I'd best go back, he thought.

But he didn't go back. He wanted so terribly to see Rose; to smell her fresh cleanliness, touch the softness of her cheek, look into the sweet, kind eyes and know how honest and loving and altogether desirable a woman could be. He had looked forward to this day for so long.

Hugh could look after himself all right. . . .

He lit the cigarette, drew the smoke deep into his lungs and went on his way.

When he reached Platt's Corner the bus was already there, drawn up by the side of The Green in front of the half-dozen sleepy shops that comprised the main street. Its polished scarlet sides and metalwork gleamed in the sun. The driver sat on the running board whistling softly between his teeth and gazing out over the valley. His white coat was spotless. His round, brown face under the back-tipped cap looked good-tempered, humorous and dependable. He nodded to Bob, who went to sit on the running board beside him.

"Warm enough for you?" said the driver.

"Ah," said Bob. He took off his cap and ran his handkerchief round the base of his throat and over his beaded forehead. His blue-checked, open-necked sports shirt was brand-new and smelled new. He wasn't very happy about the shirt. It didn't seem to go with his pin-stripe as well as he'd hoped. It would have looked better with his tweed coat and gray slacks, but they were so shabby. And a stiff collar had been out of the question if he wanted to enjoy himself.

No sign of Rose, yet.

Nobody, in fact, had turned up, barring old Crackerjack, who was loping admiringly round the big bus, staring through the windows, under the chassis, peering at the knobs and gadgets on the dashboard. Contentedly he hummed the only tune he knew: *My Bonny Is Over the Ocean.* It was the tune he crooned to himself up in the woods, when he was alone with the slender, beautiful trees shafted with sunlight, and the muted birds, and the sibilant bite of his saw. "*Bring* back, *bring* back," he would croon; and he would ease his shoulders and listen to the lovely green silence and smell the good smell of the newly sawn logs. And an immensity of longing would come flooding and tingling all through his body: a longing so sweet and vital that he never tried to find out what he longed for; it was enough in itself. "Oh, bring back my Bonny to me!"

"Bit late rolling up, ain't they?" said the driver, glancing at his watch.

"They'll be along. Plenty to do for most of 'em before they get off for the day. Been up since four myself."

"Go on!" commiserated the driver. "Lord, what a life!"

And the driver laughed again and held out his tobacco to Bob. They rolled cigarettes in friendly silence.

"You don't come from these parts," Bob observed presently.

"Ilford, that's me. That's the little old home town. But I married a Yorkshire lass, see? I like Ilford, she wants to be near her mother—well, you know how it is. She 'as 'er say and I have mine—and we're up in Yorkshire before you can say knife!" He threw back his head and laughed delightedly. "Great sufferin' ducks—women! Shockin', ain't it?"

They drew on their cigarettes and grinned in male tolerance of the shockingness of women.

There was no sign of Rose.

He hoped the old man wasn't playing up at the last minute. It'd be a rum do if they had to go without her. In that case, he thought, they'll go off without me, an' all. We'll go off by ourselves somewhere, just the two of us. And he half began to hope she would miss the bus after all, so that for one long, lovely day he could have Rose all to himself.

"Five minutes more," said the driver, "and I'll give 'em a blast that'd wake the dead, let alone a church choir."

At that identical moment the silence was shattered into a thousand shrieking atoms and the driver leaped from his seat.

"Heavens!" he yelped.

Jack leaned out of the driving seat, all smiles.

"Honk!" he said, greatly gratified.

"Beat it!" threatened the driver, advancing on him. "What's the matter with him?"

"That's okay, chum," Bob cut in. "It's only Jack. Jack's a clever lad, aren't you, Jack? There's nobody round these parts can saw logs like Jack. You come down from there an' show this gentleman how you saw the logs. Come on, now."

Nothing loth, Jack clambered down and began sawing away in the air and making the rasping note of a saw deep in his throat. The muscles of arms and shoulders strained at the cheap cloth of his jacket.

"One hundred, two hundred, three hundred," he announced importantly.

"That's right, lad," Bob said kindly. He drew the driver aside. "You don't want to worry about old Jack," he assured him. "He'll be quiet as a mouse once we've started. The lads call him Crackerjack, but he's okay."

"Here, we're not taking him along, are we!" protested the driver.

"He's all right, is Jack. He goes on all the Outings. Goes on t'buses alone, an' all. All the drivers know Jack an' they never charge him nowt. He's clean and quick and he works hard. He lives with his auntie an' she sells the logs he saws up."

"He's nuts," said the driver.

"There's no harm in him."

"Ah, well. Takes all sorts to make a world," the driver admitted. He spat and began to roll another cigarette. "Done the trick, anyhow. Here they come."

Here, indeed, they came. The parson and his wife smiling at a couple of choirboys who were playing leapfrog, being firm with a third who was throwing stones at the leapers. Joe Peck, the blacksmith, who had shut his forge for the day and had hammered and riveted himself into a suit of black-and-white check that was tight under the arms and a little baggy about the seat. With him came his wife and daughter, black-clad women of sober mien, who were drawn together less by affection than by mutual disapproval of Joe and his goings on. Miss Maddon, the schoolmistress, discreetly girlish in blue-flowered cotton, accompanied by her mother. Mrs. Maddon never allowed her daughter to go anywhere without her, even to the Choir Outing. The two Lomax girls with brand-new permanents like railway sidings and brand-new costumes of electric blue. Sam Scholey, the farmhand from Lower Staving, puffing up on his ancient bike. Harry Waterhouse, the solicitor's clerk, who couldn't make up his mind which of the Lomax girls he wanted, but was determined to find out today or burst.

The choirmaster, Mr. Walter Forsythe; retired bank manager, widower and martinet and a terrific dandy, issued from the door of Number Four, The Green, coinciding with Mrs. Phoebe Braithwaite of Number Five, The Green; buxom widow, angelic cook and most determined contralto. Miss Stacey, the Girl Guide Captain, an all-round good fellow with an Eton crop and a tenor voice and horn-rimmed glasses with broad side pieces, along with Ivy Carter, the baker's daughter, a simpering adolescent who adored Miss Stacey and hoped for no better fate than to die for her. George Fiddler, the baker's deliveryman, and Henry, his younger brother, and John William Welsh, Colonel March's gardener.

There were also present a number of youths and maidens who had suddenly remembered that they were members of the choir and thus entitled to the Outing, though everybody knew that their memories would prove most unreliable in a month or so, at the outside.

Here they all came, together with a straggle of well-wishers, and there was a good deal of heartiness and chaffing and the light badinage inseparable from such occasions.

The blacksmith, always the official wag of these outings, trolled a few bars of *On Ilkla Moor*, an arm flung round each of the Lomax girls, who slapped him and shrieked and made private faces at Harry Waterhouse to show him how vulgar they thought that old Peck was, while the female Pecks stood together looking down their noses.

And here they all were.

No, not all! For where was Rose Batley and young Les, her brother?

"Seen Rose, Bob?" inquired Mr. Forsythe.

"Any minute now," Bob said. "Here's young Les, for a start."

"Let's run," said Les as soon as they were clear of the house.

They ran up Knapswell Lane and along the Moor Cut and out on to The Green where the old gray church faced the old red hotel; where, between them, a very streamlined, very shiny blue-and-silver sports model stood warming up its engine, while a thin young man in shabby-elegant tweeds idly polished the little silver ballet girl who danced on the hood.

"Hey—look at that!" Les hissed loudly. "Look at yon car, Rose! That's him I was telling you about. Air Force fellow. He used to be a film star. Ronny Field told me. His face got all burned an' they shoved a lot of new skin on it. Fact! Ronny Field told me."

"Well, don't go staring at him."

"I'm going to have a squint at the car."

Rose called him sharply but he ran ahead. She saw him examining the car, fingering it, speaking to the thin young man; saw the man toss away his cigarette, flash his teeth in a grin at something Les said; saw Les jerk his thumb towards her and the man's glance follow the gesture.

Rose was no fool. She knew well enough that her hair waved prettily about her round face. She knew her complexion was healthy, her eyes a wide, warm gray, her teeth sound and white, her ankles good enough, her figure plump but pleasing. She knew that, although her eyebrows were unplucked, her pink frock faded and a bit tight over the chest, her hands stubby and her shoes cheap, yet nine men out of ten would be aware of her as she passed.

What she did not know was that to the tenth man she was all the youth he had forgotten, all the innocence he had lost, all the kindness he had never known. What she did not know was that the tenth man, seeing in her all these things, would love and hate her in equal proportions; that his spirit would prostrate itself before her even while his hands reached to drag her from the stars; that he would scheme to possess her and never forgive her if he succeeded; that he would never, in any case, forget her as long as breath lived in his body.

Brian Collinson was the tenth man.

He threw away the stub of his cigarette and stood watching her as she came towards him over the cropped, springy turf. Sedately yet buoyantly she walked towards him. Her brown hair lifted in the breeze. The little gray coat she wore hanging from her shoulders in imitation of her favorite film star swung to the motion of her young, pliant body.

And she smiled without coyness and said: "Good morning." And she said: "Come on, Les, it's late," and would have passed on but for the swift appeal of his outflung hand.

"Look, do you mind awfully? This boy was going to fetch me some cigarettes. It's my confounded foot, you know. Take me ten minutes to do what he'll do in a couple of shakes. Just barge through those swing doors," he went on, turning to Les. "You'll see a fellow in a white coat. Ted. Tell him I want twenty of whatever he's got. Thanks a lot."

They watched Les go running across the turf making a noise like a high-powered sports car.

Now she knows I'm lame, Brian thought. In a minute she'll notice my face, too. If she looks sorry for me she can go to hell. If she laughs. . . .

He turned and faced her, raising his eyebrows a fraction, deliberately making the most of his disability. He waited.

Rose regarded him with neither mirth nor pity. Her lips parted in a shy smile.

"Tell him to hurry, won't you? We don't want to miss the bus."

"The bus," he repeated, grinning his side-lipped grin. "And what happens if you miss the bus?"

"We don't get to the Outing," she replied, beginning to edge away.

"What Outing would that be? Here, I say, don't go for a minute. Please! There's plenty of time. There always is. Anyway, no bus would dream of starting without you—I'll take my oath on that."

"Choir Outing," Rose explained. "Young Les is singing a solo, an' he's just got to be there."

"He shall be there. And so shall you. If the bus dares to go without you I'll take you in my car. We'll pass them on the road and make rings round them, and young Les shall sing his solo before any of the others get there."

She giggled happily and a little excitedly.

"Honestly," he went on, "I'm sorry to hold you up like this. Confounded nerve on my part, I know. If I hadn't been sure you were a terribly kind person I wouldn't have dared. But you are kind." He dropped his voice to a practiced wistfulness. "As kind, perhaps, as you are beautiful. . . ."

Now what the hell, he thought, am I doing, being arch with a rustic Chloe at this hour of the morning, with the engine running sweetly and my baggage stowed away and every nerve itching to be gone! Presently she'll be giving me a shove and saying that I'm a One. . . . But how sweet she is, he thought. How young and fresh and sweet. Why haven't I seen her before?

"Why haven't I seen you before?" he said. "Where have you been all these weeks while I've been so lonely?"

"At home, I reckon. Serving in the shop, an' that." She blushed quite beautifully.

"Good lord!" Brian exclaimed, watching this phenomenon with delight. "I didn't know girls could do that any more."

"Don't be daft!" Rose laughed. She turned to go.

Les came leaping across the turf holding the packet of Players.

"Good boy," Brian murmured. He slipped a coin into the boy's hand. "Expect you'd like some candy on the Outing."

"Whee—whool!" Les whistled. For an instant shock kept him rooted to the ground. Then he gave a wild whoop and raced away without a thought for Rose.

"You shouldn't have done that," she protested.

"Why not? Fair's fair."

"He can do a hand's turn for anybody without getting paid for it, surely!"

"You're very severe, aren't you?" he mocked.

"I don't like to see kids spoiled nor good money wasted," she said soberly. "It's hard enough to come by."

The cheap shoes. The pathetic little coat swinging so jauntily from her shoulders. The faded frock that clipped her round young bosom oversnugly. . . . No, he thought, nobody's wasted much money on you, my pretty. Not yet. . . . I wonder how you'd react to a fat wallet waved under your little nose. The same as all the rest of 'em, I shouldn't wonder. The same as Beryl. . . . He stared at her wolfishly.

A motor horn blared in the distance.

"There!" she exclaimed. "I've got to go."

"Let them hoot," Brian said, staring at her. "Come in the car with me. We'll have fun. Honestly, I've been so lonely."

She moved back, almost as if she felt him groping for her.

"Ee, I couldn't do a thing like that!" Her voice held a hint of panic; but she pulled herself together instantly and said with a rather touching childish dignity: "You ought to be ashamed, suggesting such a thing. It's Choir Outing."

"Of course," he said smoothly. "I am ashamed. I'm groveling about your feet. What very pretty feet, by the way. I think they ought to run, don't you? Run away from me, Chloe. You'll be very wise, believe me."

He turned his back on her and began polishing the little ballet girl again, whistling between his teeth.

And now she knew an unaccountable desire to stay.

She gazed at the thin, stooped back in elegant-shabby tweeds, and her eyes were troubled. There was something pathetic about him. He *looked* lonely. And that, surely, was wrong. . . . He ought not to be alone, lame and scarred, while she went off unheeding, on this lovely day!

"My name's Rose," was all she could think of. "Rose Batley."

"Charming!" he murmured, polishing the little ballet girl. He did not turn round.

"Good-by," she whispered.

"Good-by. A pleasant Outing to you."

He did not turn round.

She walked a few paces and then turned, irresolute. He was still polishing the little ballet girl.

The horn blared again and she began to run. The coat slipped from her shoulders and she tucked it impatiently under her arm.

She felt awful, running away from him like this. His poor foot twisted and lame and his poor face. . . . And so brave, with his name in all the papers. . . . Months and months of pain in hospitals, and awful operations. And then—just lonely. While everybody else went off in big red buses having a lovely time.

And suddenly there was Bob standing right in her path; big and solid in the good pin-stripe suit that suddenly looked all wrong for the time and occasion, and with a rather dour expression on his face.

"Hullo," Rose panted. "I was afraid I'd be late."

"So I've been noticing for t'past ten minutes," he answered heavily.

"What do you mean, the last ten minutes!" He did not reply, and she glanced up sideways at his red-brown, impassive countenance. "I suppose I can speak to a friend if I want?" she added sharply.

"Since when have you been yon fellow's friend?" he wanted to know.

"Well, we were only passing the time of day. Les was fetching him some cigarettes. He's lame. And his face was all burned when his plane crashed, an' he's got new skin grafted on it. Pilot Officer Collinson—you remember about him, Bob. All the papers had the pictures of him."

"Aye, I remember."

"What are you being so stuffy about, then?"

"I'm not being stuffy."

"Yes you are, then—you great goop!"

He glanced down and quickly averted his face again.

"Horn went twice. You must have heard it. All of 'em's been waiting best part of a quarter hour. An' you standing there jawing away to yon fellow as if tomorrow 'ud do. . . . It's not very good manners, Rose, whichever way you look at it."

He was right, of course. Nobody knew that better than Rose. But there are few things more unpalatable than the knowledge that you are in the wrong.

"When I want learning manners," she said shortly, "I'll come an' tell you."

She looked so delicious, her cheeks pink with wrath and her little nose in the air, that Bob's heart softened.

"Nay, now, Rose. . . ."

"Don't you nay me, Bob Clough! Let me tell you—"

Whatever she wished to tell him was never told, for Les came tearing up, his pockets bulging with paper bags, his breath redolent of peppermint. He thrust two packets into her hand.

"Here you are, Rose. Liquorice all-sorts and a Mars."

"I don't want 'em, Les."

"Yes you do, yes you do! Put 'em in your pocket. You'll be glad of 'em in the bus."

And there *was* the bus, huge and scarlet and shining. And there was the driver in his white coat, doing something to its hood, with Crackerjack peering over his shoulder. And there was the choir standing in a rough half circle about Mr. Forsythe, who was glancing at his watch. And there were the Vicar and his wife standing among a score or so of villagers who had turned out to give the choir a good send-off. And the sun shining over all. . . .

A small ironic cheer went up at sight of Rose, who blushed again, laughing guiltily as she slipped into her place among the sopranos.

Mr. Forsythe gave her an admonitory shake of the head and tapped with his small black baton with the silver band, on the side of the bus.

Bob stood with the basses. Les nipped in among the other choirboys.

Mr. Forsythe tapped again, and an expectant silence fell on Platt's Corner. His tuning fork gave out a faint vibrant note and the baton lifted in the air. The choir breathed deeply, all eyes on the little black stick.

> Hail, smiling morn, smiling morn, smiling morn,
> That tips the hills with gold, that tips the hills with gold.
> Whose rosy fingers ope' the gates of day-a-a-a-a-a-ay.
>   Ope' the gates, the gates of day—
> Hail, hail, hail! . . .

As long as its oldest member could recall, the choir of Bishops Staving had started its annual Outing with this song.

They needed no music sheets. They knew each note, each ca-

[33]

dence, each diminuendo and crescendo, each pause and emphasis and sudden, knifelike halt.

They could have sung it in their sleep. They could have sung it backwards. They could, so the blacksmith often declared, have sung it upside down in buckets of whitewash. They had sung it in all weathers. Good and bad, wet and fine; with a first-class thunderstorm rolling up and in the damp folds of a moor mist; sweltering beneath a baking sun and huddled under streaming black umbrellas.

And today of all days, so fine was the weather, the good Yorkshire voices lifted and rolled and thundered and gave it all they'd got.

"Who the gay face of nature newly born," caroled Les, thinking of the puppy, and of his pockets bulging with candy. *"Who the gay face,"* boomed Bob and the blacksmith and John William Welsh.

And Mrs. Phoebe Braithwaite, that determined contralto, lifted her immense bosom and deeply uttered:

"Hail! Hail! Hail—HAIL!"

2

GROWLING in bottom gear the bus climbed steeply.

Black-faced sheep nibbling at the grass verges huddled against the stonewalls or bundled with shrill cries across the road under the very hood of the bus. The driver swore at them without rancor; then remembering this was a Choir Outing, glanced back guiltily.

The road twisted and turned, thrusting up the steep bowl of the valley. Gorse blazed along the skyline, spilled golden fire down the slopes, smoldering amongst stony outcrops. Huge white clouds moved slowly across the blue sky, trailing shadowy skirts over fields striped in yellow, chocolate, green and rust. Gulls came flying from the coast, balancing beautifully down the wind. The air was strong and fresh; the smells of leather and rubber and engine oil mingled excitingly with the freshness.

How beautiful it is, thought Audrey. How absolutely beautiful. What a long way we've come already! . . . When you get to the top of the hill you can see Staving church right across the valley.

The spire sticks out above the dark patch of elms like a needle in a pincushion . . . I wonder what the children are doing. I hope Cook's keeping an eye on them. Allegra's head is screwed on all right, and Ruth's a good little thing. If anyone falls in the pond it'll be Peter. . . . I wish I hadn't smacked Peter this morning. Suppose he fell in the pond and was drowned—and the very last thing I did was to smack him. . . . She had a swift, searing vision of Peter lying on the bank of Kathy's pond, small and limp and infinitely pathetic, with Ruth and Allegra kneeling beside him, weeping. After wallowing briefly in this harrowing scene she firmly dismissed it and made a few amiable remarks to Miss Maddon, the schoolmistress and her mother, between whom she was most reluctantly sandwiched.

"I must confess," Miss Maddon's mother was saying in a voice of regal whimsy, "that I'm hardly what you might call *partial* to chars-à-banc." (to *what?* Audrey thought, startled. Oh, lord, *chars-à-banc!* . . . Is that right? Surely not. I must look it up tonight.) Quelling a grin, she schooled her face to a Mrs. Vicar expression, politely attentive to the genteel self-pity of Miss Maddon's mother. "If you'd told me ten years ago that I'd ever go gadding about the countryside in a *char-à-banc* of all things—well, I shouldn't have believed you. I simply *should not* have believed you! Mr. Maddon always kept his own car. Didn't he, Doris?"

"Oh, yes, Mother," Doris agreed tepidly.

"Drove it himself," Mrs. Maddon continued impressively. "A beautiful car it was. Beautiful. Now what make was it? Dear me, I'm afraid," said Mrs. Maddon, "that I scarcely know a Bentley from a Hispano-Suiza, silly me!"

"It was a Morris 8, Mother," Doris said clearly.

"Oh . . . well, it was a beautiful car. Beautiful. Mr. Maddon never would allow anyone to lay a finger on it. I used to say to him: 'Why don't you let Doris hose the car down, Daddy?' I used to say. And he always said: 'Over my dead body, Agnes!' " Mrs. Maddon smirked and immediately sighed. "A most amusing man my husband was. The things he used to say—well, sometimes he had me in *fits.* Never anything *near the knuckle,* of course, Mrs. Stevens. Good, wholesome fun all the time."

(You know what good wholesome fun is? Audrey thought. No, what good is it?)

Aloud, she said: "You must miss him." And immediately brought upon herself a revolting cascade of symptoms, details of illness and deathbed scenes.

Oh, shut up! she thought violently. Shut *up*, you horrible woman! Oh, lord, why did I have to marry a parson? . . . There, that's the church spire: just exactly like a needle in a pincushion. . . . I feel rather peculiar. I hope to goodness I'm not going to be sick. What shall I do if I can't stop it? I shall just have to lean over the side and let it rip. . . . Oh, how lovely everything looks. Why can't I enjoy it? Why can't I sit next to Andy? Why do I have to be Mrs. Vicarish, when I want to sit next to Andy and hold hands and have a day out? With no cooking and no cleaning and no kids. . . . I do hope Kathy will remember about the bull, if they go past Clough's farm. How sweet Allegra looked, riding her pretend horse across The Green. Is she really as beautiful as I think she is, or do I just think so? . . . I wish I hadn't smacked Peter. . . . Oh, heavens, I *am* going to be sick! I just *can't*, so that's that. Everyone would know. . . . I could tell Andy now if only we weren't stuck miles apart. I could hold his hand and say: I'm going to have another baby, Andy; and what the devil is to become of us if we go on at this rate, I don't know! And we could have the whole thing out. . . . But we can't sit together and hold hands because we're Mr. and Mrs. Vicar and we have to be all things to all men. Andy has to talk choir and church funds with Mr. Forsythe, and I have to be polite to this awful Maddon woman, and sorry for her wretched daughter, and not be sick. I hope.

They were running along the rim of the valley.

On either side the land fell away with an awful suddenness that made the narrow white road seem to the timid traveler like a tight-rope stretched across eternity.

A bleak bit of country here, covered with harsh, wind-bitten heather and great rocks like bared teeth snarling at the sky. The wind was stronger, colder, so that coat collars were pulled closer about delicate throats and hats either jammed on more firmly or discarded altogether.

Rose Batley tied a pink scarf about her head. The blacksmith abandoned his attempt to light his pipe and began to sing: not in a respectable, church-choir fashion, but in a back-row-of-the-bus sort of way that brought the eyes of his wife and daughter slewing round to each other and pinched their mouths in even more than usual. It's beginning, they telegraphed mutely.

Between the two Lomax girls, Harry Waterhouse sat with folded arms, distributing impartial favors of word and smile. At times, the movement of the bus swayed his body so that he came in contact with one or other of the girls. He found this profoundly disturbing; inasmuch as when his shoulder touched Violet's shoulder he was sure it was Violet he loved, and when he was thrown against Pearl he was equally convinced of his desire for Pearl as a wife.

Pearl had nicer hands than Violet, and a quieter voice (though this was not saying much), but she was a few months older than himself, which was rather undesirable; whereas Violet was a year his junior and had dimples.

If only they weren't so confoundly alike, a fellow might be able to choose. . . . Anyway, they were the smartest girls of the whole bunch.

He admired their new electric-blue outfits and noted approvingly that their permanents were undisturbed by this riotous wind. Yes, they'd got style all right! Perhaps not quite so pretty as Rose Batley, if you cared about that wholesome sort of prettiness. But a fellow wanted his wife to have *style*, if he meant to get on in the world.

You couldn't, for instance, imagine Rose Batley as the wife of a rising young solicitor—as the wife of anybody but some clod-hopping farmer. Whereas Violet—or perhaps Pearl. . . .

"Daisy, Daisy, give me your answer, do," roared the blacksmith; and everybody smiled constrainedly and wished to goodness he would stop. The day was too young. They were not warmed up to that sort of thing yet.

Walter Forsythe, freely airing his views on the Gregorian Chant to the Vicar, paused to remark austerely that Joe Peck seemed in fine fettle today. And Andrew, indulging himself in a spot of wishful thinking about the roof of his beloved church being restored in miraculous fashion, without disfiguring scaffolding, argumentative architects, or the necessity for raising the money, remarked dreamily that Joe was a good fellow, a good fellow. . . .

[37]

Ivy Carter wriggled a little closer to Miss Stacey and whispered that only the close proximity of Miss Stacey saved her (Ivy) from being scared stiff on this road.

Miss Stacey roundly denied any cause for alarm. The driver was experienced, the pace moderate and the brakes in excellent order.

Ivy whined that she knew all that and it didn't make any difference.

"Hang on to me," Miss Stacey said bluffly.

Ivy thrust a limp white hand under her arm and sighed glutinously. Her head drooped against Miss Stacey's shoulder. Her eyes closed and the tip of her nose quivered pinkly. "Now I'm not frightened any more," she whispered.

Miss Stacey adjusted her glasses with her free hand and suppressed an inclination to give Ivy a violent push. Ivy was a dear little thing really, and she couldn't help looking like a rather damp white rabbit. I must have *somebody*, she thought forlornly. Ivy is better than nothing.

She thought of her three pretty sisters with their flashing engagement rings and their attentive young men, and wondered humbly what they had got that she hadn't.

And she thought of the dashing days, long dead, when she had been a Sergeant in the A.T.S., and life had been one mad whirl of work, excitement and color. "Old Staylace" they had called her affectionately. She had been popular with The Boys. Popular with everybody. She had enjoyed every minute of it; the hard work, the responsibility, the hilarious evenings down at The Bird In Hand, where she had learned to knock it back with the best of them. Leaves had been almost resented, going back an immense thrill; standing in the packed, stuffy corridors of overcrowded trains, sharing cigarettes with her neighbors, bandying jokes and language that would have shocked her dashing sisters.

She remembered the desolation of new postings. The farewell parties when she had pushed the boat out. The frantic good-bys. The fervent promises of undying friendship. *Mind you write every week, old thing. I will. And I'll run down on my next forty-eight and see the sort of mess you'll be in without me, as if I didn't know. Let's meet in Town and do a show. Try and wangle a week end soon. . . .*

Piles of equipment all strapped up. Greatcoat weighing a ton. Buttons shining. A last look in at the Mess.

"Good-by, You fellows!"

"Good-by, Staylace, old thing. If you can't be good, be careful!"

And then the new place, the new faces, the new methods and fads of the Officers. The new problems. And almost immediately the new friendships, excitements, pleasures, loyalties that made last week seem like a shabby dream. . . .

Life then had been full and rich.

There had been Laurie. . . . Major Laurence Burton of the East Whatshires, with his blue eyes and sudden melting smile, and his way of making you feel you were small and fragile and very precious. . . . Well, that hadn't lasted long.

Of course, he had been much younger than herself. It wouldn't have worked out, really. Anyway, that little Corporal Johnson hadn't given it a chance to work out, once she had poked her permanent into The Bird In Hand. . . . And after that, of course, there had been her new posting.

Oxford. . . . She'd enjoyed Oxford. City of dreaming spires, and all that. And there'd been the R.A.M.C. bloke whose wife didn't understand him. And after that old Colonel Paley, who'd called her Little Woman and had practically said he wanted to marry her. Well, *practically*. Only, of course, he drank like a fish. Like a whole aquarium, in fact. . . . And that Pole she'd sat next to, in the movies. . . .

And now, of course, there was only the Girl Guides, and the Choir Outing. And Ivy Carter breathing down your neck. . . .

Perhaps if I had a permanent, she thought, and wore rimless glasses. . . .

No. Somewhere she had read that if you were plain it was folly to disguise it. The best thing to do—the *only* thing to do—was to *emphasize* your bad points. Flaunt them. Frenchwomen did it with immense success. It was the line she had taken, the plan she must stick to. Heavy spectacles. Eton crop. Loud, hearty laugh. Goodfellow slap on the back. . . .

Somewhere, thought Miss Stacey bleakly, there must be a man who likes having his back slapped. . . .

Young Les poked about in the carton of liquorice all-sorts. He liked the round flat ones covered with tiny balls of crunchy sugar, and the fat drainpipes filled with soft white paste. He didn't care about the brown sandwich ones.

He offered a brown sandwich to the boy sitting next to him.

"Thanks a million," said that youth, proceeding to masticate noisily. He added frugally: "You didn't ought to eat 'em all now. You'll be sorry tonight."

To be truthful, young Les was already feeling a little sorry. He didn't exactly feel sick. He just wished the bus wouldn't keep going up and down so much. After a short deliberation he gave the rest of the all-sorts to his gratified neighbor, and sat quite still thinking about the puppy.

It would be brown, he decided finally. Short brown hair that wouldn't come off all over the furniture and make Mum wild. He would call it Scottie. It would have brown, bright eyes and black tips to its ears, and it would love him more than anyone in the world.

How wonderful it would be if he could train it to come and meet him from school, like Lassie in the film. Oh, whee! It would come racing over The Green and down School Lane, and all the lads would shout: "Scottie! Come on, Scottie! Good dog, here, Scottie!" But it wouldn't pay the slightest attention to anyone but him. . . .

He felt the little dog leap into his arms, the rough coat scrub his cheek, the soft tongue heal it. . . . *Scottie, Scottie. Good Lad, Scottie! Come for a walk, Scottie?* . . . *Lay down, sir. Lay down! Heel, sir!* . . . *Die for the King.* . . . *Trust. Paid for.* . . .

Les sighed; partly with ecstasy and partly in anticipation of the tussle he was going to have with Dad. Dad wasn't going to take kindly to Scottie—Les had no illusions on that score.

Not that Dad disliked dogs, but just that he disliked other people getting their own way. Dad was like that: just plain awkward. It all came of having to sit in a chair all day and feel helpless, while Mum got worn-out doing the housework and Rose slaved in the shop.

Les felt terribly sorry for Dad. It must be lousy sitting there all day feeling helpless. If he wanted to go out, somebody had to push him; they couldn't afford one of those swell invalid chairs with a motor attached.

Wouldn't it be wonderful if Scottie saved the life of a rich man, and the man bought Dad one of those swell chairs! Oh, golly!

Les saw the whole thing in glorious Technicolor. The enormous green car nosing down Knapswell Lane; the chauffeur respectfully saluting Les who stood by the door with Scottie at his feet. The rich man stepping out of the car, a diamond flashing in his tie and another on his hand. His beautiful wife, just like Audrey Hepburn, stepping out after him in a slither of silk and fur. Both stooping to fondle Scottie, who refused to leave heel until commanded to do so by Les. . . .

"Oh, isn't he sweet! Will you sell me your dog? I'll give you ten pounds for him. Twenty. Fifty. . . . Will nothing persuade you to part with him? . . . Well, you must allow us to give you the money. Oh, but you *must!* He saved my husband's life, and we want to show our gratitude somehow!" Tears by now filled the luscious eyes. "A present, then?" she pleaded. "Allow us to give you a car. A bicycle. A model airplane price two pounds seventeen and six, just like Ronny Field's, only better. . . . Then let us give your father one of those swell invalid chairs worked by a motor. . . ."

And then Dad would be able to get out of the house every day, and go mailicking round The Green in his little motor; chatting with all his old pals and having a pint at The Crown. And Mum would get a bit of peace, and Les would be able to keep Scottie and Dad would think the world of him, and everything in the garden would be lovely. . . .

He sighed again and opened his eyes.

Golly—what a precipice! And how low the stonewalls looked! If they swerved they'd crash through the wall and go toppling down the steep slope over and over, right to the bottom, and burst into flames and all be cooked to cinders! . . . He wondered if he looked as green as he felt.

To take his mind off it he knelt on the seat and looked back along the road they had traversed.

A blue-and-silver sports car had just turned the bend and was coming after them, its hood heliographing in the sun.

Bob stared glumly at the back of Rose's head wrapped in its pink scarf with the ends blowing gaily in the wind.

I've gummed the works up properly now, he thought. Why don't I keep my big mouth shut? But who'd have thought she'd fly off the handle that way! Women, thought Bob. You never know how to tek 'em from one minute to t'next. . . . All the same, she'd no call to go and plump herself down next to old Crackerjack. Hang it, I didn't come to the Outing for t'pleasure of hearing Phoebe Braithwaite yap-yap-yap in me ear all t'way!

Had it been anyone but Crackerjack, Bob would simply have tapped him on the shoulder and jerked his head in a way no interloper could possibly misinterpret. But you couldn't do a thing like that to old Crackerjack. He simply wouldn't understand. He'd just nod and grin and be right set up that folks were taking notice of him.

And of course it was quite hopeless to appeal to Rose in her present mood. He'd asked her once. "Aren't you coming by me, Rose?" he'd said. And she'd given him a cool smile and replied: "I promised Auntie Ag I'd look after Jack." And then fat old Phoebe had squashed in beside him, and that was that. . . .

Bob was fond of Phoebe Braithwaite. She'd always had a soft spot for him. Many a Bakewell tart she'd given him as a lad.

But Bob was a realist, as all farmers must be, and this was neither the time nor the place for Phoebe Braithwaite. Rose should be sitting here by his side. Her hand should be tucked under his arm. They should be talking things out and clearing the air, until they both saw the incident as the piece of nonsense it actually was, and it fell, once and for all, into its proper perspective. Then the rest of the long, lovely day could be theirs, without a shadow lying between them.

"I must say I shan't be sorry when we're off this ridge!" Mrs. Braithwaite was saying. "Ee, my word, Bob, we shouldn't half come a cropper down yon slope, if t'driver took his eye off the wheel for a minute!"

"He'll none do that," Bob comforted her.

"I remember we used to come up here for picnics when me an' my husband were courting," Mrs. Braithwaite continued. "We used to ride the old tandem as far as possible, an' when t'road got too steep, we walked. Ee, my word, I should look all right on a tandem now, shouldn't I!" She went off into a gale of laughter. . . .

It wasn't as if he'd really minded Rose talking to that Raf type. Well, not much. He didn't reckon to be one of those snooping killjoys. She'd a right to pass the time of day with anyone she'd a mind to—same as he had himself. But hang it—keeping everyone waiting like that! And then flying off the handle just because he'd dared to open his mouth. . . . Anybody'd think he'd got no rights at all.

And immediately the heavens opened and the white, blinding light of truth thrust down upon him like a naked sword.

For of course he had no rights over Rose. None whatever. And the chance of his ever acquiring such rights, always remote, had now receded so rapidly that it was a mere speck on a darkening horizon.

Panic seized Bob, turning his hefty limbs to jelly and his heart to a hollow stone.

I wish I'd never come, he thought. I wish I'd stopped on t'farm and got on with my work. I never ought to have left young Hugh to manage alone, anyhow. Goodness knows what he'll be getting up to. And that Edie mucking him about. . . . Well, she'll not get much change out of Hugh, that's one comfort. If it had been young Ben, now. . . . I'll have to watch out for young Ben when he comes home.

How could he possibly ask Rose to come and live in such a household? Well, he couldn't ask it, and that was flat. A house with two mistresses—and one of them Edie? Never on your life!

He had a devastating vision of Rose in a crisp gingham frock, working like a galley slave in the huge old kitchen at Clough's, while Edie lay on the sofa in her sluttish finery, knocking back bottles of Guinness and dropping the ash from her interminable cigarettes all over the place. Edie sneaking round corners and watching him and Rose together; trying to poison his mind against Rose and Rose's mind against him, and Dad's against both of them; either treating Rose as a servant or trying to make a friend of her, pouring filthy confidences into the small, clean ears of Rose. And later, when the children came. . . .

No, a thousand times no!

So on the whole it was just as well Rose was sitting next to old Crackerjack, while he was parked by Phoebe Braithwaite. Save a lot of trouble in the long run it would. . . .

"What's bitten you this morning, Bob?" Phoebe was saying. "Look as if you'd lost sixpence an' slipped on a banana skin, you do."

"I'm okay." He forced his mouth to a grin.

She gave a sudden tut of enlightenment.

"Well, if I'm not a fat owd fool!" Before he could stop her she had poked Rose between the shoulder blades and jerked her head commandingly. "I want a word with Jack, luv, if you don't mind. Swap seats, will you?"

There was nothing for it but to obey.

He felt Rose slide into the seat beside him, smelled the sweet fresh smell of her, trembled at the soft pressure of her arm.

Something told him that if he took her hand now and held it tightly, she would not long struggle to free it. That delicious, stony little profile would turn towards him and melt into smiles; her warmth would electrify his body from shoulder to ankle; the day would pour out upon them its glittering promises of holiday ease, of fun and excitement, of laughter in the sun and whispered ecstasy under the stars. He had only to reach out his hand. Now. He knew it quite certainly.

And then what? . . .

Then Edie making Rose's young life a burden to her. Edie prying, laughing, jeering; spoiling their privacy, smirching their decency, making a mockery of the clean, wholesome thing their marriage should be. . . .

It wasn't good enough.

Bob kept his hands folded between his knees, and Rose's profile continued its stern survey of the passing landscape.

"Rose! Our Rose!" Young Les was shouting from the back seat.

She turned and frowned.

"Don't shout, Les."

"Rose—you know yon feller with the car, who we was talking to this morning? He's coming along after us. You can see t'car now. Blue an' silver—whee! Look, Rose!"

Only too aware of young Les's propensity for keeping on, Rose turned a flaming face and nodded agreement, coupled with a private glare at Les.

Half the people in the bus craned their heads to see the blue-and-silver car, because they were on holiday and didn't want to miss anything.

Bob Clough did not turn to look. He sat quite still with his hands folded between his knees; and only the whiteness of the gripped knuckles showed that he had heard.

George Fiddler did not look at the blue-and-silver sports car, either. He was not interested in sports cars. He was not interested in anything but Getting On. If it had been a delivery truck, now: a neat, workmanlike job such as he was always trying to persuade the Guv'nor to buy instead of the ancient cart pulled by the ancient pony that caused him to take three times as long as he should take to get the bread delivered. . . .

He was always on at the Guv'nor about it, but you couldn't budge him. Not progressive—that was the trouble with the Guv'nor. When George thought of what he could do with the bakery if only he were in charge—well, it fair made him seethe! Double the profits in a year, he could.

He was bungfull of ideas that the Guv'nor wouldn't even consider; wouldn't even listen to, the silly old so-and so. "When you get a business of your own, George, you can do what you've a mind with it," he'd say. And his pink little nose would quiver in the middle of his fat little face in the way that so disgusted and infuriated George. "Things bein' as they are, what I say goes. Thee get crackin' with them loaves, or tha'll none be back until tomorrow."

It was right maddening, it was that!

He could leave, of course, but he doubted if he'd better himself that way. George had been with Mester Carter ever since he left school, and he reckoned there was summat due to him. The Guv'nor hadn't got any sons and he wasn't getting any younger. What more natural than that the business should eventually go to his faithful, experienced deliveryman, who had been with him ever since he had left school?

The trouble was that, even if the Guv'nor wasn't getting any younger, he still wasn't very old, and he obstinately showed no signs of cracking up. He might live, hale and hearty, while he was eighty, for all George knew. And even then he might go and sell the business over George's head—and where would he be then?

The word "consolidate" swam comfortingly into George's mind. I got to consolidate my position, he thought weightily.

"Grand bit of country, this," remarked John William Welsh, sucking his teeth appreciatively. "Wild. Grandest stretch in Yorkshire, I always think."

"Ah," George replied noncommittally. He wasn't interested in the country. He'd seen it. He spent his days driving up and down it and round about it, battling with dust and heat and flies in summer and mud and rain in winter. The country was an overrated sport, and that was George's considered opinion. All right on picture postcards, but an unprintable nuisance in real life.

What George wanted was to be right in the heart of the business: behind the counter; in the hot, odorous bakehouse; shut into the little office with the fat green account books and their exciting mysteries. That's where he ought to be. That's where he intended to be sooner or later, whatever the Guv'nor might feel about it.

"I got to consolidate my position. . . ."

His glance wandered across the aisle to where Ivy Carter's head drooped amorously against the stalwart shoulder of Miss Stacey. He snorted in frustration.

It might have to come to that in the long run.

He didn't want to marry Ivy. She wasn't a bad-looking kid, if you looked at her quick, though her nose was just like her father's, pink and quivery: like a rabbit's nose.

He didn't want to marry anybody. He didn't care about women. They were soft and clingy, and they were a funny shape. They were always wanting you to spend your good money on them. Or they wanted to put their heads on your shoulder and mess you about. And then they went and had babies, and complicated things horribly. They poked their noses—their pink, quivery noses—into your business and never gave you a minute's peace. . . .

But if you wanted to consolidate your position it was sometimes necessary to marry one of these creatures and make the best of it. A deliveryman, even if he had been on the job since he left school, could be discarded at will. But not a son-in-law. . . .

George sighed heavily.

There'd be one-and-ninepennies at the movies, to say nowt of bus fares into the town. There'd be teas in cafes. There'd be birthday and Christmas presents. There'd be the ring, and all the expense of getting spliced, and all the unpredictable expenses and inconveniences consequent on that rash act.

And even after all the candy and bus fares and movies and whatnot, she might go and turn him down. They said women were kittle-

[46]

cattle, and George well believed it. She might eat his candy and then laugh at him and go running back to that Stacey woman.

He glared at Miss Stacey's broad back. One thing, if Ivy and he were going to walk out, she'd have to pack that foolishness up. He wasn't going to stand any nonsense. Begin as you mean to go on.

Phoebe Braithwaite spoke kindly to Jack, asking after his Auntie Ag, and wanting to know when he was going to bring her some more nice logs for her kitchen fire. "I'll have a nice curd tart for you when you come, Jack," she promised.

Jack smiled and nodded.

"Nice logs for you, nice curd tart for Jack," he said contentedly.

Bless the boy, thought Phoebe, he's no more crackers than what I am. Less, happen! At least Jack's got his life all planned out, straight and simple. If he can't have what he wants, he wants what he can get. He doesn't go crying for t'moon, like a great silly owd buzzard. . . . I wish I wasn't so fat, she thought—though nobody, seeing her beaming face, would have suspected it. I wish I was a few years younger. . . . Nay, be your age, Phoebe Braithwaite! You can't put the clock back. Come to that, you wouldn't gain much if you could. You was never an oil painting, at your best. . . .

Ee, but I should be right set up if I could look after him properly! Mekkin' him a pie now and again and darning him an odd pair of socks isn't like the real thing. . . . Ee, I should like the doing up of them white shirts of his! And I reckon I could starch his collars a sight better than yon hussy he's got doing for him now. He always reckons as nobody can mek pastry to touch mine. . . . And that bronchitis he gets in t'winter—I can't bear to think of him lying alone t'other side of the wall, cough, cough, cough half the night, an' nobody to see to him. It don't seem right. . . .

Her eyes slid over the aisle to where he sat talking away to the Vicar fifteen to the dozen, with his short, pointed, gray-brown beard wagging up and down and his gold-rimmed pince-nez, his collar and cuffs, his tie pin, all glittering in the sun. Ee, he was a lovely man, was Walter. The sort of fellow that would do you credit.

Some men never paid you for all your trouble. Phoebe's husband, dead these ten years, had been that sort. Plenty of good suits he'd had, and looked like a stuffed dummy in all of them. No matter how carefully you starched and ironed his shirts they looked like rags in half an hour. Tie always wriggling up under his ear. . . . And sweat! Like those ads about your best friends not telling you, it had been. Poor owd Tom. He was a good sort and she'd mourned him faithfully. Black for two years and gray for another, and fresh flowers on his grave every blessed Sunday morning. . . . You could say she'd done her duty by Tom without the word of a lie. . . .

And didn't it seem daft for her and Walter to go on living in them two cottages, cheek by jowl, alone and lonely, when they could be together and comfortable?

That hussy of his was getting wed herself in a month or two, and what was he going to do then? Women were hard to get, these days. The factories paid better, an' regular hours an' all. Well, you couldn't blame 'em, really. Besides, a man was like me knife half shut without a wife.

How cosy they could be, the two of them, walking up to the church on Sunday mornings, with Walter so smart and spruce and shining; fresh, as it were, from her hands. With what cunning she would cook his meals. With what care she could guard against the insidious approach of bronchitis, and how firmly she would nip it in the bud if ever it got past her guard.

Should she leave Number Five and go in with Walter? Or would he prefer to leave Number Four and come in with her? Or would she be able to persuade him to knock down the party wall and make a decent sized place of it? That'd be far the best plan, for neither of them would want to get rid of their bits and pieces. They could make a right nice place of Four and Five put together. Parties they'd have. Musical evenings, with coffee and lemonade and three sorts of sandwiches and her special curd tarts. . . .

Mind you, he wasn't all that easy, wasn't Walter. He liked his own way. Well, she liked her own way, too. She didn't mind a bit of a set-to now and again. Made a change. Cleared the air, like. . . .

Jack pulled at her sleeve, pointed down the steep slope of fine wiry grass.

"Rabbits," he said happily.

They were scuttling in all directions, white tails bobbing in the sun. Pretty little things they were.

"My word, they'd mek a right good pie!" said the practical Phoebe.

Jack's face went dark, like a field when a thundercloud unrolls above it.

"No pie," he growled. "Pretty!" He seized her stout arm and gave it a violent pinch, so that she barely stifled a yelp of pain. "Pretty!" he insisted. "Not dead in a pie!"

My word, she thought, dismayed, I put me foot in it proper that time! She nodded vigorously. "Pretty little rabbits, Jack. We won't let anyone put 'em in a pie, will we? . . . Look, here's a bit of homemade toffee, Jack. Like it? Next time you bring me some logs I'll give you some to tek home to your Auntie Ag. Eat it up, there's a good lad." My word, I shouldn't like to get wrong side o' *yon* in a dark lane on a Saturday night! she thought. I wonder if he should ought to be put away, like that Mrs. Cope says? . . . Nay, poor soul. Whatever would his Auntie Ag do without him?

She patted Jack's arm and smiled at him. And then she sighed, and her glance returned to Walter Forsythe, talking away to the Vicar fifteen to the dozen with his trim beard wag-wag-wag against the undulating horizon.

As they descended the perilous ridge into milder country the driver drew a deep breath and began to whistle between his teeth. He was glad that bit was over.

It was all right if you didn't think about it. The old bus was okay. His nerves were okay. Of course they were. But there it was. Best part of thirty people's lives in the hollow of your hand, as you might say. And suppose a tire burst, or your back axle went or you went into a skid. . . . Well, it wouldn't ever happen, of course. The old bus was okay and so was he. He'd never had a black-out yet, and there was no reason to suppose he ever would. I got young Lil on me mind, he thought. That's what it is. I'm letting it get me down. Never felt this way before, I haven't.

He thought about his wife and the nipper she was expecting any minute now. He wondered if she'd be okay. Suppose she went and died. . . . Well, of course she wouldn't. She was okay. It'd all be over and done with in a week at most, and everything would be hunky-dory. Proper ol' woman I'm getting, he thought. Start thinking about it, you're sunk. Too much imagination, that's what I got. . . .

Once he'd got rid of this little lot and parked the old bus, he'd give himself a treat for once. He'd have a swim and then lie flat in the sun and sleep. He'd have a pint of beer with his lunch. Only chance he'd get, because he wasn't going to drink a drop before they started back—not on your life! Not with that ridge to cross again, and the sun bang in your eyes, like as not! . . .

"Can you see them yet, Fred?" asked Miss Fortune for the twentieth time that morning. And for the twentieth time her large, lazy brother gave his large, lazy smile and shook his head.

"Give over nattering, woman! They won't be here till gone eleven. Why don't you have a sit down and rest? What are those girls for, if not to do the work? Keeping a dog and barking yourself—there's no sense in it. Come on, sit down. Put your feet up five minutes. You'll be all worn to a frazzle." He patted the deck chair next his own and lay back, shutting his eyes.

"Well, just five minutes." Miss Fortune perched her spare form upright in the chair and shaded her eyes with hard, work-worn hands.

Behind them the scarlet-and-cream structure of the Good Fortune Tea Rooms shone blindingly in the sun. Striped awnings flapped and bellied in the breeze. The long trestle tables with their white cloths and polished cutlery were all ready for the lunch. Two of the waitresses were talking in rapid, high-pitched voices, back in the kitchen. "So I says to him, I says," . . . "So then he says . . ." she heard.

That was that Phyllis! Nothing but boys that girl thought of, from morning to night. Miss Fortune suspected that Phyllis was no better than she should be; but what could you do, these days! Girls were all alike. It was the war, she supposed. And things didn't seem to be getting any better. Worse, if anything. Ah, well, it would all be the same in a hundred years.

In considerably less than a hundred years, she remembered abruptly; and felt that jerk of the heart with which she was becoming increasingly familiar.

Well, it didn't matter now. It had been borne in upon her lately that it never *had* mattered as much as she had imagined. It was a great pity, thought Miss Fortune, that one never achieved wisdom until one was too old to need it. One spent one's life experimenting and blundering, trying vainly to see one's way through a brick wall. And suddenly the wall wasn't there any longer, and the way was plain to see. But by that time, of course, you were old and done for, and nothing was of the slightest importance. . . .

Her faded blue eyes rested with a gentle, aloof tolerance on her brother dozing in the deck chair beside her. He looked fat and pink and healthy. Despite the shortages his skin shone with good living. His hands were immaculately clean and well-kept. There was no streak of gray in his wavy dark hair. His flannels were pressed and spotless and his canvas shoes dazzlingly white. Those girls would do any mortal thing for Fred. Phyllis would rather press Fred's flannels any day than clean the silver. And yet she was paid good wages for cleaning the silver, whereas Fred never dreamed of giving her anything but a charming smile for her services.

Oh, well, it didn't matter. Thank goodness it didn't matter any more. . . .

She strained her eyes; but still there was no sign of the bus. They ought to be coming over the ridge by now, she thought.

As soon as she saw the bus on the ridge she would warn Phyllis to get the coffee on. It was just about half-an-hour's run from there.

They always had coffee as soon as they arrived, and then they went down to the beach for the cricket match until two o'clock, when lunch was served. Then off they went again until seven or so, when they all came trooping back for a high tea.

Ham and tongue and canned salmon with cherry cake and iced buns, canned peaches and cream.

After tea was the high spot of the day for Miss Fortune, for then came the singing.

The choir massed in a half circle and Walter Forsythe stood poised before them, pointed beard and small, gleaming baton lifted high, while Miss Fortune herself, hidden behind the piano on the balcony, struck the opening chords of the accompaniment.

The choir of Bishops Staving church was good; as good as ever Walter Forsythe could make it. It was justly famed in the county, and beyond.

Thirty years ago Beatrice Fortune had been a member of it.

She had left the village, and for a long time had lost touch with them. But then, back in 1930, she had started the Good Fortune Tea

Rooms, high up on the edge of this thriving seaside resort, and the choir had come there for its annual Outing ever since.

It was the high spot not only of her day, but of her whole year. . . .

How happy she had been in those long-ago days of her youth! Papa had been the Vicar of Bishops Staving then. She and Fred and Papa had lived contentedly together in the shabby, rambling old vicarage, and dear Nanny had looked after them all. Miss Fortune could not remember her mama, though there was a photograph of her in the old-fashioned floral album, somewhere in the attic: a narrow, delicate face with enormous eyes beneath a coronet of plaits; a lace fichu; hands folded on a Bible. . . . I'm very like her, she mused. Only a lot older, of course. How queer it was to think of that. . . .

She had been happy. She had had her music, her friends, her little romance with Walter. There had been picnics in summer; gay young people clambering about the high green bracken; taking snapshots of each other standing by the waterfall; falling in love and quarreling and making it up in the moonlight. . . . Bilberry parties in September, when the moors were royal purple, and smelled as she always thought Heaven would smell. Purple-stained mouths and fingers. Laughter and singing and a late tea at some farmhouse, and the horse brake clattering up to take them and their laden baskets home. . . . Skating on the frozen tarn in winter, hands locked, bodies swaying together in lovely rhythm. Bonfires and lanterns. . . . The carol singing at Christmas. Holly and mistletoe and new party frocks; silly games and getting a little tipsy on Nanny's Cup. . . . Lilies in the church at Easter. Massed color and scent of fruits and vegetables at Harvest Thanksgiving. . . .

So rich life had seemed, so rich and colorful. . . .

There had not been much money for the living was a poor one; how those young Stevenses managed Miss Fortune simply could not imagine, with three children already and no doubt more to come. If Papa had not had a little money of his own he could never have sent Fred to a public school and paid for her training as a pianist. . . .

Miss Fortune sighed and then smiled the sigh away. For it no longer mattered that all those hours and hours of practicing, all that good money had been wasted. It was just a dream from which she had long ago awakened.

The waking had been hard at first. Bitter. . . .

There was the day Fred had been expelled from school. Poor Papa, he had been quite stunned, but he had rallied bravely.

"Boys will be boys," he had said, and had persuaded Mr. Griffiths to take Fred into his office.

But Fred had got into trouble again so soon. Mr. Griffiths had been very kind, refusing to prosecute out of respect for Papa's cloth. But after the third time he had refused to take Fred back; and indeed Papa had not had the heart to ask him.

It had gone on like that, getting worse and worse, until Fred was more often in trouble than out of it.

It was not that he was really wicked; he just couldn't go straight. It was an illness, really; a disease, Papa said, just like any other disease. But it was poor Papa who died of it, not Fred. . . .

Everybody had been kind. Mr. Barrett had taken him on his farm, but Fred hadn't liked the long hours. Mr. Goodenough had put him in as manager of his bookshop, but that had been too slow for the high-spirited boy. He had helped Mr. Craven with his riding school, until that disgraceful affair with one of the girl pupils. And so it went on. . . .

After Papa died there was no money at all, because Fred had taken every penny.

And at that time, poor Walter was not earning anything like enough to get married on. They had thought their hearts would break; but of course they hadn't broken. Just a little bit chipped, perhaps. . . .

Aunt Florence had given them shelter for a while, but Fred had soon proved too much for Aunt Florence's endurance.

Miss Fortune had never blamed her for turning them out, even though she was Mama's only sister. It was so awkward to think of an answer when people asked: "And where is your charming nephew now?" You could hardly reply: "He's doing a stretch at Wormwood Scrubbs, thank you." Aunt Florence was very much respected and a leading light of a Kensington church, and it would have made things very awkward for her.

Somehow they had survived. Miss Fortune had given pianoforte lessons; taught in small private schools; done a little dressmaking, a little millinery; painted Christmas cards and calendars; gone through the whole gamut of such dreary, refined employments as were permissible to a genteel, untrained young person. At one period she had thrown gentility to the winds and had done some most unrefined charing, accepting with a wry smile the stale buns and left-overs proffered by kindly intentioned employers and carrying them away with real thankfulness in her little attaché case, along with her sacking apron, quite in the classic manner.

When he came out for the second time she had been shocked to see how ill he looked. His cough had kept her awake all night, and he seemed to have no life in him.

"Got any T.B. in your family?" the doctor had asked; and Miss Fortune's heart had stood quite still with fear.

But her fear was as nothing to the fear, the abject terror, the shaking, shrinking repulsion with which Fred had heard the verdict. He had gone completely to pieces; crying in her arms, coughing and crying and spluttering until she was obliged to be cruel to be kind, as they said.

She had not slept at all that night. Long after Fred had fallen asleep Miss Fortune had sat, wide-eyed and exhausted, wondering how they were going to manage, and no nearer the solution when dawn lit up the dreadful rooms they called home.

And how fortunate it had been that Aunt Florence's husband had died soon after and left her the legacy; tied up securely so that Fred could not get at it, too.

One thousand pounds! . . . It had seemed untold riches to Miss Fortune; though by the time Fred had left the sanatorium it had dwindled alarmingly. Still, there had been enough to get them started in the Tea Rooms: humbly at first, but they had proved Good Fortune indeed, and they had never looked back since that day.

The high, bracing position had suited Fred wonderfully and he had slavishly obeyed the doctor's instructions to take life quietly; had obeyed them, indeed, almost too literally, for he had never done another stroke of work since.

Miss Fortune wasn't grumbling at that. She had been quick to see where her authority lay, quick to use it in a good cause. "I shouldn't go out tonight, if I were you, there's a damp mist rising." "Don't go down to the Bell, Fred, you were coughing a bit last night. Take it easy by the fire." "Sit in the garden, Fred, it's better for you than those crowded movies. And there's the hill to climb coming back. Remember what the doctor told you. . . ."

It had been so easy, almost frighteningly easy to turn him into the pleasant, acquiescent nonentity he was today. He was such an abject coward. For the last fifteen years she had had practically no trouble with him at all. Of course, she had to keep the cashbox hidden and check up on the silver every now and again, but that was nothing.

I've done it, Miss Fortune thought dreamily, shading enormous, violet-shadowed eyes with hard, scarred, leaf-thin fingers. It has cost me my romance, my music, my friends, my health—but I've done it. I wonder if it was worth it? . . . That's the queerest part about it— it doesn't seem to matter a tinker's curse, as they say, one way or the other. . . .

And still there was no sign of the bus.

"They really ought to be in sight by now," she worried. "I hope there's been no accident. I must say, I don't like that bit across the ridge. . . ."

She leaned back in the deck chair, feeling the sun warm on her eyelids.

And almost immediately Phyllis was shaking her shoulder and thrusting a letter at her, all voluble excitement.

"Fellow in a sports car," she was spluttering. "Very swish, all blue and silver. 'Is this where the Staving choir is coming?' he says to me, Oxford accent an' all, not half! So I says 'yes,' so he says, 'I wonder if you'd give this to Miss Rose Batley when she comes,' he says, so I says 'yes,' an' off he goes in his car like a streak of lightning. Funny-looking sort of chap he was. Quite the gentleman. But sort of as if he was pulling faces at you all the time. Well, I 'ad to laugh. . . ."

"Very well, Phyllis. Put the coffee on now; I can see the bus coming over the ridge."

Well, let's hope that's exhausted the Gregorian Chant for one day, Andrew thought, as Mr. Forsythe finally ran down. I never was so sick of a conversation in all my life. I'll jolly well see I sit with Audrey coming home. . . . How sweet she looks in that green thing. Darling! . . .

Leaning forward, he caught Audrey's eye and did some peculiar gymnastics with his eyebrows. It was their secret code, meaning: *I love you. You're adorable. I'm kissing you now.* He had used it in a great variety of situations: at dull luncheon parties, across crowded halls at annual bazaars; once, regrettably, from the pulpit. . . . They called it Happy Faces. It seemed a long time since they had used the code.

Audrey gave him a cool little smile, omitting to make the correct responses. He leaned back feeling rather forlorn. Perhaps I can get a pipe going now we're off that ridge, he thought.

Mr. Forsythe cleared his throat, and for a moment Andrew feared he was going to get the Gregorian Chant again, but his fears proved groundless.

Walter Forsythe was nervous: that was why he had talked so much.

It was ridiculous to be nervous, of course. He had known Phoebe Braithwaite more years than he cared to remember, and surely, at their time of life it shouldn't be a difficult thing to say. But somehow it was. . . .

Why say it today, then? Why not poke his head over the garden fence some evening and get it off his chest? Or walking home from choir practice? Any time would do, really. He'd just got it into his head that it must be now or never. And Walter was nervous. More, he was downright scared! He hummed. He tapped a tune on the immaculate knees of his trousers. He opened the despatch case and fidgeted with the music sheets. He thought of something he hadn't already said about the Gregorian Chant and opened his mouth to say it and then shut it again.

Ridiculous! he fumed. At our time of life we ought to be able to get down to brass tacks, I should hope. . . .

The choirboys were getting restive. They wanted to get down to their cricket on the flat stretch of sands below the Tea Rooms.

"You got the bat, Ron?"

"No, you got it."

"I never! You'd got it when we got in. Les, you seen the bat?"

"It's here, under the seat. You got the ball?"

"Ron's got the ball. You got the ball, haven't you, Ron? Give us a catch, Ron!"

Ron obliged. The hard ball flew over people's heads and everybody ducked. It knocked the hat off the head of the blacksmith's wife, and the blacksmith fielded it neatly.

"Out!" he yelled jovially.

His wife shot him a bitter look. His daughter began to smooth out a broken feather. The heads of the two women bent together, muttering maledictions.

"Stop that, you lads," ordered the blacksmith with belated severity. He pocketed the ball.

"That might 'a killed me," his wife accused him.

"You're none that easy killed," he grinned.

"Coffee!" exclaimed Mrs. Maddon. "That's all I want. Just to sit on the lawn and drink coffee, and be waited on. Just like the old days—eh, Doris?"

"I don't remember, Mother," Doris said maddeningly. Really, Doris was behaving very badly today; her mother could not imagine what had come over her. Ever since she'd got up she'd been different, somehow. Mrs. Maddon hoped she wasn't sickening for anything.

Coffee? thought Audrey. No, coffee's out. The only thing that *wouldn't* make me sick right now is a strawberry ice. Gosh, how I long for a strawberry ice! It suddenly seemed that if she did not have a strawberry ice immediately life would become altogether insupportable. If I'm going to indulge in pregnant whimsies, why can't I have a passion for cheese, or marmalade, or that revolting canned hake that I stocked the larder with! There'd be some sense in that.

As soon as I've done my Mrs. Vicar act, I'll get the bus from the corner and go into the town. They're sure to have strawberry ices at Pritchett's. I might slip in and see Frances, too. No, damn. She'll be out on her rounds. And if I leave it till tonight she'll be taking the evening surgery. Oh, well. . . .

Andy was making Happy Faces. She gave him a cool little smile and turned away.

What a beast I am, she thought. Why can't I signal back and make him happy? I want to, but somehow I can't. I feel thoroughly awkward. . . . Thank goodness they've stopped throwing that missile about! I don't want to be frightened by a cricket ball at this stage of the proceedings. . . . There goes that blue-and-silver sports car! I'm sure it's the flying boy from the hotel. Who was it said he used to be in the movie business? . . . I used to think I'd do well at that, but I married a parson instead and became a pious hag. Well, a hag, anyway. I should think Allegra would film well. She's very graceful and her bones are good. Perhaps that flying boy could give me an introduction to somebody. Andy ought to bring him in to supper one night. I might work off some of the canned hake on him. . . .

The driver backed his bus carefully into position and came down from his seat whistling between his teeth, slicking his hair back from a forehead beaded with sweat.

"Well, that's that, sir! Be seeing you later."

"Why not join us," Andrew invited. "There's plenty of grub. You look as if you could swing a useful bat."

"Thanks all the same. Got a few bits of business to do down in the town. The missus give me a list. You know how it is, sir." He laughed as one family man to another, and Andrew laughed, too.

"I do indeed! . . . Well, have tea with us later, at least, and then you'll be in time for the singing."

"Thanks very much. So long," said the driver.

He caught a bus by the skin of his teeth and was rattled down into the town.

Woolworth's and Boots' and the good old Co-op. Merry-go-rounds and Bump-'ems and Walls of Death. Fish and chips. That was the sort of Outing he liked.

And a long, long drink of be-eautiful beer! Great sufferin' ducks, what he could do to a pint of beer! . . .

3

ENTRENCHED in the privacy of the Ladies' Toilet, Rose read the letter, then tore it into minute portions and flushed it out of existence. Her eyes were bright and her lips firmly folded.

What a nerve! As if she'd leave the Outing and go chasing down the road to say good-by to a fellow she'd never set eyes on until to-day, and would never see again!

Never wanted to see again, either. He'd done enough damage for one day. Let him be on his way for wherever he was bound for—and good joy go with him! . . .

She took off the pink scarf and combed her wind-blown hair; powdered her nose; pulled hopefully at the too tight frock. I look awful, she thought. I do need some new clothes badly.

She sighed impatiently, turning and twisting before the very inadequate mirror. If she did get a new frock this summer, it'd only make her coat and shoes look more shabby by contrast. What joy to possess a complete new outfit! To know that everything you wore was new and fresh—right down to your skin!

Perhaps when she got married to Bob it *could* be managed—just once in a lifetime.

And then Rose sighed again. For really, Bob was being the limit, being huffy like that, sitting mum beside her and not paying the slightest attention to her ever since they'd arrived. . . .

There hadn't been much chance, really. You couldn't get out of the cricket, not without attracting everybody's notice. Except for a few of the older ones, everybody always played cricket until lunch time. It was part of the Outing.

And she'd enjoyed it, too. Rose liked cricket. She liked to see boys swiping at the ball; running, laughing, shouting; crouching behind the wicket, intent and ready; leaping into the air for a catch; loping up with swinging arms to bowl. She liked the satisfactory sound of the ball whacking on the bat; the cries and laughter when a fielder muffed his catch; the cheers and clapping of the spectators mingled with the soft slapping of waves on firm, flat sand, and the bright sun mellowing all.

Young Les hadn't done so badly, for all he was so small. George Fiddler hadn't been best pleased when Les bowled him out first ball! And Miss Stacey had done well, too, bowling overhand just like a man, red in the face with exertion, and her deep voice booming out above everybody else's. "Come on, you boys! Put a jerk in it! . . . Oh, played, sir, *played!* . . ." Well, you had to laugh!

And the Vicar had enjoyed himself, too, making thirty-five and grinning like a boy, and saying damn when he dropped a catch, just like anybody would. That had made old Mother Peck and her daughter mumble to each other! Couple of old cats! . . . Rose felt sorry for the blacksmith, saddled with a couple of old cats like yon. . . .

How handsome Bob had looked, with the stiff coat thrown aside and the shirt sleeves rolled high up his brown, muscled arms. A proper man. . . . She'd been proud of him; ready to make it up as soon as he'd a mind.

But he hadn't had a mind, seemingly.

After the cricket he'd gone off with the other boys to wash, and she'd taken Jack round to Miss Fortune's kitchen where he always had his dinner, like she'd promised his Auntie Ag. She'd put the cat's plate against the table leg, so that if Jack poured his gravy down it wouldn't be wasted, anyhow.

That waitress they called Phyllis had made a bit of a fuss, but she'd smoothed her down all right, and Jack had behaved himself right well, and he was going to help with the dishes afterwards, like he always did.

By the time she'd got Jack settled they were all in their places singing *Be present at our table, Lord,* out on the lawn, and she'd had to squash in between John William Welsh and Miss Peck, and make the best of it. Bob hadn't kept a place for her. . . .

Rose examined her teeth. They were white, but they'd have looked whiter still if Dad hadn't made her take the lipstick off. She wondered how Mum was managing without her. Poor old Mum. . . .

I'll see she has a girl to help her, when I'm married to Bob, she thought.

She stared at her face in the spotted mirror with the advertisement for mineral waters round the frame.

"*When* I'm married to Bob," she said aloud.

The words had a hollow sound; unreal. The face in the mirror looked stupid; suddenly she had no patience with it at all.

Come on, be your age! she thought, viciously wanting to hurt that round, pink face mooning at her out of the mirror. He's never asked you to marry him. What if he has kissed you a time or two! And what if he did hold your hand all through *The Second House!* . . . You've got a nerve, my girl, expecting a man to marry you just because he's held your hand in the movies! . . . D'you think he's never

seen any other girls, all those years in the Army? You weren't much
more than a kid when he went away; I don't suppose he ever gave
you a thought. Mooning and gawping at him, acting cheap in the
movies and letting him kiss you after the Women's Institute dance,
an' going home from choir practice, an' any other time he'd a mind.
. . . Just another girl—that's all you are; an' the sooner you get it
into your thick head the better. . . .

"You're a silly fool, Rose Batley!" she said aloud, glaring at the
face in the mirror.

She swung round as the door opened to admit the Lomax girls,
who proceeded to lavish powder and lipstick on their pert faces.

"Who's in the lav?" inquired Pearl.

"Nobody."

"I heard somebody talking."

"Perhaps she was talking to herself," suggested Violet, screwing
her face this way and that, to locate any lurking blackheads.

"Happen I was," Rose said shortly.

"First signs of insanity," Pearl pointed out, and both sisters giggled
shrilly.

"Seen our Les?" Rose asked.

"Nope. Hiked off somewhere. Everybody's going some place, except old Mother Maddon, who's got her feet up on a deck chair,
giving Fred Fortune a treat. Me an' Vi's going to the Fun Fair, with
Harry Waterhouse an' Bob Clough an' Miss Stacey and Co. We
could do without the Co., only she won't take a hint. George Fiddler's coming, too. Why don't you tag along? We're going on the
Dodge-'ems."

"No thanks," Rose replied coldly. "Got something better to do than
pay sixpence to be sick on the Dodge-'ems. I can do that for nowt,
putting my finger down my throat. I'm going for a walk."

"Hope it keeps fine for you!"

Rose went out, leaving the sisters to their toilet.

"Stuck-up thing!" muttered Violet.

"Oh, she's all right," said the more tolerant Pearl. "Had a row
with Bob, I shouldn't wonder. . . . I think her hair's cute."

"Me too. Does mine look frizzy at the back?"

"A bit. Does mine?"

"Yep."

"I've a good mind to try one of those cold permanents next time. May Wilson had a beaut. Costs more, though. Wish I'd got hair like Rose's."

"Me too."

Statements which would considerably have astonished Rose, could she have heard them, as she wandered across the almost forsaken lawn, trying to give a convincing imitation of a girl enjoying herself.

I'll be waiting in the car, just down the lane. . . .

That's what he'd written in the letter.

Of course, she didn't suppose he'd meant one word of it. He wouldn't want to be bothered with her sort—even if he was lonely, like he said.

Still, there was no harm in just going to the gate to have a look. She didn't like to think of him being lonely. She was lonely herself. . . .

Young Les climbed the twisting path to the farm; quickly, so that Ronny Field shouldn't spot him and want to come too. Yet not too quickly, because now the moment was here, he was half frightened. The thought of the puppy was almost unbearably beautiful.

And what if, after all his waiting, there was no puppy? Suppose Nell hadn't had any puppies this year? Suppose she had had them and they had all died? Suppose Mrs. Mitchum had forgotten her promise and given them all away.

Overwhelmed by these dire possibilities, Les sank onto the grass verge of the lane and sat there, feeling rather sick. He thought he'd just wait a little and get his breath back. There was no hurry, after all. He'd got the rest of the day before him.

Far below he could hear the shouts and laughter of the other choirboys, fooling about as they waited for the next bus to take them down into the town. They were going to the Fun Fair. Ronny Field had seven and sixpence to spend. He always had lots of spending money, because his Dad was a waiter up at the hotel and was very rich. Ron had a bike with a three-speed gear, and an air gun, and roller skates with ball bearings. He wasn't mean with his money, either. He'd offered to treat Les to the Bump-'ems and the coconut shies, and he'd been stupefied when Les said he wasn't going into the town. "Not want to go to the Fun Fair? You must be crackers, man!"

Les liked Ron very much. He was his best friend. But he didn't want Ron just now. He didn't want anybody. Only the puppy. . . .

The shouts of the boys became shriller and then ceased. The sound of the bus engine throbbed and died away.

Everything was quiet now. Only the tap-tap-tap of a woodpecker and the distant bleating of a sheep broke the silence.

After a minute Les got to his feet and climbed up to the farm gate.

Closing the gate carefully behind him, he crossed the empty, cobbled yard. There was no sign of life anywhere, save a little group of buff hens scratching and pecking desultorily, with long-drawn craw-aw-awks of drowsy content. They made off at his approach, jerking their heads and ruffling feathers in alarm. A row of churns shone against a whitewashed wall. The air was full of the smells of manure and straw, and the spicy sweetness of stocks growing along the side of the house. The air above the cobblestones quivered with heat, so that the blue, distant hills trembled, and the strong stonewalls of the farmhouse were fluid. . . .

As he turned the corner of the house he saw Mrs. Mitchum, mountainous in a yellow-flowered overall, drinking a cup of tea in the porchway. He stopped and grinned at her shyly, lifting his cap as Rose liked him to do.

She nodded and smiled, blowing on the tea in her saucer and sipping noisily.

"Well, luv?"

She didn't remember him! . . .

His heart sank, and he swallowed with difficulty.

"The puppy . . ." was all he could manage.

"What puppy, luv?" She drank again, set the cup and saucer down and folded her fat arms across her waist. A clock struck three sonorous notes in the dim house behind her.

Les felt hollow and desperate.

"Last year. . . ." he stammered. "I came with the choir from Staving. The big sheep dog had got some puppies. You let me see 'em. You said. . . . You said you'd give me one next time I came. Next year, you said . . . you said those was all promised, but I could have one next year. So . . . so can I, please?"

Mrs. Mitchum sucked her teeth and then she laughed wheezily.

"Bless the boy! Aye, I do remember now. Well, fancy that! Nay, well, I reckon you're going to be disappointed, luv."

"Hasn't she . . . had any puppies this time?" He forced the words between dry lips. He knew he mustn't cry. He was too old to cry. But here the tears came, gathering hot and full behind pricking lids. He tried not to blink, so that they should not overflow and shame him.

"Oh, aye, she's had 'em all right! Nivver misses, doesn't owd Nell. Only you see, luv, they're all gone, only the one—and I reckon you'll none tek a fancy to *him*."

"Why not?" He blinked by mistake, and a large, hot tear rolled slowly down his cheek and trickled into the hollow under his chin.

He hoped she hadn't noticed it; but she had. She clucked commiseratingly.

"Don't tek on, luv. Nay, I blame meself! I nivver give it another thought!"

A bearded man came clanking round the corner, laden with pails. He set the pails down and wiped his face and neck with a red handkerchief.

"What's to do?"

"Little lad's come for one o' Nell's pups," his wife told him. "He came wi' t'Staving Choir Outing last year, an' I promised him one out o' this lot—an' I nivver thowt another word about it. There's nobbut the sickly one left, an' Daniel were goin' to drowned him toneet. Ought to 'a bin done at start, by rights."

"Oh, no!" Les whispered. "Oh, no! . . ."

The tears burst their dam and cascaded over his cheeks, but he was too miserable to care. "Please let me have it, instead! I'll tek care of it, I will. Our Rose'll tek care of it, an' all. She's ever so good with animals. Please don't drown the puppy, Mrs. Mitchum! I've bin looking forward to it so long. . . ."

The farmer picked up his pails and jerked his head at his wife.

"Gi' 'im the pup," he said, and departed.

"Nay, well. . . . He's in t'barn over yonder, luv, if you want to look at him, but I don't reckon you'll fancy him. He were allus a bit sickly, an' Nell took agen him, sitha. An' I must say, he's nowt to look at—

well, you'll see for yoursen. I reckon you'll do better to wait while she has next lot. Still, you can look at him, if you've a mind."

Les crossed the cobbled yard again and pushed open the door of the barn. It was cool and dark inside. Two farm carts rested on their shafts, huge and shadowy. Some bicycles leaned against one wall and straw was heaped against another. Fowls dozed and murmured overhead on a beam covered with white droppings. Dust danced madly in a beam of sunlight from a cobwebby window high up in a wall.

Les stood quite still, peering through the dimness, trying to locate the puppy.

"Scottie!" he called softly.

There was a tiny rustle of straw—no more. It might have been a mouse only. . . .

"Scottie! . . . Here, boy. Come on then, Scottie. . . ."

Silence. And then the silence was broken by a sneeze. And then another sneeze; a rustling in the straw. And then, absurdly, heart-meltingly, a growl that ended in a squeak and became the sleepiest of baby yawns.

Laughing through his tears, peering through the dimness, Les groped in the straw. His hands closed on warmth and softness. Tiny sharp teeth assailed him. A soft, hot tongue, a hot, questing nose. . . .

"Come on, Scottie. Come on, boy. . . ."

He lifted the puppy against his tear-wet throat. It snuffled and whimpered; biting his chin, his fingers; wriggling and biting and licking so that he was afraid of dropping it.

It smelled just as he had known it would smell: stuffy and hot and exciting.

"Let's have a look at you," he murmured.

He put it down by the door and squatted on his heels, staring at the puppy, entranced.

How could anybody say it was ugly! It was a lovely little puppy! . . . Its ears were queer, but Les liked its ears that way. It was very thin, but he would soon fatten it. It dragged one leg a bit, but Rose would soon put that right. Rose was good with animals.

It wasn't everybody's puppy—impartially he admitted it. That was okay. He didn't want it to be everybody's puppy. It was *his* puppy, his very own. He loved it.

"Come on, boy, we're going for a walk."

He picked the puppy up, tucked it under his coat, carried it carefully across the yard to where Mrs. Mitchum bent over the ten-week stocks.

"Well, what does t'a think on it, lad? A queer-lookin' piece, ain't it? I reckon it'd be best off in a bucket o' watter."

"Nay, it's a grand puppy," he said eagerly. "Let me have it, please, Mrs. Mitchum. You said I could, last year. It's just what I wanted, this puppy is."

"Well, some folks is easy pleased!" The farmer's wife laughed, ruffled the boy's thick brown hair, planted a loud, moist kiss on his cheek. "Nay, you're welcome, luv. Tek care how you feed him; he's nobbut a babby, think on. I'm sure I hope you'll manage to rear him. . . . Should you like a glass of milk, luv, an' a bit o' cake?"

"No, no thank you." Les was breathless to be gone now that the puppy was his. Suppose the unknown Daniel came back and insisted on putting it in a bucket, after all! He could hardly wait to be polite. "Thanks very much, Mrs. Mitchum, I'm not a bit hungry. Good-by. I'm much obliged for the puppy. Well. . . . Good-by!"

Her fat laugh followed him as he closed the gate and fled down the narrow, twisting path.

The puppy was awkward to carry. It kept slipping through his coat and he was terrified of dropping it. It whined continually.

Perhaps it didn't like being carried, wanted to walk? He put it down and walked on a few steps, giving an imperative whistle. His heart swelled to see the puppy come staggering after him, feet splaying out and tail wiggling.

It was a mousy-brown sort of color with uneven markings of black. One ear flopped and the other pricked up. There was no doubt it was very weak in the legs, especially the back ones, which frequently collapsed, so that the puppy advanced on its belly. Its brow was wrinkled. It closely resembled, in fact, a very old bank clerk, too old to enjoy his pension—though that, naturally, was not how Les saw it.

Why did it whine all the time? Wanted its mother, happen. Nay, but Nell had turned against it, Mrs. Mitchum had said so.

"You ought to be glad to leave your nasty ol' mother an' belong to me," Les told it severely. "Give over makin' that noise, now! And make up your mind what you want—walk, or be carried."

With the puppy tucked under his coat, he wandered down to the Good Fortune Tea Rooms, crossed the lawn and went down the private steps cut in the cliff to the hot beach. He found a small, secluded cove, and here he sat down, holding the puppy in his arms, rocking it to and fro, crooning baby nonsense to it.

The puppy whined and whined. It would neither sleep nor rest. He could not induce it to play.

He became aware of a wet warmth on his left leg and he put the puppy quickly aside. Good heck—it had done number one on him! First shocked and then entranced, Les scrubbed at his leg. This was coming to grips with reality. This was part of the business of having a puppy! Not only had they to be fed and loved and taken care of; they had to be trained. When they wanted to do their business, they had to wait until you opened the door and let them out into the garden. And they couldn't do as they liked in the garden, either, because Dad was nuts about his roses and his blessed old sweet peas. He'd have to train it to go a special place every time. . . .

"Behave yourself!" he said sternly. "Look what you've bin an' gone an' done!" He gave it a teeny tiny slap, to show it how stern he was feeling. The puppy yelped and he gathered it against his breast in a passion of love and remorse. "You're nobbut a little babby, aren't you, Scottie? Nobody's ever learnt you any better!"

He found a small portion of toffee adhering to the lining of his pocket. He offered it to the puppy, who licked it languidly and turned away as if revolted by the taste. Les washed the toffee in a pool of sea water and ate it himself. Particles of sand gritted between his teeth, not unpleasantly.

The puppy went on whining. The whining turned into a regular yap-yap-yap that alarmed Les. It felt very hot and its nose was dry, rough to the touch. Perhaps a little paddle in the cool water would make it feel better. Of course! Why hadn't he thought of it before!

He tore off his shoes, his gray knitted socks; turned back the edges of the gray flannel shorts, new on that day. The water rushed over the sand, creaming round his ankles, sucking back between his toes most deliciously. Grasping the puppy round its pot belly, he lowered it carefully into the water. It struggled, yelping shrilly, frantic with fear.

Les felt a spasm of impatience. Nothing pleased the puppy, nothing at all! Try as he would, he couldn't make it happy. . . .

He had imagined it chasing about the beach, barking at the waves, following him wherever he went, having a whale of a time. He had imagined it falling asleep in his arms; a heavy, trustful little burden he would gladly have borne; waking to play again, to eat and drink with him, and once more to fall asleep. But it wasn't like that at all. . . .

"All right, then—go paddle by yourself!" he said gruffly. He put it down by the edge of the water. Whining, it retreated shorewards. Very soon its back legs collapsed and it had to crawl on its belly.

Les turned his back on the puppy and began to kick the water about. He was bitterly disappointed.

It was not that he minded the puppy being backward, odd, weak in the legs. He had been warned of all these things, and he hadn't minded. Had the puppy been content in his arms, how gladly he would have carried it all day; nursing it tenderly while it peered at the new, strange world; sitting quiet as a rock while it slept.

But it was quite clear that the puppy neither trusted nor liked him, and that he could not understand. The thought filled him with desolation, darkened his day.

Should he take the puppy back to Mrs. Mitchum and explain that it hadn't taken to him?

No. Oh, no! For then Daniel would inevitably put it in a bucket. Better it should hate him and live—a thousand times better!

It was very upsetting. . . .

Far along the shore he could see the piled roofs, the tall hotels, the flashing windows of the big town. The sands below the town were black with people. Faintly he could hear the music of a military band. Ron and the other lads would be right in the thick of the Fun Fair by now. . . . Swooping and yelling on the Scenic Railway, sloshing coconuts, sucking ice-cream cones, cracking rifles and blowing squeakers into people's faces. . . . He'd only got sevenpence left out of the two bob that flying chap had given him. But Ron would have treated him to the Bump-'ems and the coconut shies, anyhow. He could have had a wonderful time.

And here he was, saddled with a sickly puppy that didn't even *like* him!

It was very upsetting. . . .

He turned to whistle to the puppy.

His eyes popped and his mouth fell open.

The puppy was nowhere to be seen!

He began to wade back to the beach. "Scottie! Scottie!" he yelled. He felt as if he would choke.

The water rushed backwards. Caught in a tangle of seaweed, half covered with yellow, scummy foam, he saw the puppy; a dark, shining bundle battling helplessly against the sucking tide.

He grabbed, and missed, grabbed again and fell to his knees, cutting them on the sharp stones.

But he had the puppy in his hands. He had it out of the water, sneezing and spluttering, clutched against his heaving chest. He had saved the puppy. It was alive. . . .

He began to run over the hot sand. His soaked clothing chafed and dragged at him. He picked up his shoes and socks, climbed up the cliff steps and ran up the lawn into the kitchen of the Good Fortune Tea Rooms.

Miss Fortune was sitting there alone, drinking a cup of tea. She stared at his white little wedge of a face, startled, but only for a moment. Then she took the puppy from him and put it in front of the fire.

"Strip off your clothes," she said crisply. "All of them—don't be silly. Here, wrap yourself in this towel and have a rub down. Yes, yes, we'll see to the puppy in a moment. Now rub. Rub hard! Get yourself in a glow and you'll take no harm. I'll rinse the salt water out of your clothes and they'll be dry in an hour with this sun and wind. My, just *look* at those knees! We'll have to get the iodine. You won't mind if it stings a bit, a big boy like you."

"My puppy!" Les quavered.

"The puppy will be all right," Miss Fortune said firmly. She raised her voice and called for Jack, and Jack came loping into the kitchen, grinning expectantly. "Will you dry the little puppy, please, Jack? And then wrap it in the piece of blanket you'll find in that drawer. Keep it very warm, Jack. Poor little thing, it fell in the water, but you'll look after it, won't you, Jack? . . . Now you keep on rubbing your hair," she went on to Les, "and I'll get you a nice hot cup of tea. Dear me, you have had an adventure, haven't you?"

Les drank the hot tea, stoically suffered the iodine. He tried not to look at the puppy. He was sure it was going to die. Oh, poor little puppy! Poor, *darling* little weak-legged, backward, unhappy puppy! He couldn't bear it to die. It was all his fault. He hadn't been patient enough. It was going to die, and it was all his fault. . . .

"There there," murmured Miss Fortune, pretending not to see his tears. "Have another cup of tea, and a slice of cherry cake. I'm sure you like cherry cake! I'll just go and see to your clothes now. Help yourself."

It was a lovely cake—full of cherries. The tea was very hot and sweet, very comforting. He kept his back to the puppy, stuffing himself with cake and dabbing at his eyes. He didn't want old Crackerjack to see him crying. He felt silly, wrapped in this blanket, and hoped none of the waitresses would come in.

Les cut himself another slice of cherry cake: she had told him to help himself. He felt warm and comforted and his tears dried up.

Old Crackerjack was singing behind him, very softly, under his breath. Singing without words; but Les knew the words well enough. "*Bring* back, *bring* back; oh, *bring* back my bonny to me . . ." he was crooning.

Surely he wouldn't be singing if the puppy was dead?

Cautiously Les turned his head.

Old Crackerjack was sitting in front of the fire with the puppy, wrapped in the warm blanket, on his knees. Very gently he was rocking his body from side to side. He gazed down at the puppy and smiled as he crooned. And the puppy lay quietly on Crackerjack's knees, comfortable and content.

Les went and stood by the puppy, bent over it. But Crackerjack scowled at him and said, "Sh!" and gathered the bundle closer.

"*Bring* back, *bring* back . . ." crooned Crackerjack.

And the puppy whimpered once, and went to sleep with its mouth open, showing the tip of a pink tongue.

Ivy was being mulish in the Fun Fair.

She clung tightly to Miss Stacey's arm; dragged on it, whining and protesting, refusing to join in the jollity. The crowd pushed her this way and that. Her toes got trampled on. A nasty man with a false nose burst a balloon in her ear, and only laughed when she screamed. She was too hot in her coat, but argued that if she took it off she would only have to carry it. In the end Miss Stacey carried it for her, and Ivy wept and moaned that she was a nuisance to everybody—which was incontestably true.

"Brace up, Ivy!" Miss Stacey urged.

"I didn't want to come with all this lot," Ivy protested. "I only wanted you. We could have gone somewhere nice and quiet, all by ourselves. I never seem to get you alone!"

"Silly-billy!" Miss Stacey's voice was robust; but in spite of her irritation she felt a spasm of tenderness for the silly, clinging little thing. It was something to be wanted, if only by Ivy. "Come on, we're going on the switchback."

"Ow, I couldn't!" Ivy squeaked.

"Yes, you could. You'll love it! Come on, now, buck up. Don't spoil the party."

"Let me sit by you, then. Ow, I know I shall be sick; I won't go on if I can't sit by you."

But Ivy *did* go on the switchback, and she did *not* sit next to Miss Stacey. Whether by accident or design, Miss Stacey and Bob Clough sat together, and Ivy found herself, shivering with fright, in the seat next to her father's deliveryman, George Fiddler.

"Lemme get out!" she cried shrilly. "I got to get out!"

"You can't," George stated implacably. "It's started." The thought flashed through his mind that this sounded almost like a prophecy. . . .

"Ow—Miss Stacey!" Ivy yelled; but her voice was lost in the crescendo of shrieks that arose as the crazy little car plunged downwards, gathering momentum with every foot.

Ivy shrieked louder than anybody. She flung her arms blindly about George Fiddler and buried her quivering little pink nose in his chest.

And George consolidated his position by gripping her grimly against his side.

Down they swooped, and up; toppled over the dizzy brink and down again, and up and round and down. . . . It seemed as if earth would never be reached.

And when at last they arrived, Miss Stacey immediately shouted: "Let's have another basinful!" and up to the pay-box they pounded, Miss Stacey and Bob and Harry Waterhouse and Pearl and Violet Lomax; without so much as a thought for Ivy, whose nose had begun to bleed, or for George Fiddler who was landed with the job of staunching it with his best silk handkerchief.

"You don't want another go, do you?" he suggested.

"I should think not!" Ivy gasped. "Oh, dear—*look* at it! Oh, I believe I've burst an artery or something!"

"You don't keep arteries in your nose. What you want's a cold key down t'back of your neck. That's what Ma always did to our Henry. Stops it in two shakes."

"I haven't got a key," Ivy said peevishly.

"I have."

"How shall I get it back?"

"We'll think about that afterwards," George declared resourcefully. "Come on out o' this crowd, unless you want to bleed to death or something."

Still Ivy hung back, mopping at her ridiculous nose and moaning, ruining his best silk handkerchief.

"I'd better wait for Miss Stacey."

"Why? *She* don't want you," George said brutally.

And indeed, that seemed only too true. For here they came again; swooping, screaming with fright and enjoyment; and none more oblivious than Miss Stacey of poor Ivy and her bleeding nose. Downright heartless, that's what it was!

"I'll buy you some chocolate peppermints," George offered—stoical, even in his anguish.

"I couldn't eat a mouthful, not while me nose stops bleeding," Ivy whined, suffering herself to be led away.

It was a bit rough, George reflected, when you had to put your key down a girl's back for the doubtful privilege of buying her chocolate peppermints. . . .

After the fifth basinful, Miss Stacey drew a gusty breath, wiped her hot face with a manly handkerchief and called it a day.

Nobody was more relieved than Harry Waterhouse.

It was all right for Miss Stacey—she had only herself to pay for.

Harry had three to pay for. It never seemed to occur either to Pearl or Violet to contribute towards any expenditure; and as they invariably stuck together, as thick as thieves, taking the Lomax girls out was apt to be an expensive amusement.

They had extraordinary staying power, too. They could have stayed on the switchback all day and felt none the worse for it. They could sit for hours in a rowing boat at goodness knew what an hour, on the choppiest day, and not feel sick. They could sit the program twice round in cinemas simmering with germs and heat, or keep you talking for hours on corners in the teeth of a January northeaster and apparently keep warm. They never seemed to feel tired and they never had colds, and they never, never dreamed of forking out a ha'penny of their own money if there was a male in sight to pay for them.

It was Pearl who suggested ices, and Violet who laughed their escort to scorn when he hopefully suggested that they were all a bit overheated for ice cream. "Pearl and me can eat ices while the cows come home!" she declared vigorously.

"I don't want to upset your physical equilibrium," he said gallantly.

"We had one, but the wheel came off," Pearl agreed.

So Harry Waterhouse, fingering his wallet and doing some rather apprehensive mental arithmetic, followed in the wake of his charmers and tried to console himself with the reflection that such robustness, shattering in a fiancée, would definitely be an asset in a wife. . . .

"Should you like an ice?" Bob Clough asked Miss Stacey.

"Not for me, thanks. I'd rather go on the Bump-'ems. What about you?"

"Suits me."

"Righty-ho! Come on, Troops!" Miss Stacey made for the pay-box and Bob followed, grinning; grateful for the unglamorous presence of Miss Stacey; grateful for the crowds and the heat and the noise; the violent movement that gave him no chance of thinking coherently about anything. Especially of Rose. . . .

So Bob and Miss Stacey went on the Bump-'ems and the Roundabouts and the Ghost Train, and into the smelly, depressing little Zoo. And a fortuneteller informed Bob he would marry a dark woman and go to South Africa and have seven children, while Miss Stacey learned that a great deal of money was coming to her very shortly and that she would move in Exalted Circles. They weighed themselves and tested their strength by punching a ball and won five packets of very nasty cigarettes between them, which they found a great embarrassment. And at last even Miss Stacey showed signs of wilting and gasped: "What about a cuppa?"

They made their way out of the Fun Fair and along the crowded promenade to a little tea place perched above the swimming pool, its tables shaded from the glare by gay umbrellas of striped orange and black.

Refreshed by tea and cigarettes and by the cool splash of water below, they sat in companionable silence for a while, thinking their own thoughts.

Bob wondered gloomily where Rose had got to, and what she was doing, and Miss Stacey wondered rather guiltily where Ivy had got to, and what *she* was doing.

And after a while, by a natural sequence of ideas, Miss Stacey found herself thinking not of Ivy, but of Rose, and wondering how any girl with eyes in her head could behave so stupidly to a decent fellow like Bob Clough, who was the salt of the earth. And Bob was marveling that a nice body like Miss Stacey could waste a moment's thought on that sniveling little Ivy Carter.

There were no strawberry ices at Pritchett's. There were none at Grigg's. There were no ices at all at Shepherd's.

I'm being thwarted, Audrey thought disconsolately. I'm sure it's bad for me.

Trailing through the hot streets she came to the crowded end of the town, beloved of tourists. And there, like a heavenly messenger, a fat man in a straw hat pushed a barrow, yelling: "Strawberry and vanilla ices! They're lovely!"

"I'll take three, please," she said, fumbling eagerly in her purse.

"That's right, luv. Give the kids a treat."

"They're all for me, thanks."

"Aye, well, you're only young once," agreed the fat man. He winked at her jovially, and in a sudden gust of lightheartedness, Audrey winked back.

She found a secluded corner behind the showcase in front of a jeweler's doorway, and she stood there, licking at the ices with immense relish. They had not been within bowing distance of a strawberry—that was immediately apparent. But they were pink, they were cold, and indubitably they contained seeds of a sort. . . .

Mr. Forsythe pattered past the shop, but his brow was corrugated in thought, and he did not glance at the jeweler's window.

Miss Maddon, escorted, rather surprisingly, by John William Welsh, drifted dreamily down the street. They paused for a moment to gaze silently at barometers, and passed on. Audrey started on her third ice with increased pleasure. I wonder what dear Mrs. Maddon will have to say about *that!* she thought. A nasty common gardener, living in a poky little lodge by the Hall gates. Shades of the Hispano-Suiza! . . . One thing—there won't be room for Mother! We're going to have fun! . . .

"What are you grinning about?" said a voice. "And what on earth are you eating!"

Audrey whirled round.

"Oh, *Frances!* How lovely. I was going to ring you, but I didn't expect you'd have a minute to spare. Are you doing your rounds? And can I come with you and hear all the juicy bits?"

"If you've quite finished your revolting meal," Doctor Frances Hill replied, eying the violently pink concoction with extreme distaste. "I suppose you know that's probably seething with germs?"

"And they keep it under the bed. I know. And I couldn't care less. I've eaten three, and loved them to the last lick!"

She followed her friend to the parking lot; watched in silent admiration while she maneuvered the car out of the crowded place and through the narrow, winding streets, across which children darted and old folks jay-walked with maddening unconcern. I shall never drive as well as Frances, she thought. She always did everything better than me, even at school. Exams. Hockey. Tennis. Being a prefect. . . . And look at us now. Me in a pinned-up, last year's frock, married to a poor parson, with three children and another one coming, and no money and no hope of any, either. And Frances looking like a million dollars, with a handsome doctor-husband, a honey of a car, a lovely modern house run by an efficient housekeeper, and all the trimmings. . . .

[75]

"There's nothing urgent for an hour or two," Frances said, turning the car into a broad, tree-lined avenue. "We'll go home and have some tea. That is if you fancy any tea after all that muck."

"I had to have it," Audrey said somberly. "I mustn't be thwarted."

Frances shot her a swift professional look.

"High time, too," she commented. "Those twins must be rising four."

Drooping a suede-gauntleted hand from the window, she drew the car over to stop outside a green-painted door in a high stonewall. On the door a shining brass plate announced: DR. DONALD HILL. DR. FRANCES HILL; each name followed by a plethora of letters.

They went up through a steeply sloping garden. Rolled gravel, lawn like a bowling green, bright, disciplined herbaceous borders. The room opened onto the garden; a beautifully proportioned room of deep settees, thick pile carpet, bowls of flowers mirrored in polished wood, books galore and the dark gleam of a grand piano.

"No place like home," Frances remarked, smoothing her handsome, already graying head.

"Be it never so humble," Audrey agreed dryly.

"Well, I have to do a lot of entertaining. And this carpet was second-hand, anyway."

"Okay. I'm just being dog-in-the-mangerish. . . . I love this green and cream! I'm saddled with baskets of roses tied up with blue ribbons, and sweet little blue-birds flying madly about amongst them. The vicar-before-last papered it himself, and nobody's been able to afford to tear it off, so far. Fortunately, we live mostly in the kitchen, so it doesn't worry us unduly."

"I'll give you a look-over if you like," Frances said. She pressed a bell, and a smooth, clean woman in a white uniform came smiling in. "Will you bring tea here in half an hour, please, Miss Cole? Come along, Audrey, let's get it over, and then we can take our back hair down."

When they returned, tea was waiting on a low table by the French doors. The room was an unrippled pool of sunlight and green shadow. It smelled of roses and newly baked scones.

"Well, that's that!" Frances said with maddening professional cheerfulness. "Now you can put your feet up on that settee and eat enough for two—or even three!—with a good conscience. While I pick at a sandwich because of my figure."

Audrey swung the blind cord peevishly.

"Of course, *my* figure doesn't matter! I'm just a brood mare! . . . Frances . . . I suppose you couldn't . . . do anything about it?"

"Don't be an ass," Frances said briefly. And then, more kindly: "Somebody has to have the babies."

"But not you," Audrey retorted.

"But not me," Frances agreed after an infinitesimal pause. She put a cushion behind Audrey's back and poured tea. "Cheese and to-mato, I think," she announced, peering at the sandwiches. "And cucumber. And these are scones."

"I may be Exhibit A," Audrey snapped, "but I can still recognize a scone when I see one, thank you, Frances . . . I feel sick," she added, suddenly swept by self-pity. "And I think I'm going to cry."

Frances bit crisply into a cucumber sandwich.

"A lot of this sickness is self-induced, you know. To a certain ex-tent it can be controlled. And if you cry I shall probably slap you fairly hard. It wouldn't be the first time."

Audrey managed a watery grin.

"Do you remember hacking my shins with your hockey stick, be-cause that yellow-haired Games Mistress liked me better than you?"

"People had a habit of liking you better than me," Frances re-plied in a noncommittal tone. "Andrew did."

"Oh, well, that was a long time ago. We were only kids," Audrey said uncomfortably.

"Yes. We were only kids. Have another scone."

"And look where it's got me!" It was an effort to sound tragic be-cause, in spite of regretting the strawberry ices, and feeling sick, and wanting to cry, Audrey was enjoying her tea, and fully intended to eat more than enough for two—or even three.

"I am looking. It looks pretty good to me."

Audrey glanced curiously at Frances.

She sat in full sunlight, gazing over the rim of her cup into the gay brightness of the garden. The linen suit was perfectly cut, the stockings sheer, the suede shoes immaculate. Her well-kept hands curved round the bowl of the cup, steady as a rock. There was not a hair out of place in the graying, upswept curls. She had big bones, big features: handsome rather than beautiful. The horn-rimmed glasses framed dark, intelligent eyes beneath a smooth, broad brow. Handsome, clever, successful Frances, sitting in the rose-scented coolness of her green-and-cream drawing room—why should she stare into the poverty-stricken muddle of Audrey's life and say: "It looks pretty good to me!"

"It's easy to talk," Audrey said, "when you've got everything."

Slowly Frances turned her head. Audrey was shocked to see the dark eyes full of pain. But her voice was quiet and controlled as ever.

"People are always likening love to gardens," she said in her rather precise manner. "The garden of love. The garden of flowers. Roses, roses all the way, and all the rest of it. There's an awful lot of rot talked about love. . . . If love is like anything, it's like the earth: good black soil, teeming with life. Flowers come and go, and they're beautiful. But they couldn't bloom without soil. There's more beauty in a handful of black, crumbly, fruitful earth than in any bed of roses. . . . It holds the secret of life, the whole meaning of existence. . . . You've got it, this beauty, this miracle. You and Andrew hold it in your hands. All the beauty of the world. All the wisdom. All the boundless happiness, the sweet suffering; the laughter and trust and hope and fear. . . . All life. It's yours. Yours and Andrew's. . . . Are you surprised it looks pretty good to me?" She flicked a crumb from her lap. "Another cup of tea?" she said evenly.

Audrey shuffled uncomfortably.

"But Frances, surely. . . . You and Don. . . ."

"I'm very fond of Don," Frances said calmly. "I'm proud of his looks and his brains, and I'm very grateful for my nice home—though that's my doing as much as his. We earn quite a lot of money between us. We make a good team. We respect each other. I'm not grumbling. I didn't marry for love. I loved somebody else—somebody I couldn't have—and Don knew. I made no secret of it. I married because I wanted children. . . . Only I can't have them, you see."

"*Frances*—are you sure?"

"Quite. I've been into it fairly thoroughly, I can assure you! . . . So it's a good thing Andrew did prefer you, isn't it? It would have been such a waste. Such a shocking waste."

Audrey stared at her hands. At the small red scar where she had burned her thumb on the stove. At the roughness of the forefinger that never would come perfectly clean. . . .

"Frances. . . . I'm sorry, but I've got to know. Do you still feel that way? About Andy, I mean?"

Frances considered this dispassionately.

"No, I don't think so, Audrey. I shall always be fond of Andrew. He's a terribly nice person, isn't he? But I'm unfertile ground, you see, so it's all pointless. . . . You don't like that, do you? It's not nice. . . . Believe me, my dear, Nature's very far from nice. Love isn't nice. Love's nothing more than the overpowering urge to produce children. Sorry to smash your pretty dreams, but you might as well face it."

Audrey swung her feet to the ground, smoothed last year's green-and-white voile which was getting decidedly crumpled.

"There's more to it than that," she said soberly. "You're clever, Frances, but you don't know everything. . . . You might just as well say that a ship has no other purpose than getting you from one shore to another. But there's fun and happiness and sheer delight in sailing a ship, even if you never get to the place you set out for. Frances. . . . I'm sorry about you, but you've got it wrong. You've taken the truth and twisted it somehow, so that it looks different. . . . I can't explain, I'm not clever enough. But I just *know*."

"Well, go on thinking that way; it's probably good for you. Certainly it's good for the population." She glanced at her wrist watch, got up and stretched. "I must throw you out now, it's nearly surgery time. I have my uses in this pretty garden of life. I may not be good earth but I'm a nice solid rock for sick people to lean against. . . . Be a good girl and do all your doctor tells you—though you should know all the answers by this time. You have Cartwright, don't you? He's a good man. Nice and handy, too. You'll be all right. I shouldn't wonder if you had a dozen before you've finished—lucky you!"

They went down the sloping garden together and kissed casually, as women do. The green-painted door closed behind Audrey. It was like a door closing in her life. Suddenly she felt breathless and frightened, as if she had narrowly escaped some frightful danger.

I want Andy! she thought.

She began to hurry towards the nearest bus stop.

She had forgotten about feeling sick and she no longer wanted to cry. She just wanted Andy. . . .

Walter Forsythe pattered along the crowded street, dodging erratic perambulators, truculent iron spades and melting ice-cream cones. He dodged and edged and muttered; glaring at people who bumped into him; glaring at people into whom he bumped, even while raising his hat in punctilious apology.

Mr. Forsythe had taken the bus into town for the express purpose of having a word with his old friend Booker, who kept the music shop on the corner of Market Street; and now he was regretting it. For not only had he been confronted among the pianos and the gramophone records by a perfectly strange young man, but he had learned to his astonishment and dismay that Booker had taken unto himself a new young wife, and was honeymooning with her among the green hills and silver waterfalls of Bettws-y-coed.

And, as if this news had not been shattering enough, the strange young man had given it as his opinion that Booker was off his rocker —and him with one leg in the grave; and had rounded off the conversation with such a lewd and luscious wink that Mr. Forsythe had hurried from the shop in deep offense.

Dodging and recoiling and glaring and raising his hat, Mr. Forsythe precipitated his small, dapper person down the crowded street and out into the comparatively open spaces of the Lower Front.

It was cooler here than in the street, but still too hot for comfort. The glare off the sea was blinding. The noise was terrific. Children yelled in the shallows. The vendors of ice cream, shrimps and cockles shouted their wares. The funny man of The Swallows Concert Party was approaching apoplexy in his efforts to control a vast, sweating, enthusiastic audience who were packing up their troubles in their old kit bags, and not caring how flat they became in the process. Boatmen besought Mr. Forsythe to take a trip round the lighthouse. Photographers pestered him to pose. A fat woman pushed a bunch of inflated balloons in his face. A young harpy with crimson talons and no eyebrows shrilled the perfections of a lurid pile of pink-and-white rock. An elderly gentleman with a green frock coat and a frightful, matted beard, demanded to know what Mr. Forsythe intended to do should his soul be required of him that night; adding with gloomy relish that in the midst of life we were in death. And over all the mechanical music of the Fun Fair laid its inescapable blight.

Mr. Forsythe pattered steadily along, wishing he had never left the green peace of the Good Fortune Tea Rooms.

One leg in the grave, indeed! . . . Booker was two years younger than himself; and if anyone had a leg in any grave, it was not Walter Forsythe. No, indeed!

Nevertheless, he certainly felt a great deal older than he had felt an hour ago. He had a pain in his left knee and the beginnings of a headache, and the cucumber he had eaten at lunch, so unwisely, was definitely not agreeing with him. He was very hot and his feet ached and he wanted a cup of tea.

That's it, he told himself. I want a cup of tea. That's all that's wrong with me.

All along the Lower Front a number of small tea shops flourished exceedingly, their rooms filled to capacity and the pavements in front broken out into a rash of little iron tables under colored umbrellas.

Mr. Forsythe directed his aching feet towards Maisie's Place, which seemed less crowded than most.

He was about to be seated when he noticed a familiar hat bent over a teapot. Its wearer was peering inside, intent on adding the exact amount of hot water.

Mr. Forsythe was no more familiar with the garments of women than most men. Nevertheless, one can hardly sit within touching distance of two bunches of bobbing red cherries and a brown velvet bow, Sunday after Sunday for the best part of three years, without becoming aware of them.

The hat, as Mr. Forsythe knew very well, belonged to Phoebe Braithwaite. . . .

He wanted to sit down, he wanted a cup of tea, and he wanted to speak to Phoebe. The time, the place and the loved one—in a manner of speaking—all together. Was ever moment more propitious!

Mr. Forsythe did not hesitate. He walked smartly past Maisie's Place and jumped onto the first bus that came along. . . .

All the way back to the Good Fortune Tea Rooms he blamed himself for this rash act. It had been a heaven-sent opportunity to get what he had to say to Phoebe off his chest. But it was too late now.

Tomorrow he would clip the hedge that divided Number Four from Number Five. Phoebe, no doubt, would bring her knitting to the door, as she often did, and he would work the conversation round as naturally as possible.

Having come to this decision Mr. Forsythe felt immensely relieved and hopped off the bus in quite a sprightly manner.

One leg in the grave, indeed! . . .

All he needed was a cup of hot, steaming, fragrant tea, and Beatrice Fortune would give him one.

Strictly speaking, only morning coffee, lunch and high tea were catered for; but he'd known Bee Fortune a good many years now. Twenty? Thirty? . . . He couldn't remember. Why, once he had imagined himself in love with her!

But she had been the Vicar's daughter then, and he a mere gangling bank clerk, with nothing to offer except his heart. . . . And then, of course, there had been that business over Fred, and then the Vicar had died and Bee had taken Fred away. And soon after that he had met poor Louise. . . .

Twenty years? Thirty? . . .

Good heavens, how old that made him feel! One leg in the grave. . . .

He could see Fred now, lying in a deck chair. And by his side Mrs. Maddon reclined with her feet up and her hands, still genteelly encased in gloves, clasped in her lap. They were both fast asleep. Giving thanks for this small mercy, Mr. Forsythe pattered across the lawn in search of solace.

"When did you first know you loved me?" Miss Maddon said dreamily.

John William Welsh pondered deeply.

"I reckon it were four years ago, near as no matter," he decided finally.

"And you never told me until yesterday!" Miss Maddon reproached him softly. "Oh, John William!"

"When did you?" he asked, gruff with shyness.

Miss Maddon hesitated. If she told him the truth and said: "Yesterday," wouldn't that make her seem rather cheap? As if she had jumped at the chance of marrying him? Which, of course, she had.

She would have jumped at the chance of marrying almost any man in order to get away from her mother.

Incredible as it may seem, at thirty-eight Miss Maddon had never had a lover; never been kissed by a man; never had the slightest liberty taken with her maiden modesty. She was not unattractive to look at. She had dark hair and eyes, a pale, clear skin, a thin body that just escaped angularity, and a pleasant voice. Had they been aware of her existence, a number of men might have thought her desirable. The trouble was, she had lived her whole life in the deep shadow of Mrs. Maddon's gentility, and nobody had noticed she was there.

"Can't you think on, luv?" John William prompted. His plain, brown, furrowed face bent to her kindly.

"No," she whispered, seizing gratefully at this life line. "No—I can't think on."

They sat on an iron seat on the Lower Front, in the full glare of the sun. People surged on every hand. Voices shouted, sang, screamed and scolded. They sat in the midst of pandemonium, wrapped in the isolation of their love, and were happy.

John William squeezed her hand, then lifted and gazed at it with reverence. By contrast with his own calloused, earth-stained palm it looked fragile as a flower.

"A lady's hand," said John William weightily. "Too good for my owd paw. Don't seem right as it should have to sweep and wash and scrub for the likes of me."

Miss Maddon cradled the paw on her lap, and smiled tenderly. "It won't be the first time I've swept and scrubbed and washed, my dear. I just want to be your wife, and live in the lodge by the Hall gates with you, for the rest of my life."

"It's a bit dark," he worried, "an' inconvenient, so me mother allus used to say. An' there's too much heavy, owd-fashioned stuff in it. An' t'stove doesn't draw as well as it might."

"I like tackling problems," Miss Maddon said happily.

"I've asked the Colonel time an' time again to have summat done about yon stove, but he allus puts me off. He's hard put to it to mek ends meet, what with all this taxation an' things being the price they are."

"I'll tackle the Colonel, don't you worry, dear."

[83]

"I don't rightly know what would happen if the Colonel had to pack up. Reckon I'd be out of a job."

"Not for long. And anyway, we'd have each other."

John William turned his stolid, weathered face towards her, and it was filled with love and humility.

"Reckon I've got nerve, asking a lady like you. . . ."

"I'm no fine lady, John William," Miss Maddon said firmly. "Let's get this straight right at the start, and then we shall know where we are. . . . Mother likes to pretend we've come down in the world since Father died; but it's not true, for we were never up! To hear Mother talk, you'd think we were County folks living in a great house full of servants and I don't know what. The truth is, my father kept a corn chandler's shop in Rochdale, and he drank like a fish! The car Mother brags about was used mostly as a delivery truck, and we never had a servant at all except a charwoman now and then, when Mother's veins were bad. . . . As long as ever I can remember I've known how to wash and scrub and bake and polish, and I've had to do it, too! I can make my own clothes, and quite a lot of yours. I can whiten ceilings and paper walls, and I know how to use a soldering iron and mend fuses, and if things come unstuck, I don't yell for a man, I mend 'em myself. . . . I'm a working woman, born of working-class parents, John William, and I'm going to make a success of being a working-man's wife. I'm sick of teaching. I want a home of my own. And the sooner the better, John William," she added, her voice quavering but valiant.

There! . . . It was off her chest, and they knew where they were!

Had she lost something by her honesty? Some shade of reverence, of worshipful gratitude?

Maybe.

But she had gained something, too. She felt it in the urgency of his hands, heard it in the quickened breathing, felt it in the way his arm went round her, pulling her against him quite roughly. . . .

For weal or for woe, Miss Maddon had emerged into the broad daylight of ordinary life. And the view seemed to her beautiful past the telling.

Miss Fortune had dried his clothes and pressed them. Les looked respectable again.

He thought he would take the puppy into the garden and play with it; but very gently this time, much more patiently.

Old Crackerjack sat before the fire with the puppy in his arms, still asleep in the blanket.

"Thanks for looking after him," Les said. "I'll take him now."

"Sh!" Jack frowned and held the puppy closer.

"Come on, Jack, give the puppy to Leslie. It's his dog, you know," Miss Fortune said brightly.

"Jack's puppy," said Jack stolidly.

Les put out his hand, and Jack struck at it swiftly.

"Hi, you!" Les exclaimed, nursing the hand under his arm.

The puppy woke, yawned and stretched deliciously. Jack's face broke into an adoring smile.

"Now Jack," said Miss Fortune, "you heard what I said. The puppy belongs to Leslie. Put it down on the floor at once, and let it go to its master." She smiled at him kindly. "You and I are going to have a nice cup of tea and some cherry cake."

A hurt, bewildered look came over Jack's face. He looked pleadingly at Miss Fortune, but she gave a peremptory nod. He unwrapped the puppy from its warm blanket and put it gently on the floor. It began to yelp.

"Come on, Scottie," Les encouraged it. "Here, good boy! Come on!"

The puppy staggered a few steps towards him. Then its back legs collapsed and it crouched there, whining and shivering. Les picked it up, cradled it in his arms. It licked his chin, but it was restless and unhappy.

"Careful!" Jack said angrily.

"I know. It's my puppy, isn't it? I know about my own puppy."

"Jack's puppy."

"It's not yours. Mrs. Mitchum gev him to me. Didn't she, Miss Fortune?"

"That's right, Leslie, she did. But quite honestly, if it were mine, I should give it back to Mrs. Mitchum before I got fond of it. You see, Leslie, it's a very delicate puppy. I don't say it might not grow up strong and healthy, mind you, but it would need a great deal of care and attention. I'm sure your mother would rather you had a healthy puppy. Come, now, don't cry, a big boy like you!"

"If I give it back, their Daniel will put it in a bucket. Mrs. Mitchum said so," Les snuffled.

Jack rose to his feet and grabbed the puppy.

"Not in a bucket!" he roared, red in the face with wrath. He wrapped the puppy in its blanket again and began to rock it gently on his knees. "Jack make it well. Jack's puppy."

The puppy stopped yelling and lay quietly on its back. It chewed Jack's finger, stared up into his face, relaxed and trustful.

Les watched it miserably. It was *his* puppy. . . .

Mr. Forsythe came into the kitchen, wiping his forehead with a handkerchief of dazzling purity.

"Ah, there you are, Beatrice! I've just escaped from that awful town. I couldn't stand it another moment. The heat! And the noise! . . ." His eyes rested hopefully on the teapot and the brown, delicious-looking cake studded with cherries. "I think I must be getting old," he said pathetically. "One leg in the grave!"

Miss Fortune smiled and poured milk into a cup. Her placid voice soothed the three ruffled male creatures who cluttered up her kitchen.

"What nonsense, Walter! What you want is a cup of tea. Jack and I were just going to have one. Leslie's had his. He fell in the water and had to be dried off, so he missed going to the Fun Fair with the other boys. I was just thinking, there's still time to go, if he caught the next bus down. What do you say, dear?"

Les looked at the floor, his face red with embarrassment, and Miss Fortune smiled sympathetically. She reached for her purse.

"Just in case your budget doesn't work out," she said, slipping a bright half-crown into his hand.

"Bless me," said Mr. Forsythe. "Mine never did, I well remember." He added another half-crown. "And mind you get all the lads back in time for the singing," he warned. "Don't forget, you're all to meet at the bus stop by six-thirty. Mr. Welsh is going to wait for you, so see you don't give him any trouble."

"Oh, golly! . . . I say, thanks ever so!"

Without another glance at the puppy Les scampered off across the lawn and down the lane, leaping onto the bus as it moved off, whistling happily as he clumped up the stairs followed by abuse from the conductor.

Five whole blooming shillings to spend! Nearly as much as Ron Field had had at the very start of the day! Ron would be spent right out by now, and Les would treat him to the Bump-'ems instead of Ron treating *him*. It made Les feel important, restored his self-respect. He pushed behind him the thought of the puppy lying contentedly in Jack's arms, and he jingled the two fat silver coins in his pocket.

4

BRIAN braked sharply, turned off the engine and lit a cigarette.

"Like it?" he grinned.

Rose blew out a long breath. She unwound the pink scarf and shook her head like a little animal.

"I never knew anything could go so fast! I don't seem able to catch me breath back, and I feel deaf. . . . Where are we?"

"I haven't a clew."

They gazed around, rather awed by the sunlit solitude, the silence, the feeling that they had been catapulted into a completely strange world.

It was a world entirely their own. As far as the eye could see there was nothing but moor and sea and sky. Not a human habitation broke the undulating line of land. Not a sail, not a drift of smoke moved on the dark blue water. Not a bird's voice sounded in the silence. Not a wing beat across the cloudless sky.

The bracken was breast-high, lordly and strong, its spreading fronds turned golden at the tips. The smell of it was hot and exciting.

They went across close, springing turf to the cliff's edge. The cliff was very high, falling sheer into the sea.

They stood silently. The colored world spread all around them, high and deep and wide; empty, enchanted. The spell enfolded them, touched them with majesty, so that they knew how small they were, how alone and helpless, of how little account.

I wish Bob was here, Rose thought. And Brian thought: Beryl, I want you. My love, my dear love. . . . Knowing her false and

[87]

worthless, yet longing suddenly for the known and familiar, the beauty he could touch and hold and understand.

Their hands reached out; met and clung together as children clasp hands when they are afraid. It was Bob's hand and Beryl's hand they reached for; and as if each were aware of it, they turned and briefly smiled, swung their clasped hands lightly and let them fall apart.

"Quiet, isn't it!" Rose whispered.

He laughed down at her, the distorted mask of his face hiding a sudden compunction, a tenderness he barely comprehended.

"I don't suppose you've any idea how beautiful you look!"

She gazed up at him, pleased and startled.

"Do you really think so? Ee, I'm glad!"

Had she drawn back, afraid, distrustful; had she turned coy at his words, his mood might have snapped; tenderness have turned to intolerance, liking to lust. But she stood there smiling, happy in her beauty, her innocence, her touching youngness, grateful to him for his tribute. Her sweet gray eyes were filled with friendliness for him.

This is the girl I brought here to seduce! he thought wryly; and knew himself powerless.

"I've got to get back," she said, half regretfully.

"Not before tea," he protested.

"Tea? . . . Where do you think we're going to get tea in a place like this! There's not a house for miles."

"There's a tea basket in the back of the car."

"Oh! . . . Oh, how kind of you to think of it! You didn't ought to have bothered. But really, I ought to be going. They'll be wondering where I've got to."

Brian threw a pebble over the cliff's edge. The silence took it, swallowed it.

"By 'they' I suppose you mean that imitation thundercloud in the gents' natty suiting, that you were in such a hurry to meet this morning?"

Rose looked faintly troubled.

"That's Bob. Bob Clough. He's a grand fellow."

"Your young man?"

She hesitated. She blushed delightfully.

"I don't rightly know how things are between Bob and me. We had a few words this morning. . . ."

"Over me?"

Rose slid the cheap silver bracelet up and down her arm.

"I kept 'em all waiting, you see," she evaded. "I shouldn't have done it, I know, but that weren't enough to send him off t'deep end like that. I reckon Bob's worried a bit. He's got a lot to worry him. Everything's on his shoulders, like. The farm, an' his father lying there helpless, an' that stepmother of his that's no better than she should be. And then there's his two younger brothers. Ben's a wild spark if ever there was one. And Hugh's an idle young monkey.— So it's all on Bob's shoulders as you might say."

"You certainly might!"

She talked like a middle-aged woman, he thought, amused, yet pitiful. And yet she was ageless. Younger than Beryl had ever been in her life, probably. Older than Beryl would ever be. . . .

They sat in a bracken-ringed hollow and had their tea.

He offered her a cigarette, which she refused.

"I do smoke sometimes," she assured him anxiously. "Only some-how——"

"What?"

"Well, somehow I think it meks me look a bit daft."

He lay back, laughing, hands clasped behind his head. He knew his face was grotesque in the searching light, but he did not care. Rose would be neither callous nor overpitiful. She would accept it. Just as she accepted Bob's troubles with the farm and the two young brothers and the stepmother who was no better than she should be. Just as she accepted her own poverty, the too tight dress stretched across her small, pointed breasts. . . . His eyes rested on them now with pleasure, but not with desire.

"So you're going to be a farmer's wife?"

"I hope so," she said simply.

"And work hard all your life—is that it?"

"I shall do that anyhow, I reckon, what with the shop, an' Dad being queer, an' all."

"Not necessarily."

"How d'you mean?"

He blew three perfect smoke rings, eyes screwed up against the glare. Steady, Barker! he thought. Keep on the beam!

"I mean. . . . You might, after all, take a fancy to somebody else. Somebody who didn't have to get up at crack of dawn and clump about wet fields until he was too tired to do anything but fall into bed. Somebody who wasn't hedged about with young brothers and stepmothers and sick fathers, and masses of creatures with foot-and-mouth disease, or staggers, or what-have-you. . . . Somebody who'd buy you a lot of pretty frocks and take you places: London, Paris, even Hollywood—why not? . . . A nice, quiet, fairly respectable Raf type, for instance, who might make quite a decent living writing scripts, even if his face wasn't photogenic any more. . . ."

In the silence that followed Brian blew another smoke ring; watched it widen and waver and finally disappear.

He turned his head, squinting through the glare at her sweet, un-ruffled profile. What the hell! . . . he thought. She doesn't even know she's been proposed to! And part of him added: Thank God. And part—the greater part—knew a forlorn emptiness in the middle of which his heart lay like an unconsidered stone.

But suddenly her eyes swerved to his; startled, incredulous. And again that slow, delicious blush.

"Don't talk so daft!" she exclaimed, softly but vigorously. And she laughed. He laughed. Their laughter mingled and went forth and died together on the silence.

"Tell me about you," she said.

"There's nothing worth telling."

But he found himself telling her, all the same. . . . His childhood in the Worcestershire market town where his father was a doctor. His school days and college days. The row there had been when he had preferred films to medicine. His fun, his fantastic struggles as a film extra. The staggering excitement of being noticed, given a small part, mentioned by the critics. The heady importance of being signed up. . . . He even told her about Beryl; tried to convey the sleek, cool loveliness, the poise, the groomed, glamorous enchant-ment she had thrown about him, and the ruthless breaking of that enchantment—but not, alas, his longing for her beauty. . . .

He tried to stop then.

But he couldn't stop. Now he must tell the whole thing. Now he must speak of the unspeakable. . . .

The crash. . . .

The awful, blinding light and the intolerable heat, and the little navigator screaming for his mother. . . . Beatty scrabbling along the ground with no legs . . . the queer, dead, fortunate heap that was Donaldson. . . .

And then the nightmare seized him again; flung him on his face, sobbing, his body writhing under the searing lash of memory suddenly become actual.

Light scalded his eyeballs. Fire licked about him; shot upwards, roaring into a scarlet column of terror. The little navigator screamed and screamed again until he thought his eardrums would burst. "Shut up!" he sobbed, tearing at the smooth turf. "Oh, Christ, shut up! Shut up! . . ."

And then he felt her arms around him; felt himself pulled upwards until his head lay on her breast. Her breast was soft and firm, her arms strong and heavenly kind. She held him as presently she would hold the babies she would bear; close and safe against the bourn of her body, one strong little hand cupping his ruined face and her cheek resting against his head.

And it seemed that she held not only himself, but Donaldson and Beatty and Kent and the little navigator with the freckled face. She held them all in her arms, together again; whole and silent and at peace. . . .

When the trembling was quite gone, Brian sat up and smiled at her, dried his eyes, unashamed, and smoothed his hair.

"Bad show," he apologized, lighting another cigarette.

"It's all right," she said softly.

They sat for a long time in silence.

"I ought to get back," Rose remembered.

He got to his feet at once, pulled her up after him. He bent and kissed the hand that had cupped his face so kindly. I wish I were good like Rose, he thought suddenly, childishly. I wish I hadn't done the things I have done. . . . No, I don't. It's been fun. . . . Oh, hell, I don't know what I wish! I don't even know if it matters. I've never thought about it much. I wish I knew more about it. . . . Perhaps if I talked to some parson. . . . That one at Staving didn't look a bad sort, but it's too late now. . . . He kissed her rough little hand again. "Black sheep saying thank you!" he said.

"Go on with you!" Rose exclaimed. And this time she did actually give him a little push. They smiled at each other and went back to the car.

The engine spluttered and roared, settled into a steady hum. It died away into the distance. A bird beat up from the bracken in alarm, circled the air a few times and dropped again from sight.

Moor and sea and sky once more lay silent, enchanted, wrapped in a timeless solitude, untroubled and serene.

Phoebe Braithwaite put twopence under the plate and left the welcome shade of the striped umbrella for the hard glare of the Lower Front.

Phew—it was hot! That was the worst of tea; it made you hotter than ever, just for a bit. Still, there was nothing like a cup of tea, say what you might.

She wiped her steaming face and exchanged a few words of badinage with the cockle seller, whom she had known from childhood. She bought half a dozen balloons. They came in handy for the neighbors' children.

A pity Walter had gone past without seeing her. They could have had a nice tea together and a bit of a chat. She'd called out, but he hadn't heard. For a moment she'd wondered if she'd been mistaken. But that was Walter all right! She'd have known his back in a thousand.

Silly to mind, really. They could drink a cup of tea together any day of the week. Still, she was alone, and he was alone; and why be alone when you could be together?

Phoebe hadn't started out alone. There'd been a whole crowd of them on the bus. Joe Peck and his wife and daughter, Miss Maddon, John William Welsh, young Henry Fiddler and Sam Scholey and herself.

There'd been some talk of the Fun Fair. Joe Peck was all for it, but those two women of his had scotched that. Phoebe would have given a good deal to see them two owd buzzards coming down t'water shoot! But they'd gone off shopping at finish. Joe's wife, it seemed, was set on buying a new hat, and Joe'd got to fork out for it. Somebody'd given the one she'd got on a bash with the cricket ball. Pity, thought Phoebe, it hadn't given her head a good bash, an' all! Joe was a handful, and no two ways about it; but a fat lot of use it was for Addie Peck and that Minnie of hers going about with faces like fiddles, forever in their blacks, as if they'd just come from one funeral and were off to another. It was enough to drive a man to drink. Not that Joe needed a deal of driving.

Yet Phoebe could look back forty years and remember Addie Peck —Addie Simmonds she was then—as the prettiest girl in the village, and head over heels in love with Joe, as he was with her. They'd had to get wed a bit sudden, like, but nobody had held that against them. Queer how that Minnie should have been the result, and the only result, at that! A plain, awkward child she'd been, and she'd grown into a plain, awkward woman. And young Addie had become a shrew, and Joe had taken to the bottle. . . . Nay! thought Phoebe, the things life does to folks! She sighed and wiped her hot face again. I reckon I'll get the bus back. Even talking to Mrs. Maddon's better than talking to nobody.

"You've got a lucky face, dear."

The voice issued from a hut painted in violent colors, with the name MADAME VERONA in black and gold. A bead curtain clashed faintly in the doorway. A grimy claw covered in rings pushed the curtain aside, disclosing a gray plate of a face pierced by two black holes and a magenta gash.

"Come in and hear yer luck, dear. Two and a kick, and an extra bob for the crystal."

No fool like an owd fool! Phoebe thought, as she pushed her way into the hut.

The hut smelt strongly of cheap scent, but not strongly enough to disguise the reek of the fried fish with which Madame had recently been sustaining her psyche. Indeed, a vinegar bottle still stood on the dirty little table, and the seer was even now pursuing operations on a hollow tooth with the aid of a bobby pin. This she now replaced in her head, smiling professionally at Phoebe, who was blowing into her best kid gloves before submitting her hands to fate.

"There's something you want very badly, but things aren't turning out like you hoped," Madame Verona muttered, staring into Phoebe's fat palms.

Well, of course that was a thing you might safely say to almost anybody, Phoebe thought. Still, it made her sit up a bit!

"Will it come right in the end?"

Madame sucked her teeth loudly.

"I don't see it," she admitted. "I think there's a disappointment in store for you. You're crying for the moon, dear, that's what you're doing. You've got good health, a nice home and enough money, but you're not satisfied. You're crying for the moon, and you won't get it." She sucked her teeth and leaned back, staring glassily at Phoebe.

"What else?" Phoebe inquired.

"What more do you want! Good health and enough money and a roof over your head—and all for half-a-crown!"

"I knew all that, without paying out half-a-crown," Phoebe said loudly, with rising color.

"There's nothing else written in your hands. I can't read what's not there, can I, dear? I could look in the crystal for another bob."

"No you don't!" Phoebe picked up her purse and gloves. "And I'm not paying no half-crown for that swindle, so you needn't think it! I'll give you a bob and not a penny more—an' think yourself lucky!" She slapped a shilling on the table and glared at Madame Verona, bracing herself for a row.

But Madame seemed to bear no ill will. She pocketed the shilling without a flicker of resentment in her flat, gray face. She groped for the bobby pin and recommenced operations on the hollow tooth.

"Hard to please, aren't you, dear? I reckon you've got all you want in this world—bar the moon. . . ."

Halfway through the bead curtain, Phoebe stopped and faced the woman again.

"This disappointment . . . can't you tell me what it is?"

"Another one-and-six," Madame said nippily.

Phoebe opened her purse and slapped the money down on the table. Madame whisked it into her pocket without delay. Her dead black eyes slid over the homely features, the stout figure, the work-stained hands grasping the bulging purse.

"Reckon it's summat to do with one of yer children, dear. More I cannot say. You a widder?"

Phoebe nearly burst with wrath.

"Yes, I am a widder, these many years! And I haven't got any children, an' what's more I never had none!"

Madame Verona was not in the least put out.

She transferred the bobby pin to pastures new, and her only comment was: "You should worry, dear! I got seven, and a precious set of baskets they are, too! You ain't missed nothing."

"What about a dip?" demanded Miss Stacey.

"No trunks," Bob objected.

"We can hire things. Come on, me for the briny! It looks marvelous. We'll go in off the top board. I'll show you my swallow dive. You'll laugh yourself sick and I shan't mind a bit."

"Water's often cold when it's hot on shore."

Once in the water, however, he began to enjoy himself immensely. Miss Stacey was a fast swimmer and it was pleasant to discover that he could beat her. The swallow dive made them hilarious. They began to fool about in the water like a couple of adolescents. Miss Stacey splashed and screamed, Bob splashed and shouted. He seized Miss Stacey by the shoulders and attempted to duck her. Miss Stacey proved unexpectedly agile and it was Bob who took the ducking. They spluttered and laughed and pushed each other about. They flung themselves full length on the hot, white tiles above the swimming pool. Miss Stacey pushed Bob back into the water with a mighty splash and Bob rose gasping to the surface, seized Miss Stacey by the legs and pulled her in after him.

"Oo! . . . Grand, isn't it!" Miss Stacey cried. "Nothing like sea water for washing your cares away. At this moment I feel about sixteen, and I haven't got a worry in the world!"

But even as she spoke her eyes lighted on a familiar figure standing on the promenade above the swimming pool, gazing down at her with deep reproach. Oh, dear! thought Miss Stacey, who had forgotten all about Ivy.

Assuming a nonchalance she was far from feeling, she waved to Ivy, mutely inviting her to join them in the water. But Ivy's narrow little face stared bleakly down at her, unresponsive; and after a moment it turned and was gone, lost in the crowd.

In spite of the hot sun Miss Stacey shivered.

"I think I'm for in."

"Oh, rot! A day like this you could stay in for hours!" Bob protested.

"No. I go cold suddenly, and then I'm finished. But don't you come out. I ought to go and find Ivy Carter."

"Whatever for?"

"Oh, well. . . . I feel sort of responsible for her."

"Don't talk so daft," Bob said bluntly. "A fine lass like you wasting your time on a sticky little image like yon! Anyhow, she was with George Fiddler. I saw 'em."

Miss Stacey suffered and instantly squashed a faint, disturbing jealousy.

"She's fond of me, at least," she said defensively.

"Aye, same as a leech might be fond of you."

Miss Stacey pulled herself up to the hot white tiles again, slicked the water out of her cropped hair till it lay close and smooth as a seal's coat.

"Sometimes," she said slowly, "I wish the war had never stopped."

"Then what did you want to leave the Army for?"

"I was demobbed, of course."

"You could have signed on again."

She stared at him stupidly.

"But. . . . There's Dad to think of."

"Well, you've got three sisters. Isn't that enough for him?"

"But they're all going to get married!"

"All the better. Three homes for him to choose from. If ever a woman were free to please herself, I should think it's you!"

She stood there staring, shivering in spite of the sun. Her arms were goose-pimpled, her face and neck unbecomingly scorched, her thick, strong legs planted wide apart on the wet tiles.

Bob thought how pretty Rose would look after a swim.

And suddenly he'd had enough of Miss Stacey. She was a good sort, but she wasn't a woman. . . .

"Well, I'll have another five minutes, I think. So long. Be seeing you."

He plunged back into the water and began to swim to the other side.

Miss Stacey went into the cubicle and began to towel vigorously.

Her face no longer looked stupid. It shone with hope, with relief, with a dazed astonishment.

It never even *occurred* to me! she thought, incredulous. Never once! . . . Tomorrow I'll go. I'll go straight away, before I start thinking. I'll go. . . . I won't take any notice if they kick up a fuss. They shan't stop me. . . . I'll get my stripes again in no time. I might try for a Commission. . . . I can stay in for years. I can stay in all my life! . . . Oh, boy! rejoiced Miss Stacey, scrubbing away at her heavy thighs. Look out, you boys, here I come. Old Staylace—remember? . . . *Left, Left, Left,* right, *left.* She'll be wearing pink pajamas when she comes, pom, pom. She'll be wearing pink pajamas when she comes. . . .

As she made her way from the swimming pool along the promenade, Miss Stacey marched with a military air, head up, back straight, arms swinging from the shoulders, so that several people smiled and turned to watch her.

Miss Stacey didn't see them. And if she had she wouldn't have cared. She saw nothing but a long, gray-brown column of girls beating the dust up with their Service shoes, swinging their arms, singing. As far as the eye could see the column stretched; before, behind. It was all Miss Stacey ever wanted to see. . . .

Ivy glanced slyly up at George Fiddler. Her sharp little elbow rapped into his ribs.

"Did you *see* them?"

"Aye, I saw 'em," George replied stolidly.

"Slapping each other about in the water, and him pulling her by the legs that way! Disgusting I call it." Her pink rabbit-nose quivered horridly. "I never thought I'd live to see the day!" It was a favorite remark of her mother's and came in very aptly at this point. "Never thought I'd live to see the day, I didn't!" she repeated, relishing the phrase.

"Well, you a'nt dead yet," George pointed out.

Ivy began to cry.

George stared in front of him. He was fed up.

He was having a lousy day. He had paid for tea and cakes at the Kardomah and had discovered that Ivy's appetite was out of all proportion to her size. His best silk handkerchief was in a shocking state. And his key was still down Ivy's back.

Rather a high price, George felt, to pay for the consolidation of any position.

And to cap all, Ivy had sniveled and whined for the best part of an hour and a half.

Ivy continued to cry.

And indeed, she now had good cause for depression. For it was time, and more than time that she spent a penny, and she had nothing less than half-a-crown in her purse. True, she might ask George Fiddler to lend her a penny, but Ivy's whole nature revolted against so unmaidenly a gesture. In any case, they were walking in the wrong direction for the Ladies' and Ivy lacked courage to suggest turning back.

With Miss Stacey no such problem would have arisen. And how Ivy yearned at that moment for Miss Stacey! But she hardened her heart. No one who behaved in so loose and abandoned a fashion as Miss Stacey had behaved in the swimming pool had any claim on Ivy's devotion. And with a man, an' all! . . .

Men were so horrid. They had no consideration for a girl. Look at George Fiddler. She had wasted the whole afternoon on him, and all she had got out of it—bar her tea and a few chocolates and the use of his hanky—was a beastly great key down her back, which was even now causing her a good deal of discomfort. Without so much as a by your leave, he had slapped the cold, hard thing down her shrinking back, and there it was. And there it seemed likely to stay unless she could find some privacy in which to unburden herself of it.

The courage of desperation came to Ivy.

"Well, so long, George," she said. "I can't stop with you any longer. I got a date."

Well, that was okay by George. Not that he believed it for a moment, but it was okay by him. He'd had about as much of Ivy as he could stand for one day, and any further consolidating could wait for some future date.

"Okay. I'd better have my key, then."

Ivy began to panic.

"I can't give it you now. I can't get at it."

"I can get at it."

"No you don't! You leave me alone!"

"I put it down," George persisted stolidly. "I reckon I can get it up."

"Don't you lay a finger on me, George Fiddler!" Ivy said shrilly, "or I'll tell me father."

"Well, I got to have me key, haven't I?"

"I'll give it you later on."

"All right," he said reluctantly. "See you don't go losing it. There won't half be a fanfare if me Gran'ma has to get out of her bed an' let me in."

He turned on his heel and left her, walking back towards the more populated part of the town.

He glanced down at the swimming pool. Miss Stacey had disappeared but Bob Clough was still there, floating on his back with closed eyes, his hands idly cupping the clear greenish water. And with him was another fellow whom George soon identified as the driver of the bus.

The driver dived, swam beneath Bob's body and came up on the other side, spluttering. They both had brown, strong limbs and deep chests with dark hair running down the middle. Whatever their private problems they were both, at that moment, completely happy.

George did not envy them. He thought swimming a silly waste of time, and uncomfortable at that.

He went down the steps of the promenade onto the beach and strolled, thinking his own thoughts.

The whole day was a waste of time, come to that. Holidays weren't all they were cracked up to be. Just another excuse for chucking away the good money you had sweated to save. The best way of spending a day off was to lie flat on your bed and sleep, which was cheap and health-giving and caused the minimum of trouble to everybody.

If it had not been for the singing George would never have come to the Choir Outing. But if he could be said to love anything besides money, he loved a good sing. He had a strong, clear voice and he was proud of it. He never missed a church service or a choir practice. He had never yet missed an Outing.

There was always a crowd to hear the singing. Miss Fortune threw open her gardens and people came from all the houses near-by, and quite a number of visitors from the town, too. The annual Outing of the Bishops Staving choir had become quite an event in the place.

But there were still some hours to while away before the singing, and how to spend them George was unable to decide.

It was, however, decided for him, and in no uncertain manner. The Lomax girls, prancing along the promenade, leaned over the railings and called his attention to their presence by a shower of small sharp stones and stinging sand.

"Yoo-hoo! Georgie!" they yelled in unison.

"Now then!" George responded, picking sand out of his ears.

"Can we come, too, Georgie?" they caroled.

At that moment George desired nothing more devoutly than to be rid of all females forever and ever; but he was too wary to show it. The Lomax girls were, by this time, slap-happy with excitement. Their cheeks blazed, their eyes were brightly brazen. They made crazy gestures. They sang loudly. They shrieked with meaningless laughter. Their electric blue costumes were in considerable disarray. The rigid waves of their permanents were crowned by round white hats reminiscent of the American Navy, adorned by remarks of a peculiarly personal nature. *Hold me tight, Baby,* said Violet's hat; while Pearl's declared openly: *Yours for the asking!*

From past experience George was aware that, in this mood, Pearl and Violet were liable to go to lengths that did not bear contemplation. So he made no protest when they leaped over the railings, showing a shocking amount of leg, and joined him, each flinging an arm round his neck, laughing immoderately and guiding him, slowly but surely, towards the entrance to the Pier.

"What've you done with Ivy, George—drowned her?" Pearl wanted to know.

"Happen the little lambs have et her," said Vi. At which both girls became quite incoherent with mirth, though George couldn't see it was all that funny.

"What have you done with Harry, come to that?" he demanded.

"Oh, he got on our nerves, didn't he, Vi? He's a dope."

"England's Number One Drip," Violet agreed. "He's sissy, too. He wouldn't come on the Pier and play the slot machines, like we wanted. So we gave Mr. Sissy Waterhouse the air, didn't we, Pearl?"

"*And* a couple of raspberries! . . . So we'll all go on the Pier now; Me and Vi and little Georgie-Porgy, shall us? There's a swell tearoom where you can get ices. And we'll have a peek at What the Butler Saw, and the Execution. You any good at skittles, Georgie?"

George broke into a gentle sweat. This was going to cost him a pretty penny! This was going to cost the earth!

He had no illusions about the Lomax girls. He knew he was going to fork out for the whole shebang. Short of running away from them at top speed, there was nothing to be done. And he couldn't run a step; for Pearl had fast hold of one arm, and Violet clutched the other; and even now they were approaching the turnstile to the Pier.

He was in for it.

In the dignified, male atmosphere of the Gentlemen's Outfitters', Harry Waterhouse was buying himself a tie.

He chose a sober gray with a faint stripe to match his suit. Harry liked things to match.

"Mind if I put it on now?" he asked.

"Certainly, sir. If you would kindly step this way."

Harry would and did step that way into the cloistered privacy of a small cubicle that contained a full-length mirror, in which he surveyed himself with considerable disfavor.

Discarding the stringlike object which hung around his neck, he put on the new tie, paying strict attention to the set. Taking a small comb from his pocket, he breathed heavily on it and slicked his hair back into a neat, becoming wave. He also removed from the region of his chin a small, but quite recognizable splodge of lipstick. (No wonder the assistant had grinned!) He flicked the clothes brush over his suit, thus disposing of a quantity of sand, dust, face powder and several long, reddish-brown hairs of feminine origin. He flicked his handkerchief over his shoes, picked up the discarded tie and reentered the shop.

He laid the tie on the counter and requested the assistant to dispose of it, which he readily agreed to do.

"Seems to have had its day," was the assistant's cautious comment. "Looks to me like this tie's been through quite a bit. You might almost say it'd been salvaged."

"You might," Harry conceded, pale and stern. "And you'd be perfectly correct."

As he stepped out of the shop he bore a distinct resemblance to the Harry Waterhouse who had set forth so hopefully that morning. In reality, he was a changed man.

Had anyone warned him then, that the Lomax girls, so neat and pleasant with their new electric blue costumes and their sculptured heads, could change in the course of a few hours into a couple of screaming, brazen, *common* hussies, Harry would have refused to believe it. But he had seen it happen, he had felt and heard it happen, he had suffered most cruelly from its happening; and he was shocked to the very core.

He was more than shocked—he was apprehensive. For a very terrible thing had happened to Harry.

It had happened just after he had refused to go on the Pier, and was urging their return to the Good Fortune Tea Rooms. Pearl and Violet, already silly with excitement, had become quite violent and unmanageable.

It was Violet who had wrecked his tie, Pearl who had bestowed the lipstick. They had both pulled him about, messed up his hair, mauled and slapped him in ferocious playfulness, shrieking with laughter; making a proper exhibition of themselves and him. Passers-by had stared, grinning. Some had shouted comments.

It had been bad enough with strangers. But suddenly, who should have come strolling along the Lower Front, staid and respectable in Panama hat and white linen jacket, but Mr. Venables, the head clerk of the firm of solicitors to which Harry was articled.

And there were Pearl and Violet, in those awful hats they had made him buy—*Yours for the asking; Hold me tight, Baby*—screaming with silly laughter, messing him about and shouting: "Oh, don't be such a drip, Harry, we want to go on the Pier! Come on, let's go on the Pier! WE WANT TO GO ON THE PIER! . . ."

Mr. Venables had pretended not to see him. But of course he'd seen him right enough! You couldn't *not* see an exhibition like that. And it was good to tell he wasn't best pleased. . . . There'd be a few words about that when next they met! Harry could already hear that dry, precise voice: *"I understood it was the Church Choir Outing with which you were associated, Mr. Waterhouse. Correct me if I am mistaken. . . . I can hardly say that the—er—trio I was privileged to hear and—er—witness, was in the best interests of this firm . . ."*

It would be useless for Harry to protest that he was shocked, astonished and grieved beyond words at the behavior of his companions. It would cut no ice at all. In any case, it simply was not done to indict one's lady friends. A gentleman took the blame on his own shoulders, and Harry hoped he was a gentleman. Though he very much doubted it at this moment, so violent was the revulsion of his feelings towards the Lomax girls.

No. He would simply have to prove to Mr. Venables by the integrity of his conduct and close application to duty, that he was truly a worthy future member of the firm of Watkinson, Humply and Blair.

Live it down. . . .

Cherchez la femme, Harry thought bitterly. Or, in this case, *les femmes.* And with a heavy heart he turned his face towards the Good Fortune Tea Rooms, taking a circuitous route that led him well away from the Lower Front and the region of the Pier.

When he judged himself far enough from the danger zone he turned seawards once more, with the intention of climbing back along the cliff path. The way to this path lay through a small coppice. It was pleasant in the shade of the trees, and Harry sat for a while in the cool, green gloom. He lit a cigarette and thought how nice it was to be alone, and how much older he felt than he had felt this morning. Older, more experienced, more responsible; but not, Harry decided, entirely and finally disillusioned regarding women.

Terrible though his experience had been, he was glad to find that he could still think kindly of women as a whole. He had kept a sense of proportion. All women were not like Pearl and Violet.

There were plenty of girls who knew how to behave in public; who dressed smartly, who were good-lookers, who would be glad of the chance of marrying a rising young solicitor, and would be fully aware of all that was due to such a position.

Some day, somehow, he would meet such a girl, and then they would have to see. . . .

In the meantime, it was pleasant to be among the green trees, with a glimpse of blue sky above their interlocked branches and a glimpse of blue sea beyond their towering trunks; and to be most blessedly alone. . . .

He blew smoke at a hovering cloud of gnats. He listened to the small sounds of the gnats and the léaves and the infinitesimal life that went on busily among the thick, curving grasses.

There was another sound, and for a long time he could not place it; but presently, and with a rising sense of panic, he recognized it as a human sniff.

Someone—probably some female, and quite close to him—was crying. . . .

Harry's immediate impulse was to go while the going was good. Rising cautiously to his feet he began to step carefully, with no thought but of escape.

But the acoustics of trees are notoriously misleading; instead of walking away from trouble, Harry walked right into it. In fact, he nearly fell over a small female figure who, on her knees, went round in circles, grubbing in the long grass and giving alternate sobs and sniffs at regular intervals.

He saw at once that it was Ivy Carter.

Harry's heart sank into his shoes.

A stranger he might have ignored and passed by. But not Ivy. Not a member of his own choir, obviously seeking that which was lost, laddering, in all probability, her best stockings, and weeping most drearily in the process.

Besides, Harry was, normally, a kind-hearted young man, and the sight of Ivy's damp little wedge of a face lifted in the greenish light of the coppice gave him pause. It made him think suddenly of a small fish he had once caught in his very young days; and he remembered how his pride had turned to pity, and he had unhooked the fish and thrown it back into the stream, and had never gone fishing again.

So now, he supposed, he must unhook Ivy from whatever circumstance she was caught on and, if possible, set her free.

"Hello," he said awkwardly. "I say, is anything the matter?"

"I've lost a key," Ivy muttered, and sniffed loudly.

"A key?" Harry was at once the practical male. "What sort of a key?" Easing his nicely creased trousers at the knees, he bent and began poking and prodding in the long, cool grass.

"A great long black iron thing, the sort you open back doors with. Weighs about half a ton," she said resentfully.

"Where did you put it?"

"If I knew that I shouldn't have to be seeking it, should I?" she observed waspishly.

"No, of course not. Silly thing to ask. How did you come to lose it?"

"It was down me back."

"Down your *back*? What for?"

"George Fiddler shoved it down."

"*Fiddler*? . . . What did he do that for!"

Ivy gulped and sniffed; she peered at Harry over her handkerchief and her thoughts darted about like tadpoles in a rather muddy pool.

"Don't talk to me about George Fiddler!" she begged, shuddering realistically.

"Ha! Getting fresh, was he?" Harry's bosom swelled with indignation. Ivy might be a poor fish, but that was no reason why bounders like Fiddler should be allowed to muck her about. No reason at all. Harry knew—none better!—what it was like to be mucked about, and his sympathy went out to Ivy. "Why did you go off with Fiddler, anyway? I thought you always stuck with Miss Stacey."

"Don't talk to me about that woman!" Ivy wailed, beginning to sob anew.

As there seemed to be a paucity of subjects on which one could talk to Ivy, Harry occupied himself with searching for the lost key; which, and in a place he had already scrutinized a score of times, he presently found and presented to Ivy.

"Oh, thank you, Mr. Waterhouse!" Ivy cried, sniffing damply. "Oh, I do think you're ever so kind!"

Mr. Waterhouse. Harry approved of that. It showed a very proper sense of the fitness of things in Ivy; for they were not well acquainted, Harry being a comparatively new member of the choir and this his first Outing.

It occurred to Harry that he and Ivy had a great deal in common. They both approved of polite behavior. They had both suffered from the lack of it in others. They had both, it would appear, been deceived in those for whom they had cherished feelings of friendship and admiration, if nothing warmer.

Not that he believed half the things some folks said about Ivy and Miss Stacey. Of course not. Still. . . .

Watching covertly as she did small, feminine things to her hair and face, with the aid of a mirror the size of half-a-crown, Harry decided that Ivy wasn't a bad-looking piece at all when you got a good look at her. Her pale hair was limp and rather scanty, but would look much better waved and worn swept up instead of shoulder-length as she now wore it. Her skin was quite good; a bit pasty and damp-looking, perhaps, but clear enough and fine. Legs thin but shapely—and anyway, he liked 'em on the thin side. It was a pity about her nose, but even that was greatly improved by the application of powder. Her clothes were nondescript: she ought to go in for more definite colorings; not so much of this beige and wishy-washy pastel. . . .

Narrowing his eyes and twisting his head to a visionary angle, Harry saw an Ivy transformed. Bright, upswept hair; smart black suit; nylons and four-inch heels. Matching accessories. A bit of veiling somewhere. A touch of perfume, a touch of lipstick. . . .

Yes, with a bit of trouble you could make Ivy look a bit of all right! Smart, and at the same time modest. Dignified; with a proper sense of what was due to her as the wife of a rising young solicitor, yet grateful to him; not above working and saving for him and—naturally—waiting for him until he actually *became* a solicitor and had begun to rise.

People could call her a white rabbit if they liked. Harry didn't care. As a boy he had kept white rabbits with pink, quivery noses, and had been devoted to them. He still liked them very much indeed.

"Look," he said, "what about a spot of tea?"

And Ivy, with a mendacity that would have deprived George Fiddler of speech, declared that tea was just what she had been longing for, all the afternoon.

"Come on, then," said Harry. He pulled her up from the long grass, dusted her down, folded her coat over his arm and took her by the elbow. "By the way," he added, "I think *I'll* give that key back to George Fiddler!"

He held out an authoritative hand.

Ivy squeaked and wriggled and protested. But presently, and not without a secret relish, she took the key from her handbag and put it into Harry's hand.

Feeling and looking like a bull in a china shop, Joe Peck clumped cautiously across an acre of green carpet and lowered his tightly clad carcass onto a plush stool. He ran his handkerchief over face and neck, and blew gustily.

"Now then," he said, "get thysen a hat, and not all day over it, neether. I don't want to stuff indoors, day like this."

His wife, Addie, and daughter, Minnie, stood together: two black, alien birds in the gay flower garden of hats.

"They'll none be cheap," warned his daughter.

"Who said owt about a cheap one?" Joe demanded. "I'm buying the bally hat, a'nt I? I can do as I've a mind wi' me own money, can't I? Or can't I?" he exploded, glaring at his daughter, who clutched her black handbag, moving closer to her mother.

Mother and daughter glanced at each other, blinking and wordless. They had come into this shop to escape a scene in the street. They must get out without a scene, if that were possible.

It was just like Him to drag them into the most expensive shop in town. At Spanner's, on the Lower Front, they could have bought a hat for half-a-guinea, even in these times. Here, they'd be lucky if they got out under twenty-nine and eleven—and then not the sort of hat they were accustomed to.

"Nobody's serving, seemingly," Addie said. The two women took a tentative step towards the door, but Joe sat still.

"Shop!" he roared suddenly. His great fist thumped on the mahogany counter; and a tiny, frivolous affair of forget-me-nots and veiling toppled and fell to the floor.

"Nay, Pa, give over!" Minnie whispered, crimson and agonized.

A startled female face popped round a screen; gaped and giggled and retired. "Miss Dawson!" a voice was heard summoning.

Addie Peck bent and picked up the little foolishness of forget-me-nots.

It was light as a feather in her hand. The flowers were heaped about a narrow brim of black velvet, rakishly a-tilt. A black velvet ribbon was fixed to hold the trifle becomingly in place on the fortunate wearer's head.

Addie Peck turned the hat this way and that on her black kid-gloved hand. Her eyes devoured it.

"Nay!" she muttered. "Did you ever see owt sillier!"

Her daughter's elbow jogged her ribs.

"Girl's coming, Ma."

Addie slapped the forget-me-not hat on its stand with unnecessary emphasis. The price ticket swung into view. It cost three pounds ten and eleven. . . .

"Nay!" she muttered again.

"Can I help Moddom?"

A pert miss was standing by her side, bored and supercilious.

"Aye, you can," said Addie sharply. "And not afore time, neether." She put the hussy in her place with a glare. "I want a black hat for best. A straw. Not too fancy an' not too dear. Just a bit o' ribbon, an' happen a feather."

"What does t'a want wi' another black 'un!" the blacksmith grumbled. "Black, black, black, the two on you, all t'while! Life might be one long funeril! Why not go in for a bit o'color for once in yer life? Look, I'll stand thee both 'ats, if tha'll lash out an' get a red or a puce or summat, for a change."

They neither listened to nor looked at him.

From a drawer the pert miss produced a number of dreary hats of varying sizes and shapes, which Addie proceeded to try on before the long mirror. She looked precisely the same in all of them. Minnie watched the performance somberly. The pert miss watched contemptuously. The blacksmith watched fretfully.

"For goodness sake, mek up thi mind, wilt t'a!"

"I'm tekkin' me time," Addie announced firmly.

"Then I'm for off! I can think of better ways of spending t'day than sitting here while tha gets ready for t'corpse."

He winked at the pert miss. As he passed behind her she stifled a squeak; whereby his wife and daughter surmised, correctly, that he had done more than wink. "See you later," he called, making a bid for freedom.

"If he gets in t'pub, we shan't see him again while tomorrow," Minnie whispered, much agitated.

"That's right. You'd better go with 'im," Addie agreed, gloomily surveying the effect of a boat-shaped creation, complete with crepe sail. "It wants an hour to opening time yet, but we'd best not lose sight of him, or we shall never get him to t'singing in time."

"You can't choose your new hat without me," Minnie objected.

"Why not? I chose 'em before you was born, didn't I?"

"Very well. . . ." Minnie wore a martyr's smile. "Don't blame me if you get done. It teks two to choose a hat, as you've allus said yourself, think on."

"It teks two dozen to get yer pa out of a pub, once he's in—as he will be, if you don't shift yer stumps!"

Minnie scuttled away, clutching her black handbag. Her mother watched the narrow, stooping figure out of sight. Then she laid the boat with the crepe sail back on the counter and fixed the pert miss with a forbidding eye.

"I saw a hat in the window. Black chip with a high crown and two velvet bows. I should like to try it on if it's no trouble. It's right in t'front on t'left side."

"No trouble at all, Moddom," snapped the pert miss, slaying Addie with a look.

Well, Addie reflected, not without a wry humor, that had got rid of the lot. Now she could act as daft as she'd a mind, and nobody to laugh, only herself. . . .

She lifted the forget-me-not hat from its stand again and turned it around and around, feasting her eyes. She'd always had a fancy for forget-me-nots. . . .

Once, long ago—nay, more than forty years ago!—she had worn a hat trimmed with forget-me-nots. It was when Joe had been courting her. She remembered with a faint sense of astonishment the things Joe had said about the forget-me-nots and her eyes. . . . A rare lot o' rubbish he had talked in those days, and best forgotten; just as Joe had forgotten them and all they had meant—if ever they had meant anything.

As soon as she had set eyes on the little hat something had gone *click* in Addie's mind. All the time she had been trying on first this suitable model and then that, with Joe grumbling and Minnie mumbling, and yon hussy looking as if she'd just smelt summat nasty, Addie had been staring in the mirror at a girl with blue eyes and dimples and bright brown, tumbled hair under a hat wreathed in forget-me-nots.

Addie Simmonds, the prettiest girl in the village. . . .

It had been a sort of vision.

And then the vision had faded and she had seen herself and Minnie standing side by side: black and bitter and awkward: unlovely and unloved, save of themselves.

It had given her a shock, that.

Addie seldom looked in mirrors nowadays. Not for years had she seen herself and Minnie thus, standing side by side, and she had forgotten, if she had ever known, how awful they looked: fat and thin, squat and stooped; sixty-odd and forgotten of love, thirty-nine and unknown to love; and black, black, black. . . .

Black as two thunderclouds. Two mutes. Two carrion crows. . . .

How on earth had they come to get that road?

Of course, she'd always spoiled Minnie, right from the start.

Minnie had been a love child. Well, and what of it? She wasn't the only one in the village—not by a long chalk she wasn't. She'd been a difficult child; delicate, shy and—even to her mother's partial gaze—awkward and homely. Addie had loved her all the more to make up for it. Minnie hadn't liked playing with other children, so Addie had played with her. Minnie had been jealous if her pa and ma went out together, so Addie had stayed at home with Minnie, and Joe had gone out. Minnie had been frightened to sleep alone. So Addie had slept with her. . . .

Joe had lost patience. There had been ugly scenes and loud, frightening rows; and Minnie had cried and had to be comforted.

And after a while, Joe hadn't cared enough to bother with rows. Except on Sundays and choir practice nights, he had spent his leisure hours at The Crown; and Minnie had helped her mother put him to bed when he fell into the kitchen, long after closing time. Addie had never asked where he had been since closing time. . . .

Minnie had grown up very suddenly, jumping, it seemed, straight out of adolescence into middle age. She had copied her mother in all things: in her work and speech, in the way she dressed, in her attitude towards Joe. They were less Mother and Daughter than two life-long cronies. The bond between them was strong, but now it was fashioned of need rather than love, of habit rather than the ties of blood.

They were bound together, as two states band themselves together against the third, the aggressor state. . . .

It shouldn't have got this way, Addie thought bleakly.

She was still Addie, wasn't she? Still the girl with the dimples and the forget-me-nots? . . . Even if she were over sixty, and had grown stout and screwed her hair into a gray knob at the back of her head; even if she had forgotten how to laugh, she was still Addie; Joe was still Joe. . . .

With an almost ritual gesture she lifted the little hat and set it straight on the top of her head. It wobbled. She fastened the black velvet ribbon under her bun. She tilted it this way and that. She pulled it forward over her right eyebrow. The veiling obscured her vision, tickled her nose.

She looked awful. Awful! She looked a figure of fun. A sort of Aunt Sally. . . .

It wasn't because she was old and stout and gray. There were women as old as herself—aye, and older!—who could wear a silly hat and get away with it. This hat had less to do with body than with spirit.

The body of Addie Simmonds—Addie Peck if you liked—was still here, sound and whole and healthy. The spirit of Addie was dead: had been for a long, long time. It smelled of corruption. . . .

Suddenly she became aware that Minnie had returned.

Minnie was standing just behind her, staring over her shoulder at the Aunt Sally in the mirror. Minnie was sniggering; jerking her shoulders about and covering her mouth with black-gloved hands.

"Oh, for goodness' sake, Ma, tek it off! You look a proper sight, don't you! Get it off before t'girl comes back."

Addie lifted the forget-me-not hat from her head and put it back on the stand.

"Where's yer pa?" she asked.

"He went in t'George and Dragon."

"They're not open yet."

"He went round t'back. I called out. He poked his head out an' told me to go to hell." Minnie's top lip was down, her shoulders hunched, her hands gripped round the black handbag.

Addie smoothed her hair and put on her old hat. The broken feather lolled ludicrously.

"You stop here," she told Minnie. "When the girl comes back, tell her I've changed me mind, I don't want a hat. After that you can go where you've a mind, so long as you're back in time for t'singing."

She began to walk away over the vast green carpet.

"Ma!" Minnie yelped sharply. "Here, Ma!"

Addie paid no attention; neither to Minnie, nor to the pert miss whom she met on the stairs, carrying the black chip. She walked steadily down the stairs and out of the shop, down the hot, crowded street and into the back yard of the George and Dragon.

Joe was sitting on an empty beer cask in the yard. He had a couple of sleek fawn grayhounds between his knees, and he fondled their narrow muzzles. The landlord of the pub leaned against the wall picking his teeth. Both men were laughing heartily.

When he saw Addie Joe stopped laughing. Addie distinctly heard him mutter: "Oh, cripes—here's t'missus!"

"Better go quietly," grinned the landlord, turning away.

"All right, all right," Joe said, glaring at his wife, "I'm nobbut going to have a pint. What d'you want to come barging in for?"

"Same as you, Joe," Addie said, more calmly than she felt. She seated herself on another cask. "I just thought I could do with a port an' lemon."

5

THE wind had dropped and the sun had gone in.

Down in the town the air became stale and oppressive. The Fun Fair smelled of sweat and food and dust and gasoline fumes. Tempers were apt to be brittle. Parents slapped indiscriminately. Babies wailed and slept, sticky and exhausted, sagging over adult shoulders. Children fought and kicked and occasionally threw up, to the improvement of their spirits but the detriment of the general scene.

It was the slack hour of the day. Those who had been spending were spent out. Those who had hoarded their money for the evening had not yet begun to spend.

In the booths and tents of the fair, and in all the little teashops, and behind the stalls of whelks and cockles and sweating pink rock along the Lower Front, there was a general relaxation of effort. Proprietors refreshed themselves with mugs of strong tea, or sat staring glassily across the water, or frankly put up their aching feet, tilted straw hats and indulged in a nice little spot of shut-eye. The balloon vendor and Madame Verona sat together behind the bead curtain discussing their operations with somber pride and drinking gin.

The town yawned and wilted.

Residents went about their lawful occasions keeping themselves *to* themselves. Hotel guests gathered on balconies, tapping tired feet to sweet rhythm and drinking weak little drinks out of expensive bottles; wondering, sometimes audibly, why they hadn't stayed comfortably at home. Trippers, thinking of the hot trains awaiting them, began collecting spades, thermos flasks, left-over food, funny hats and defiant children. Car owners kicked their tires and peered into radiators. Streets began to empty and pubs to fill up.

Rain fell suddenly. Hot, thick splashes fell on the just and the unjust with a splendid impartiality.

It fell on the choirboys, racing for the six-thirty bus back to the Good Fortune Tea Rooms; to the grand meal that awaited them and the singing afterwards.

Their spirits, which had suffered from the heat and noise and violent motion of the Fun Fair, rapidly revived. They pushed each other about, clowning at the heavy raindrops, shouting and laughing.

Young Les clowned with the best of them, but his heart was heavy, because now he remembered that the puppy belonged to Jack. It would go home cuddled up in Jack's arms. Because it loved Jack, and it didn't like him, Les, at all.

So his laughter was shriller, his clowning less restrained than all the others'. And passers-by, glancing indulgently at his antics, murmured what a thing it was to be young and happy and carefree. . . .

The rain fell on Miss Maddon's blue-flowered cotton; and John William Welsh immediately took off his coat and wrapped it round her shoulders with a calmly proprietorial air.

"Oh, John William!" she exclaimed, pink and girlish, "you can't go through the streets in your shirt sleeves! You'll get soaked!"

"I'd go through t'streets in me skin, sooner than see thee get wet, luv," John William said warmly: which piece of romantic extravagance gave Miss Maddon the biggest thrill of the whole day.

The rain fell on Harry Waterhouse and Ivy, just as they were about to emerge from the coppice. So naturally, the only thing to do was to stay in the coppice, until the rain stopped.

And if you had to shelter under a tree it was surely more sensible to sit down?

And if you were sitting, why not be comfortable and sit close together?

Harry's arm, in the most delicate manner possible, crept round Ivy's narrow little shoulders. And Ivy's head, in a ladylike, somewhat gingerly gesture, descended upon Harry's shoulder. And there they were, all hunky-dory; as comfortable as one could wish, yet refined withal, and everything in the best possible taste.

I never thought I'd live to see the day! reflected Ivy who, deeming all men vile, had hitherto yearned for no shoulder other than Miss Stacey's.

And Harry, fingering the key in his pocket, felt that nothing short of a punch on the nose could bring home to George Fiddler the enormity of his behavior towards so small and helpless and ladylike a creature as Ivy Carter.

The rain fell on George who, having profitlessly carried his mack through the heat and burden of the day, now found it snatched from him as a covering for the newly waved heads of the Lomax girls.

Down the Pier they pounded: Pearl and Violet screaming under the billowing canopy of mackintosh and George stamping sourly after them to the narrow haven of a shelter already crammed with damp, disconsolate holiday-makers.

"Whatever shall we do?" wailed Violet. "It's gone six. We shall miss the bus!"

"We shall miss tea," added Pearl.

"We *can't* miss the singing," they chorused.

For the Lomax girls, despite all evidence to the contrary, possessed high, sweet voices of surpassing tenderness; and they loved to sing.

"It'll have to be a taxi," Pearl decided. "George, be a pet and go and find a taxi. Here—you can have your mack," she added generously.

George put on his mackintosh with judicious promptness.

"I'll get the taxi," he announced grimly. "You'll pay for it."

They stared at him with bright, hard eyes.

"Fancy!" Violet laughed shortly, "for one minute I thought you said: 'you'll pay for it.'"

"That's what I did say," George replied stolidly. "I'm spent out. I've not got a penny-piece in me pockets. Not even t'bus fare! So you've either got to walk, or else I get a taxi and you pay for it. Suit yersens."

He turned his back on them and glared at the ocean, its glassy surface now chapped and roughened by rain.

He heard them muttering together. He heard the chink of coin and the rustle of notes. The sounds made him grit his teeth. He turned his head sharply. His eyes popped at the bulging purse of Pearl, the padded notecase of Violet.

And they'd let him pay for every single thing. Every single perishing thing!

"Well, I don't know!" he muttered feebly.

"Okay, George. You get a taxi and we'll pay for it," said Pearl.

"We'll give you a lift, an' all," Violet said kindly.

Simmering, George departed.

By the time he had persuaded a taxi to acknowledge his signals of distress he had, however, cooled off considerably, in every sense of the phrase.

After all, you had to hand it to 'em. They knew the value of money all right, those girls! George had a deep respect for folks who knew the value of money.

He suddenly remembered, moreover, that old man Lomax had a very snug little oil and color business down in Lower Staving; that the deliveryman was equipped with a motor van such as George had for years dreamed of in vain; that the said deliveryman, having injudiciously got himself mixed up with a German bomber on Dunkirk beach, was now stumping around with an artificial leg which not only impeded his driving but necessitated time off at regular intervals for hospital treatment.

He remembered, moreover, that old man Lomax was a widower and that Pearl and Violet between them ran, not only the house but the business, too; their father having irons in other fires, necessitating frequent absences from home.

Taking it by and large George decided, once having consolidated one's position with the daughters, it would be a comparatively simple matter to wangle the old man. In fact, you might almost say it would be as good as done!

"Whoopee!" George murmured reverently; in much the same voice as he intoned Amen after the prayers in church.

The rain fell on Miss Stacey, striding up the cliff with arms swinging from the shoulders and head erect.

Miss Stacey could not have cared less!

"She'll be wearing wet pajamas when she comes," sang Miss Stacey.

And at the back of her mind she thought; I must remember that. It'll get a laugh some time when The Boys feel they can't march another step.

The rain fell on Phoebe Braithwaite, standing in the queue for the bus, bitterly regretting her last-minute decision not to bring an umbrella.

This'll finish me hat, she thought glumly. Serve me right!

An umbrella clicked up behind her. Turning to make a neighborly comment on the English summer, Phoebe found herself staring into the bleak countenance of Minnie Peck.

"Well, there, you're a god-send, Minnie! I were just thinking as me hat would be ruined. Got room for a little 'un?"

Minnie accorded grudging hospitality to the two bunches of red cherries and the brown velvet bow. Her face was forbidding; but Phoebe had known her from childhood and was not in the least intimidated.

"All on yer own, luv?" she inquired cheerfully.

"Yes," said Minnie.

"Well, it's not often as you an' yer ma's parted, I must say! Regular Siamese twins, you two."

"I know when I'm not wanted," Minnie said hollowly.

Phoebe kept eyes front. She did not need to glance at Minnie to know that she was crying. There were damp, small sounds, and the smell of mothballs as a handkerchief was brought out to deal with the situation. Eh, dear! thought Phoebe. Now what!

"It's a job getting a hat, these days," she remarked soothingly. "Such silly bits o' things they wear now; just a couple of inches of straw an' a bit o' veiling. How they keep 'em on beats me! I like summat as you can get your head into. And the price is summat fierce! I reckon yer ma's got her work cut out, finding what she fancies."

"Nay, Ma's got her hat all right," Minnie said. "I've seen her in it." She hiccoughed and blew her nose so passionately that Phoebe felt obliged to turn commiserating eyes upon her and pat her bony arm. "You know where I saw her wearing it?" Minnie shrilled. "In the public bar of the George and Dragon—that's where! I looked through the window, an' I saw 'em! Her an' Pa, settin' on them high stools by the counter an' laughin' away fit to bust. . . . An' Ma had got this hat on, an' I saw it with me own eyes!"

She blew her nose again with shattering venom.

Phoebe, compassionate yet intrigued beyond words, continued to pat her arm.

Minnie's voice dropped suddenly to a tragic whisper.

"It were one of them paper hats they sell along t'Lower Front, an' it had got: *Thrilling and Willing* written round the front of it. Now then!"

They stared at each other; Phoebe's jaw slack with surprise, Minnie's grimly clenched.

If the bus had not at this moment come rolling up, Phoebe had no idea how she could have coped with this astonishing revelation. But fortunately it did come, and the queue surged forward and Phoebe and Minnie were torn apart, so that no further conversation was possible.

The rain fell on Mrs. Maddon sitting alone in thundrous majesty in a deck chair, on the lawn of the Good Fortune Tea Rooms. It did not improve her temper, which was already strained to snapping point.

The whole afternoon she had been alone. Absolutely alone, for the whole long, boring afternoon! For of course, Fred Fortune did not count. What Mrs. Maddon meant by being alone was being without Doris.

Of course, she *had* mentioned that all she wanted was to sit on the lawn, but naturally she hadn't meant that she wanted to sit there alone. She hadn't meant that Doris should go gallivanting off in that peculiar fashion, without so much as a by your leave! She would have some very pungent remarks to make to Doris when she did turn up!

Mrs. Maddon put up her parasol and hoped the shower would be only a short one, for it was quite a business getting out of these deck chairs, once you got set; she had been sitting so long that she felt part of the chair, part of the lawn, part of the cliff on which the tearooms were built.

Really, thought Mrs. Maddon, the manners of people, these days! That Fred Fortune plumping himself down in the chair next to hers, and going bang off to sleep with his mouth wide open. . . . Well, actually he was already plumped when she happened to come and sit next to him—but that didn't make it any better. Gone bang off to sleep, he had, while she was in the very middle of telling him about the trip to the Lake District she and her husband had made in the car, twenty years ago. And when at length he had waked up, had he apologized? Not he! He had yawned and grinned and gone off across the lawn muttering about tea. Not tea for Mrs. Maddon, mind you. Oh, no. Tea for himself, the lazy, selfish wretch, with never a thought for anyone else. . . .

The rain fell more heavily. Mrs. Maddon eased her joints, preparatory to heaving herself forwards and upwards and into some place of shelter. Her mauve marocain was brand-new, and clothes were clothes.

Where on earth *was* Doris! It would serve her right if she got wet through; though that would mean a bad cold, which Mrs. Maddon herself would catch. Not that anyone would care if she got pneumonia and died, as far as she could see. . . .

The rain fell more heavily. With a vast heave Mrs. Maddon

achieved the perpendicular and lumbered across the lawn to shelter.

Encountering Phyllis, she inquired for Miss Fortune and was curtly informed that she was engaged; which was pure nonsense, for Mrs. Maddon had marked with her own eyes Miss Fortune's departure up the lane, not half an hour ago, accompanied by Walter Forsythe. "If it's tea you're wanting," Phyllis added quite rudely, "you can get it in the tearoom, through the white gate yonder. There's a rare long queue waiting."

"I am a friend of Miss Fortune's," Mrs. Maddon said stiffly. "I came with the Staving choir."

"That's right," Phyllis agreed indifferently. "Afternoon tea extra. Through the white gate, please."

Well, really! What people were coming to, Mrs. Maddon simply dared not think! It was a sure thing Walter Forsythe hadn't stood in a queue for *his* cup of tea.

And come to think of it, just what was Walter Forsythe doing, gadding up yon lane with the Fortune woman? Rather queer goings on at their time of life! If they'd got anything to say to each other, surely they could have said it here in the open, without creeping up dark lanes in that hole-and-corner fashion!

Oh, dear, if she didn't get a cup of tea soon, she would drop. If Doris had any sense of duty she'd be here now to cope with this queue business. Doris was far too old to go gallivanting off with a crowd of youngsters. On the other hand, she was quite young enough to stand in queues.

And here came that idiot fellow—Crackerjack, or whatever his name was—with a bundle in his arms.

Mrs. Maddon gestured imperiously, and Jack ambled up, bobbing his head and grinning.

"Jack's puppy," he said softly, bending to show her the bundle, his face alight with love and pride.

"Put the dog down, Jack, and go get me a cup of tea. Here's tuppence to buy a nice cake for yourself."

Jack shook his blond head.

"Jack's puppy asleep. Not put him down."

"Don't be silly," Mrs. Maddon said firmly. "The dog won't take any harm and I want a cup of tea. Here, give it to me, I'll mind it for you."

She reached to take the puppy. Jack struck her hand quite a violent blow.

"Don't touch!" he growled. "Jack's puppy!" He shifted the bundle tenderly on his arm and strolled away, humming his tune like a lullaby.

Well, really! It had given Mrs. Maddon quite a turn, that had! It was about time that lad was put away, and if she'd said so once she'd said it a dozen times. Attacking her like that! He wasn't safe, and that was a fact. She'd tell the Vicar so and insist that something was done about it. . . .

Doris ought to be right down ashamed of herself, leaving her mother to starve and be drenched to the skin and sauced by servants and attacked by dangerous lunatics. . . .

This is the last time I come with Doris to a Choir Outing! she thought viciously.

And only Doris and John William Welsh knew how true that was.

The rain fell on Miss Fortune and Walter Forsythe, as they strolled up the lane together in pleasant companionship.

"Dear me!" Walter exclaimed, staring in dismay at the lowering sky.

"We'll shelter in Mitchum's barn," Miss Fortune said placidly. "It's only a few yards farther on."

Walter was anxious.

"I hope this won't spoil the singing!"

Miss Fortune smiled.

"It won't spoil anything, Walter. It will be over long before the singing. Here is the barn, and here is plenty of nice straw to sit on. So we can be comfortable while you tell me what is troubling you." She sank down on the fragrant straw and looked at him in calm expectancy.

Walter lowered himself carefully, easing the knees of his trousers, giving his nervous cough.

"Do you mind if I smoke?"

She laid a cautionary finger on his sleeve.

"In a straw barn, Walter? And you a country boy!"

Walter slipped the silver case back, laughing shamefacedly.

"It's a long time since I was a boy, and you the Vicar's pretty daughter. A lot of water's gone under the bridge since then, Bee. . . . Do you remember we fancied ourselves in love in those days?"

Beatrice regarded him serenely.

"It wasn't fancy with me, Walter. I was head over heels in love with you."

"Eh? . . . Oh, well, I suppose I was, too. Yes, indeed, I'm sure I was. But we were very young. We got over it, didn't we?"

"Yes, we got over it, Walter."

"Such a long, long time ago!" he sighed.

Miss Fortune rearranged a fold in her frock.

"Surely you did not bring me all this way to tell me how old I have become, Walter?"

"My dear Bee! . . . Besides, it would scarcely be true. You have worn a great deal better than I have, if I may say so. It was brought home to me only this afternoon that I have one leg in the grave; while you are still blooming. Like the rose. . . ."

Beatrice smiled faintly and folded her hands, glancing covertly at her wrist watch. She could not leave Phyllis for long.

"Thank you for those gallant lies, dear Walter! And now, what is wrong?"

Walter sighed impatiently.

"It's Phoebe Braithwaite, Bee. I want you to tell me the best way of approaching her on a rather delicate matter." He coughed and fingered his tie. "You see, Phoebe and I have been friends and neighbors for a very long time. . . . Have I said something amusing, Bee?"

Beatrice composed her features.

"I wasn't laughing at you, personally, Walter. Just at men in general. You're so silly, all of you, when it comes to dealing with women. Don't you understand that women—especially women of Phoebe's sort—don't need to be 'approached.' All you have to say is: 'I want to marry you, Phoebe, how do you feel about it?' And then she'll tell you either yes or no, and it's all over. You need not lose a night's sleep over it, my dear."

"But Beatrice!"—Walter was aghast, quite stupefied—"it's nothing to do with marriage! Whatever put that into your head? Great heavens, woman, *marriage*, at my time of life! Nothing could be further from my thoughts!"

In that same instant he recollected that his friend at the music shop was even now honeymooning at Bettws-y-coed.

"Then what is it, Walter?" Miss Fortune tried to be patient. But she had such a lot to attend to, and really, Walter had become such a little bore. And such a dandy, with his gold cuff links and his creases and his funny little beard. . . .

She recalled the twenty-year-old Walter: such a sweet, gangling, awkward, lovable creature, and with such wild, romantic notions! Why, she seemed to remember that he had even urged her to leave everything and go away with him to some far Pacific island, where they would live on love and bananas, or some equally indigestible diet. And when she had refused to abandon Fred, Walter had exclaimed quite violently: "To the devil with Fred!" and had gone so far as to mention blowing out his brains. Walter's, not Fred's.

Their parting had been quite tragic. . . .

"What's wrong with Phoebe, Walter?"

"It's her voice," he groaned. "Oh, that bellow of Phoebe's! My choir is all I have to live for, Bee, and Phoebe's bellow is ruining my peace of mind. And I can't tell her. I just haven't the courage. . . ." He blew his nose noisily. "Twenty years ago her voice was rich and mellow, an asset to any choir. Ten years ago it was still good. Five years ago it wasn't too bad. But now. . . ." He shuddered, laid his hands over his ears in an extravagant gesture. "She's been a good friend and neighbor to me. My wife was fond of her. I was fond of her husband. How can I tell her?"

"You want me to tell her, Walter?"

"No, Bee. Good gracious no! It's my responsibility and I must do it. But tell me how. Tell me how!"

Miss Fortune shook her head, smiling faintly.

"There's only the one way, my dear. Complete honesty. It hurts at the time, but in the long run it doesn't hurt nearly so much as prevarication. Make up your mind which means more to you, your choir, or Phoebe's feelings, and act accordingly. You will have to be quite ruthless, of course."

He poked the straw about with his cane. He frowned slightly.

"That doesn't sound like you, somehow, Bee."

Still smiling, Miss Fortune's eyes rested on the ragged golden edge of the cloud that was sailing overhead, leaving the horizon washed and bright. The storm would soon be over, as she had prophesied.

"It doesn't sound like the me who loved you all those years ago, I agree. It doesn't sound like the me who gave up everything—love, marriage, children, a career—for the sake of a worthless brother, if that's what you mean, Walter. But *was* that me—the real me? I don't know. Sometimes I have thought it was and sometimes I have been quite sure it was not. It is only just lately that I have been certain of one thing—that it doesn't matter one way or the other."

"I have always thought," he said, "that your life has been a very noble one, Beatrice."

She gave a swift grimace.

"Noble! . . . Perhaps. What is the result of my nobility? Instead of being a pianist I run the tearooms. Instead of being a drunkard and jailbird, my brother is a hypochondriac. . . . Was it worth it? Wouldn't it have been better to be quite ruthless at the start, and make one of us, at least, a success?" She made a flicking motion with her thin fingers. "It doesn't matter now, one way or the other. Shall I tell you something, Walter?"

He turned a troubled face towards her.

Miss Fortune smiled at him, but as if she did not see him.

"I'm going to die, Walter. Quite soon, I think. This is probably the last time I shall play for the Outing."

His face paled and then reddened. His little beard quivered up and down in distress. She thought he looked funny, quite ridiculous. Poor little Walter, it was a shame to shock him so.

"Bee!" he spluttered. He grabbed her thin hand. "Bee—I don't be-lieve that! Tell me you don't mean it!"

"Don't distress yourself, Walter. We all die sooner or later."

"You must see another doctor."

"I've seen three. They all told me the same."

He brought out the snowy handkerchief again.

"They could still be wrong." He blew his nose repeatedly. "What is it? What do they say it is?"

"It's my heart." She laughed suddenly. "My poor heart was always my downfall, wasn't it, Walter? They want me to sell the business and take life easily. Lie about the place and look pathetic. But I won't do that. I don't want to leave this place. I like to be high up, to be able to see a very long way. I like to watch the gulls sailing

[123]

down the wind and the sea piling up against the cliffs in stormy weather. And the sun on the hills in the early mornings. . . . And I like the wet, smooth sands at low tide, and the little creatures in the pools, and the sea pinks in the grass. . . . And in the winter I hear the ships out at sea calling through the fog. . . . I shall stop here until the end. . . ."

"Is there much pain?" he got out.

She nodded.

"Sometimes. They've given me something for that. I'm not afraid. I think it will be quick and sudden when it comes."

He could not bear it. He seized her work-worn hands and laid his forehead on them. She was Bee, the Vicar's pretty daughter, and he was the young bank clerk, and they were in love. . . .

"No," he cried. "No! Marry me, Bee. Marry me now, and I'll look after you. I won't let you die. I'll live here if you want me to. We'll be together—like we should have been all along."

She tried to withdraw her hands, but he held them fiercely. She could feel his tears on them, trickling between her fingers.

"Dear Walter!" She smiled at the bald, pink spot on his crown, but her nose wrinkled a little, too: she didn't like men to be bald. "What a pother all about nothing! People do die. You, too, Walter,"—she was amused to see his quick recoil—"but not for a long time yet, I hope," she soothed. "Why, what would the choir do without you! It's quite unthinkable, isn't it? You will have many more Outings in this place, I hope. . . . And maybe I shall still be here in spirit; flying above the roof with the sea gulls, or sitting amongst the sea pinks on the edge of the cliff. . . . I shall see you standing there, beating time with your baton, and I shall smile at you, and you will remember me for an instant. . . . I wonder who will play your accompaniments then, Walter? Be sure I shall keep an eye on her, too!"

He drew away from her. Such talk was distasteful to him.

"You have shocked me—shocked me profoundly!" he muttered miserably. "How can you speak of it so, Bee! Surely it is not a subject for levity?"

"If our religion means anything, I can hope, at least, for a better time in the next world than I've had in this one." Her voice was matter-of-fact, almost gay. "Come now, Walter, save your severity for poor Phoebe and her bellowing. . . . It's time I got back. Look, the rain is over. Here comes the sun. Look—oh, look, Walter, how the sea shines! What a lovely, lovely world!"

She went down the lane, hands and face lifted to the sun's warmth. Sad and perplexed, Walter pattered after her.

The rain fell on Audrey. She stood under the close-leaved branches of a tree for shelter.

It was not far from the bus terminus to the gate of the tearooms, but the rain was heavy and she wore no coat. Her green-and-white voile frock would be soaked in two seconds—for, of course, she must not run, now.

She suddenly wanted quite terribly to run. To go running up the lane and jump fences, and climb trees and roll over and over down grassy slopes, as she did when she was a child. She wanted to shout and sing and push people about; to stand on a swing and tug at the ropes, urging her body backwards and forwards, till she was flying high above the sea, above the trees; higher than the whole world; alone in clouds. . . .

But she must not run because of the baby.

She was caught again. Caught in the trap of life, of experience. Her youth struggled rebelliously in the toils. *O, Thou, who didst with Pitfall and with Gin beset the Road I was to wander in. . . .*

Once, she had been able to repeat the whole of the Rubáiyát from beginning to end, but she doubted if she could do it now.

> Awake! for Morning in the Bowl of Night
> Has flung the Stone that puts the Stars to flight. . . .

What magic. What utter sorcery the words distilled! All her life in moments of stress she had fled to the old Persian rebel as others fly to the Bible, to the *Financial Times,* to the radio.

She shut her eyes and leaned back against the rough bole of the tree, groping in memory for lovely words, stumbling through half-forgotten verses, suddenly remembering whole pages correctly. Her copy of Omar had been a very precious one, bound in brown suede, beautifully illuminated, with illustrations by Frank Brangwyn. She hadn't set eyes on it for a long time. Whole piles of beloved books lay stored away in dusty trunks in the attic. What time did she have for reading nowadays? What time would she ever have again?

> The Bird of Time has but a little way
> To fly—and Lo! the Bird is on the Wing. . . .

Sadness poured through her; sadness and beauty intermingled. The bird is on the wing. And here am I, stuck in a country parsonage with three children and another one coming. And no maid. No money. Nothing. . . .

Tears burned behind her closed lids. She allowed them to trickle down her cheeks. One fell into the hollow beneath her chin and she felt its erratic course down between her breasts.

> One Moment in Annihilation's Waste,
> One Moment of the Well of Life to taste—
> The Stars are setting and the Caravan
> Starts for the Dawn of Nothing—O, make haste!

A sob caught in her throat.

I'm enjoying this, she thought. I'm having a lovely time. I hope nobody comes along and spoils it. I just want to lean against this tree and say my lovely words and fairly drip with self-pity. . . . If Frances could see me now she'd get me psychoanalyzed. Andrew would be terrified. . . . I don't care. I want to be alone, like Thingummy, and just wallow. . . .

But she was not alone.

A twig snapped behind her. There was a human grunt, a human sniff. There was a tiny whimpering. Somebody said: "Sh! . . ." and began to croon a wordless song.

Audrey peered cautiously round the tree.

Jack was sitting among the heaped, twisted roots, rocking a blanketed bundle in his arms. He glanced up and laid a finger on his lips.

"Jack's puppy," he whispered. "Asleep."

She nodded and stood still, gazing down at the small, absurdly touching little face between the blanketfolds; eyes not quite shut, showing the whites; shell-pink tongue protruding between needle-sharp milk teeth; one ear up, one flopped.

She did not offer to touch the puppy, for she sensed he would resent that, and she sympathized. People were always poking at your babies, breathing in their faces, rousing them from placid slumbers with shrill cries of admiration.

"It's a lovely puppy!" she whispered.

He beamed delightedly.

"Poorly," he volunteered. "Jack make it well."

He will, too, she thought, watching his gentle movements as he shifted the bundle higher on his arm, put back a fold of blanket to give the puppy more air.

She looked at him more closely than she had ever done before. Old Crackerjack. The village idiot. Why, what rubbish! He's no more an idiot than I am, she thought with surprise. His face was alight with tenderness. His hands, surprisingly well-shaped, showed precision and delicacy. And they were so clean. He was clean all over: the odd, patched items of his clothing, the back of his neck, the thin, blond, silky hair, the ridges of his ears. . . . He was clean and kind and gentle and strong. He was a worker. And he loved small, helpless things. . . .

Audrey talked about the puppy, speaking in a whisper, not to wake it. But she thought of other things. Of the tumble-down cottage whose rent, small though it was, was still more than Auntie Ag could afford, and of the many shut, unfurnished rooms in the Vicarage. Of the comfort of having Auntie Ag always at hand instead of only two half-days a week. Of logs piled high in the shed, of nicely weeded paths and well-cut lawns. Of the relief of knowing that the children were being watched over, kept out of mischief, taken for walks when she was too busy to give the time to them. . . .

Some people would call it a crazy notion. Kathy would, for instance. Kathy was terrified of anything the least bit out of the ordinary. But Kathy hadn't seen Jack nursing his puppy. She didn't matter, anyway. She had never had to make do and go without and grin and bear it. She didn't know what it was like being Mrs. Vicarish and polite when you were feeling completely hellcat and longing to murder everyone in sight. She hadn't the faintest notion of what it took to have three children and another one coming and a vast old house in a shocking state of unrepair, and a husband with his head in the clouds and his toes poking through carpet slippers, and no money.

No money.

Well, there you were. Even if Auntie Ag and Jack lived rent free in the vicarage, they still had to eat and be clothed.

No money. Hell—no money!

If I'd stuck to teaching, she thought, instead of getting married, I'd be sitting pretty now. Holidays abroad. Clothes like Frances's instead of bargain basement remnants, and pinned up at that. . . . When I'm through with this baby I'll go out teaching again, and Andy can lump it. The village can lump it. The Bishop can lump it. . . . No, I couldn't leave the children. Nobody else would understand Allegra. And Peter would never have dry feet. Oh, hell. . . . I can teach *them*, anyway, for the first few years. That'll be a saving. There's nothing but the village school for miles. . . . Maybe I could start a kindergarten in the big south room with the veranda. We could do it up ourselves and get desks and things on installment. . . . The two boys at the Hall. Mrs. Patman's girls and the Moore child. John and Philly Waterhouse. Barbara Prescott. Our three, and the baby coming on, and other people's babies always coming on. . . . Gosh! Her eyes shone. Why haven't I thought of it before? It'll be a riot. There'll be a waiting list as long as your arm. And I could afford Auntie Ag and Jack, too. . . . Why is my neck wet? Oh, yes, I was crying. What for? I must find Andy at once, I can't wait to tell him.

She leaned over the sleeping puppy, kissed one finger and laid it delicately between the half-shut eyes. Jack liked that. He did it, too. The puppy slept on, unaware of its importance in the scheme of things.

The rain had stopped.

Audrey smiled at Jack and slipped away to look for Andrew.

The rain fell on Andrew, woke him from a pleasant dream of undergraduate days to the realization that he had walked much farther than he had intended, and looked like getting uncommonly wet.

He sat up in the small, turfed hollow on the moor and looked about for shelter. There wasn't a tree in sight. What a nuisance. A farm about a mile down the road sent up a finger of smoke, but he'd be soaked to the skin long before he got there.

Well, it couldn't be helped. Of course, he ought to have brought his raincoat; but who could have dreamed of rain on such a day! Anyway the raincoat leaked pretty badly.

He eyed his blazer and flannels with misgivings. Did grass stains come off readily? Audrey got upset so easily these days. They'd have to go to the cleaner's soon, anyway, but such items were not allowed for in the domestic budget. It was all very worrying.

The trouble is, he thought contritely, it's Audrey who does the worrying, not me. I can shut things out so easily. Too easily, maybe —I don't know. She worries about all of us all the time. She's always in the thick of it. I can get away and forget.

He pictured the cool, dim interior of his church; smelled the smells of old stone, old wood and fading flowers. Even up here on the empty moor with the rain on his face and the sky darkening about him he could recapture something of the peace, the ecstasy he knew when he knelt alone before the sunshot dimness of the altar amongst the familiar smells, the silence that was full of infinitesimal sounds, the shadows compound of color, the light dropping richly from the rose window onto the ancient gray stones of the chancel, worn by the knees, the feet of a hundred living, a million dead.

Morning and evening he knelt alone in the dim little church and surrendered his soul to peace. This was his kingdom, this his escape. This he shared with no one, not even Audrey.

Not even God. . . .

Abruptly Andrew halted at this thought. Its impact was chill and impartial as the rain on his down-bent head.

Was that true? he wondered, dismayed.

It could not be true. What of the joy he experienced, the ecstasy, the passion of peace; the feeling he sometimes had of being upborne by powerful wings? These things were surely of God. . . .

But were they? How could he be sure they were not the result of autosuggestion? Hadn't he often been irritated, even angered by the intrusion of another worshiper? That was the word—intrusion; and it was the measure of his failure as a priest.

But I love the services, he thought, justifying himself. I love the people. At least, I think I do. . . . I work for them, with them. I enter into their joys. I visit the sick, comfort the dying. I do the work to which I was dedicated. What more is required of me?

The rain ran coldly down his face. He wiped it away with the back of his hand in a helpless gesture.

"Don't let me be a failure, Lord," he prayed; and was immediately ashamed. There I go, shifting my responsibility. That's the sort of prayer God hates, I should think. . . . Perhaps I'd better take my blazer off. Shirt, too. . . . No, I can't go lolloping round the country half naked. I'm the parson, not a man. Better keep going. I expect Miss Fortune can dry me off somehow. . . . I wonder where Audrey is. I've hardly spoken to her since we started. She must have slipped away into the town while I was talking to the boys after lunch. Might have told me she was going. I think she's rattled about something. She's been rattled an awful lot just lately. I wonder if I'm a failure as a husband, too. . . .

He sneezed violently twice; and for a short space allowed himself the luxury of thinking about double pneumonia and funerals with floral tributes, and being appreciated too late. But he was snapped out of this by the sight of a sports car approaching at a great rate.

He leaped to the side of the road. There was a loud report. The car shot past him, swerved violently, turned a complete circle and came to rest with its hood pointing in the direction from which it had come.

"Hell's bells!" complained a voice from under the hood.

A head poked out and regarded the flattened tire with deep dislike.

"A neat bit of driving," Andrew complimented.

An odd, tight, surprised-looking face peered at him from under a down-snapped brim.

"I was going to stop, anyway. Aren't you the parson from Staving?"

"Yes. And you're the Pilot Officer who's staying at the hotel."

"Ex-Pilot Officer. And ex-guest of the hotel. I left this morning, as a matter of fact."

"You haven't got very far."

"No."

"Been having engine trouble?"

"No."

They watched each other warily. The rain hung between them like a gray curtain.

"I'll give you a hand with this," Andrew offered.

"No need, thanks. Probably be quicker alone, if you get me. Anyway, you're soaked."

"I am rather. I expect they can fix me up at the tearooms."

Brian threw away the stub of a cigarette.

"I've got plenty of clothes," he said diffidently. "Take my case and walk fifty yards farther on, and round the bend there's an old barn with an open front. You can rub yourself down—there's a towel of sorts stowed away somewhere—and take what you fancy. It's all shabby and most of it foul, but at least it's dry, and we're much of a size. I'll drool her down and change the wheel under cover. Okay?"

"It's very good of you," Andrew mumbled, ashamed to accept such kindness from one towards whom he had failed, he told himself miserably, in his obvious duty.

The barn was waterproof and surprisingly warm. Andrew shed his dripping garments and did a few brisk exercises. Then he opened the suitcase and took out a towel. It was perfectly clean. He carefully averted his eyes from certain scarlet markings which made him dreadfully afraid that it was the property of a famous hotel in Droitwich, and concentrated earnestly on the parable of the Good Samaritan, while briskly scrubbing.

By the time the car had edged its way gingerly into the barn he was glowing with warmth and good-fellowship, ready with the offer of his tobacco pouch, fortunately dry.

Brian explained that he couldn't hold a pipe any longer because of the things they had done to his mouth; and once again Andrew felt ashamed, because he ought to have seen that without being told.

"Funny how good you feel without any clothes," he exclaimed, puffing clouds of smoke up to the rafters. "I wonder if that is the solution to all this war business. If everybody took off their clothes I feel sure they'd stop sending ultimatums to each other."

Brian's grin tore his face into a ghastly caricature of mirth.

"We should all die laughing at each other—so it'd be the same thing in the long run."

Brian jacked up the car and attacked the wheel with practiced ease. Funny, he mused, even without his clothes you'd know he was a parson. . . . Not a bad sort of fellow, really. Not the hearty back-slapping type. I wonder if I could talk to him. Wonder if it'd do any good. Probably not. . . . What is there to say, anyway? I'm adult. I'm capable of distinguishing between right and wrong without the help of any parson. Rose has made me feel sentimental, that's all it is. . . . Rose, sweet Rose. How kind her arms were, how soft her breast. Sweet, sweet Rose. . . . But what's the use of talking? I don't really want to change. At least, I shouldn't if I wasn't fed up and disfigured and out of a job. If there is anything to this God business, is seems a bit low-down to start sucking up just because there's nothing else left. . . . "Sorry those bags are so foul," he threw over his shoulder.

"Not at all," Andrew assured him. "I'm more grateful than I can say. If you'll give me an address, I'll have them cleaned and sent on to you." And that means two pairs at the cleaner's, he thought, but at least it'll be cheaper than pneumonia.

Presently, clothed and warm and puffing steadily, he stood at the door of the barn watching Brian's movements with respect.

"Can't think how you handle it so easily," he commented. "I'm an awful duffer with cars."

Brian grunted, stood up, wiped his filthy hands on an oily rag. "Nothing to it."

"I'm afraid I'm not very practical."

"Well, I'm not very spiritual."

They grinned shyly at each other.

Now, Brian thought. Now is the moment, if you want it. You'll never get such a chance again.

And Andrew thought: I wonder if there's anything I can do to help him? He doesn't look happy. This is just the sort of opportunity I ought to welcome. Probably his trouble goes much deeper than plastic surgery or the horrors of war. . . . I'm a parson, aren't I? A word from me might do incomparable good. Or irretrievable harm. . . . I ought to chance that. That's what I'm *for*. If I let him talk it might help. I should hate him to think I was prying. . . .

He gazed steadily at a patch of blue that was struggling through the clouds beyond the barn door.

"You probably think I'm a queer sort of parson," he managed, picking his words slowly and with difficulty. "You've been on my doorstep, as it were, all these weeks, and I've never even spoken to you. You've been through a pretty bad time, I believe? . . . I've often wished to speak to you. I've wondered if there was anything I could do to—to help, if you see what I mean."

He hesitated, embarrassed.

Brian stared past him at the rapidly brightening sky.

"The church was there, if I'd wanted to come."

"But it's my job, you see. I'm not supposed to wait till people come, if they are in trouble, in need of help . . ."

"Round 'em up, like a sheep dog—is that it?"

"I'm not good at it," Andrew confessed. "I hate to pry, to poke my nose in. I haven't got a thick enough hide, that's the trouble with me. I dream dreams and see visions and avoid personal contacts unless they're thrust upon me. In fact," he admitted, turning a troubled gaze on Brian, "I don't think I'm a very good parson."

Brian threw the oily rag into the car and lit a cigarette.

"Be all the same in a hundred years, I expect," he said indifferently. "It's clearing up fast."

Snubbed! thought Andrew. And serve me right! Of all the clumsy approaches . . . but he stuck at it doggedly.

"The fact remains that I really should like to help you, if you want help. If you feel you would like to talk to me, get things off your chest. . . . Sometimes it does help, just to talk to another person, you know. You could forget I'm a parson. Wash that out. . . ."

Brian's eyes glimmered under the snapped-down brim of his hat.

"What would you like me to tell you?" he asked politely. "I have a large variety of sins to my credit, both of commission and omission. Some are more entertaining than others, naturally. Shall I start with a certain week end I spent in Cairo? Or one of the less hectic, but more frequent Paris episodes?"

Andrew's ears were red. He bent and knocked out his pipe on a stone.

"I suppose I deserved that," he said wryly. "Now you see what I mean when I say I'm a bad parson."

"Oh, I wouldn't say that. But you're not so hot as a psychologist, are you? . . . Let's take it that I *don't* want a heart-to-heart, shall we? That lets us both out."

"If you say so," Andrew said slowly.

"I do say so." He slid behind the steering wheel. "Hop in and I'll run you back to your flock."

Andrew folded his length tidily into the other seat.

"You'd make a better parson than I," he said abruptly.

"Maybe you'd make a better job of acting than I did."

"I might, at that!"

Brian grinned and let in the clutch.

Outside the barn the earth was once more bathed in sunlight. A lark bored up ecstatically into the blue, shrill with praise.

"What sort of choir have you got?" Brian asked. "The usual squeaks and rumbles, with the postmistress sawing away at a harmonium?"

"Good heavens, no! It's good—exceptionally good! We have quite a name in the county; and Yorkshire folks know what they're talking about when it comes to singing, don't forget. You'd hear a sample this evening, if you'd care to stay. We always 'gi' 'em a tune' after tea. Miss Fortune throws open her private lawn and people come from all over the town. We're quite famous for our annual concert. Why not stay and listen? Come as our guest—I'm sure Miss Fortune can manage an extra knife and fork. Of course, not if you feel you ought to push on," he added quickly. And he thought: There you go, spoiling it! What does it matter if he thinks you a bore?

"Well, I might, at that. But no food, thanks. I'll just lurk on the edge for a few minutes, if I may. I don't take very kindly to crowds, at the moment. . . . There's a kid who sings solos, isn't there? Nice kid they call Les. I'd like to hear him do his stuff."

"Oh, yes, young Les and his sister, Rose, are two of our best. Nice children, both of them. Mr. Forsythe—that's our choirmaster—has written a descant to *The Day Thou Gavest*, and Leslie will sing it. It's really rather fine. If you never believed in angels before you'll do so when you hear Leslie sing his descant."

"Rose," said Brian. "Yes, I know Rose. . . . As a matter of fact I've been with Rose all the afternoon."

Andrew turned his head sharply.

"You and Rose Batley have been together all the afternoon?" he repeated. His voice had taken on an edge. "Alone, may I ask?"

"Alone." Brian grinned suddenly, wickedly under the brim of his hat. "No, I didn't seduce her. That, I may tell you, was the general idea when I started out, but it didn't work out that way. . . . As a matter of fact, I asked Rose to marry me." He glanced obliquely at Andrew and grinned again. Mouth set and ears flaming—he'd got the parson in a flat spin all right! "She turned me down, of course," he added easily. "There's a lot of common sense in our pretty Rose. She didn't want fine clothes or good times or foreign travel. She didn't want anything the wicked stranger tempted her with. All she wants, it would appear, is to marry some farmer fellow who hasn't got horse sense enough to ask her. It's a queer world, isn't it?"

"Bob Clough," Andrew told him, his voice stiff in spite of himself. "An excellent fellow. He's been in love with Rose a long time."

"Then hell, why doesn't he marry the girl and give her a break?"

"It isn't as easy as all that. And of course, Rose is only twenty; there's no hurry. Bob has a good deal to contend with, poor fellow."

"Such as?"

"Shortage of labor, for one thing. There's only one hired man at present. Everything falls on Bob's shoulders. Then there's his father —he's lying helpless from a stroke. The mother died some time ago and there's a stepmother who leads them an awful life. She met up with him when he was crazed with grief over his wife's death. They met in some pub one market day, when he'd had too much to drink. He married her—God knows why! I believe she was actually on the streets, or as near as makes no difference. Not a local woman. It was just one of those things that do sometimes happen. Anyway, he married her."

"Made an honest woman of her, in fact. You ought to approve, parson!"

"Well, I don't," Andrew answered sturdily. "The whole thing was a tragedy from first to last. If you ever go into The Crown you'll know what I mean; she's in there every night until they turn her out. She has to be seen to be believed. . . . Not a very inviting household for a young, innocent girl, you'll agree!"

"Why doesn't the fellow throw her out on her ear? Or get a divorce, or something?"

"They're lawfully married. And as far as anyone knows, she's been faithful. Knows which side her bread's buttered, I expect. Of course she drinks like a fish and keeps the place filthy, and they have vile, degrading scenes. . . . But you can't divorce a woman for those things."

"Separation, then?"

Andrew shook his head.

"The husband is a helpless invalid. He can't do anything about it. Actually, he's not the one who suffers most. It's Bob, and those young, impressionable brothers. And, indirectly, of course, Rose. . . . That woman's safe, and she knows it."

"He could pay her to go away."

Andrew laughed shortly.

"With what? Farmers don't have money, they have land and crops and stock. Everything they make goes back into the land. Even if he could do it, she'd bleed him white. . . . No, she's safe enough while the old boy lives. One can only hope it will not be too long."

Silence fell upon them. The car began to descend a steep, winding lane. Brian braked, sounded a long blast on the horn.

"Good thing if she ran off with somebody," he said. "Good out of evil, and so forth. Or wouldn't you approve?"

Andrew sighed.

"That's one of the questions people are so fond of springing on us parsons. Can good come out of evil? How do I know? How does anybody know? Right and wrong, good and bad, black and white . . . the longer I live the less I know about them. Like you, I've often wished somebody *would* run off with her—God forgive me for it," he put in worriedly. "But I'm afraid there's not much chance of that. You haven't seen her. She's not even *clean* . . . I want Bob and little Rose to be happy, but as far as I can see they'll have to wait for it." He sighed again. "I seem to be thrusting my problems on to you, instead of helping with yours." The car slid to a standstill and Andrew climbed out. "Sure you won't come and join us now?"

"I'll get a bite in some quiet pub," Brian said, "and come back for the singing. But I'll say good night now, if you don't mind. I'm pretty hopeless with masses of people. Besides, I probably shan't be able to stay to the end. I ought to be on my way."

"Good night," Andrew said, "and thank you for the clothes. Where shall I send them?"

"Oh, give 'em away," Brian said easily. "I'm sure you know somebody who'll be glad of them. My good deed for the day! You get soaked, so some lad gets a pair of pants for nothing—so good can come out of evil, you see!"

Andrew smiled.

"Good night, then."

"Good-by."

They shook hands.

The car backed and turned and shot away. Andrew watched it

out of sight and then went slowly through the gate of the Good Fortune Tea Rooms.

The rain fell on the driver as he lay on the beach, having a nice little bit of shut-eye after his swim.

It fell for some minutes before a large drop splashing in his open mouth brought him sitting upright, dazed and belligerent.

"Darn it!" he muttered, half awake.

He scrambled to his feet, shaking himself like a large dog.

He was nice and wet!

The beach was deserted, save for a few figures tented behind mackintoshes and umbrellas against the sea wall. Paper bags and newspapers, sodden and hideous, strewed the sand, along with orange peel, banana skins and ice-cream cartons. A small wooden spade floated in the moat of an abandoned sand castle.

"Great sufferin' ducks!" he muttered, scrambling up to the promenade and making a beeline for the nearest pub.

As he pushed open the swing doors the noise and the heat were terrific, but he welcomed them. Good old England. Good old damp, safe, crowded, shockin' old England! The wrong part of England, maybe; not so good as Ilford; but not so bad, at that. He elbowed his way through the crowd and ordered a bitter. He took a long, satisfying pull, lit a fag and turned to survey his fellow creatures.

There was a figure he recognized. Big boy in a comic check outfit. He'd been on the old bus, along with a couple of womenfolks in black, like molting crows. Blacksmith, so the farmer had told him. Had about enough, by the looks of him, too. And that woman on the stool beside him, her in the paper hat—goodness, that *was* one of the old crows in person! Well, well! Whaddyer know! the driver thought, grinning.

"What are *you* grinning at?" said a voice.

And there was the farmer bloke, lining up beside him, tankard in hand.

The driver indicated Joe Peck with a jerk of the head.

"Looks like we're going to have fun when the parson sees that little lot."

"Ah," Bob agreed. "I been watching 'em. Joe's okay. It teks a hell of a lot to put Joe out cold. It's his missus I'm thinking on. I can't sum it up, her being in here. She's bin giving the old man hell about the drink for thirty years—an' look at her! You seen what's on yon paper hat she's wearing?"

"No, what?"

" 'Thrilling and willing.' "

Their eyes met. Their brown faces creased into delighted grins.

"That's a good 'un!"

"Worth another?"

"Not for me, so long. I got to drive you home. What about you?" Bob shook his head.

"I'd better get the two of 'em on t'bus, or we're all going to miss us teas, let alone the singing. Stand by, in case I need a hand?"

"Okay."

They drained their tankards, slapped them down on the smeary bar.

"Same again?" asked the barmaid, preening her brassy curls at Bob.

"No, thanks, just off."

The driver winked at her and received a haughty glare for his pains.

Bob tapped the blacksmith on the shoulder and was accorded a bellowing welcome.

"What you drinking, Bob lad? Hey, there, driver an' all! What's yours, lad?"

"Time we were off, Joe."

"Nay, bags of time," Joe protested. "Come on, lads, gi' it a name. Bitter for thee, Bob?"

"Nay, I'm finished. Come on, Joe, tea starts in twenty minutes an' tha'll be wanting a wash up an' that. Better get a move on."

"Who wants tea!" demanded the blacksmith.

"I do," Bob said stolidly. "I want a good meal inside of me. I'm right hungry. Don't come now, tha'll happen miss the singing," he added, "an' we're short on basses as it is."

Addie Peck clutched the edge of the bar and levered herself carefully off the high stool. Her color was deeper than usual, her hair a little disordered, but she was perfectly steady on her feet, Bob was thankful to see.

"Bob's right, Joe, it's time we was off."

"Thee get back on t'stool," ordered her husband. "We're havin' one for t'road."

"Nay, Joe, I've had three already!" Her eye caught Bob's and she glared defiantly. "And enjoyed 'em above a bit, I have."

Bob gave her a friendly nod. Mrs. Peck looked more human than he'd ever seen her. He wondered where Minnie had got to. He never before remembered seeing Mrs. Peck without Minnie tacked on.

"Don't forget our storm, Joe," he said. "That bit where you an' me come in: *Pom per-om per-om pom; Pom, Pom, POM.* I shan't be able to manage that bit on me own. I shall sound about as much like a storm as a couple of peas rattling in a tin."

"Sweep across the bosom
Of—the—DEEP . . ." bellowed the blacksmith, nearly bursting his collar. "Aye, it's a grand bit, yon!" He wiped his mouth on the back of his hand and sang it again. Bob hummed in harmony. Several people turned and listened, smiling.

"No singing, *if* you please!" commanded the barmaid.

"An' then sopranos an' tenors comes in," the blacksmith continued with rising enthusiasm; and his voice soared into a grotesque squeak: "Dee, dee, dee, dee; deedle dee, dee, dee. . . . An' then me an' Bob comes in again, fair thundering it out: As I swee—ee—eep across the bosom Of The DEEP. . . ."

"You 'eard!" the barmaid cautioned, glaring at the driver.

"Great sufferin' ducks, miss, I never opened me mouth!" he protested.

"Aye, it's grand, that!" gloated the blacksmith. "That's what we're goin' to sing tonight, folks," he informed the room. "Up at the Good Fortune Tea Rooms. Number Four bus. No charge for admittance and all are welcome. The Bishops Staving choir at its best. Come an' hear us, all on you. No charge for admittance. Number Four bus to the Good Fortune Tea Rooms." He glanced at his watch and frowned. "We're goin' to be late," he accused his wife. "How much longer I got to wait for you?"

He began to shoulder his way out, Bob behind him, grinning. Addie made haste to follow with the driver.

As she came into the street she pulled the paper hat from her head, smoothing her hair self-consciously.

"He wanted me to wear it," she explained in a pinched voice.

"And very nice, too, Ma'am!" the driver replied gallantly.

They caught the bus by a hairsbreadth.

6

How grand the tea table looked with its weight of good food, shining crockery and bright, branching flowers! Young Les could hardly believe his eyes.

All down the middle of the table stood tall vases of yellow and white daisies, fringed with fern, alternating with earthenware pots of geraniums, radiantly aflame. Tablecloths were snowy white, cutlery gleaming and tall tea urns winking in the sun. Salad bowls were heaped with color: green, scarlet, yellow, white, and the dark wine of beetroot. There were plates of ham and tongue. There were brown fortresses of pork pie. There were mountains of bread-and-butter and immense teacakes split and buttered with no grudging hand. Red and yellow jellies jostled piles of cherry cake, seed cake and sponge sandwich sparkling with sugar. . . .

"Golly!" whispered young Les. "Oh, golly, golly, golly. . . ."

They crowded round the tables. The choir kept eyes on Mr. Forsythe's little black baton with the silver band. Miss Fortune mounted the veranda and sat down at the piano, waited for Walter's nod and struck a chord. The baton lifted, paused, fell.

"Be—present at our ta-a-able, Lord . . ."

The choir led and everybody followed. The blacksmith thundered. Young Les and Ronny Field shrilled eagerly, eyes on the food. Mrs. Maddon mouthed with genteel restraint, glaring at Doris, who, for some unimaginable reason, had got herself wedged at the far end next to Colonel March's gardener. Phoebe Braithwaite folded her hands across her middle and gave it all she'd got, watching Walter's face, which looked tired, she thought. Ee, he wanted looking after! Singing with mechanical lustiness she wondered if that Madame Whatever-her-name-was really had seen anything in her palm. Crying for the moon, she'd said. But surely Walter wasn't as inaccessible as all that! Living right next door to her, and all alone, and not getting any younger. . . .

"Bring back, bring back . . ." chanted Jack, rocking the puppy in his arms. He was very happy.

They had put him right at the end of the table where Miss Fortune would be dealing with the tea urn, and on his other side, Rose, who was always kind to him. He hummed throatily, delighted to be singing with the others. He was having a lovely day. Such a lot of good food, and the ride in the bus, and the puppy and everything. . . . The puppy opened its eyes and sneezed and went to sleep again. Jack held it close in a passion of tenderness. "Bring back, bring back . . ." He was very happy.

Fred Fortune listened, hands in pockets. Lazily he wondered how much Bee thought she was going to make out of this do. As far as he could see she'd be well down on the deal. Not that he could care less. As long as he could eat, sleep in the sun or by a good fire and take care of his health, he didn't give a damn. It did sometimes occur to him that if Bee were to get sick of looking after him, or die or something, he'd be in a bit of a spot; but it didn't worry him. Bee was the sort that lived forever, and never got tired of being a mug.

Minnie Peck stood silent, too. She kept her eyes on her plate, but she missed nothing. She knew that Pa was flushed and boisterous and Ma was flushed and nervous. She knew that Ma wasn't wearing any hat and that her hair was all over the place and looked a proper sight. She knew that Ma kept sending glances of apology and invitation down the table; but she wasn't going to sit by Ma—not if she went down on her bended knees, she wasn't! On the other hand, she had no wish to stay in her present position, with that Pearl Lomax jammed against her on one side and that Miss Stacey on the other. There was no need to crowd and crush. There was plenty of room. Mrs. Maddon had an empty chair, right next to her. As soon as Grace was over, Minnie decided, she would move over and sit by Mrs. Maddon—and Ma could nod and hiss and beckon as much as she liked, and lump it.

"Bless these Thy gifts. . . ." sang John William Welsh and Doris Maddon, holding hands quite shamelessly and letting their love shine in their faces for all to see.

"Bless these Thy gifts. . . ." sang Andrew. And he looked across the table at Audrey, his wife (for once again they had not been able to sit together), and made the motions with his eyebrows that were as clear to her as speech. *I love you,* he signaled. *I love you. . . .* And his heart lifted with gratitude for the gift of Audrey, who was making return signals to show that she understood and approved.

". . . and grant that we
  May feast in Pa-ra-a-dise with Thee."

They all sang these words, and to each they meant something different.

To Miss Fortune they meant simply that she would fold her hands and let somebody else think about food. To Bob they brought thoughts of Rose with her sleeves rolled up, dimpled, floury arms, baking bread in his kitchen. Mrs. Maddon had a confused vision of golden plates balanced precariously on a marble parapet above the clouds. Miss Stacey thought of the warm, noisy sergeant's mess, with the radio going full blast and all The Boys drinking innumerable cups of char. George Fiddler imagined himself installed in the parlor behind old man Lomax's oil and color shop in Lower Staving, with Pearl (or Violet) getting his supper while he checked up on the day's takings.

To the choirboys, however, Paradise was simply here and now, with all these lovely eats; and no sooner had they shrilled *Amen* than they were in their seats and hard at it.

George sat between the sisters Lomax, gallantly plying them with food.

It was astonishing how much those girls could eat! Didn't seem to put an ounce of fat on them, either! "Sooner keep you a week than a fortnight," he remarked, as Pearl reached for her third tea-cake.

It was meant as badinage and taken as such.

"Oh, we can eat, me an' Vi. And why not? We work for our food, an' nobody can say any different. You don't do so bad yourself, George Fiddler, come to that!"

"I'm a worker, an' all. I like to see folks eat hearty if they work for it, I will say that."

"Me, too."

He warmed slightly to Pearl.

After all, you couldn't judge a girl by the way she acted on holiday. And it was true she was a worker. They were both workers: in the shop and in the house behind the shop. They both knew the business, and they both knew how to cook and clean and sew. They were both superlatively healthy and thoroughly understood the value of money—especially other people's money.

It seemed to George, reaching for a quivering glass of red jelly for Violet, that if you had to marry, you might do a lot worse than marry Violet—or Pearl—and be done with it. He thought longingly of the bright, clean, double-fronted shop in the High Street of Lower Staving, and of the smart green delivery truck standing outside. Just the job!

His eye lighted on Ivy, who was sitting next to Harry Waterhouse across the table, quirking her little finger in the air and picking at her food as if she wasn't made of real flesh and blood. He thanked his stars he hadn't gone too far with Ivy.

To think that he had even contemplated spending the rest of his life with that quivering, pinkish nose, that whining voice, those finicking ways! Drive you crazy they would!

He suddenly remembered that Ivy still had his key.

He tried to catch her eye, but Ivy wasn't having any. He hissed across the table, and Harry Waterhouse gave him an old-fashioned look and asked him if he happened to be wanting anything.

George said stolidly that he only wanted a word with Ivy.

Ivy kept her eyes on her plate. She nibbled the edge of a curd tart and shrank a little nearer to Harry, as if for protection.

"Afterwards," Harry promised George; and his voice had an ominous ring.

Slight as it was, the verbal and visual exchange had not been missed by the Lomaxes. Their eyebrows arched at each other across George's body.

"Pity he never sat by Ivy if he wanted to talk to her all that bad," Violet remarked.

"I didn't want," George said dourly.

"Pity nobody never told him it was bad manners to sit with one party and shout at another," said Pearl.

"I never shouted," George protested.

[143]

"Whispering, then. Whispering an' making signs. That's worse, isn't it, Vi?"

"Much worse. Come to that, there's room between Ivy and Mr. Welsh, if everybody shoved up a bit. Can't think why he doesn't tek his plate an' go an' sit by her, an' have done with it. I'd just as soon have his room as his company."

"Sooner," said Pearl.

Surreptitiously George wiped damp hands on his trousers. This wasn't doing much to consolidate his position!

"I don't want to sit beside nobody," he declared, "only you."

"Were you addressing me," Violet inquired politely, "or our Pearl?"

"Both of you," said George; and added with poetical recklessness: "a rose between two thorns, eh?"

"That's not a very nice thing to call us!"

"Well, you know what I mean," cried the goaded George. "I mean t'other way round!"

"Make up your mind," Pearl advised coldly.

George ate doggedly and in silence. He knew that whatever he said now would be the wrong thing, so he might as well say nothing. But that need not stop him making a good meal. It seemed to George that, before this day was done, he was going to be thankful for the strength given by a bellyful of good nourishing victuals. He felt it in his bones.

"What do you fancy, luv?" asked John William Welsh. "A queen cake, or some of yon sponge?"

Miss Maddon indicated the sponge with a blush that delighted her lover's eyes and caused his knee to press against hers beneath the table. Which, in turn, caused her to blush ever more brightly.

"Give over, John William!" she whispered, trying to look severe. "Whatever are you thinking of!"

"Shall I tell thee, luv?" he whispered ardently.

"No, of course not," she said hurriedly. "Get on with your tea, do, Mrs. Braithwaite's looking at us."

"She's welcome. Old Phoebe's none the sort to grudge anyone a bit of happiness. Ee, by gum, I'm enjoying me tea; this is a right good sponge, isn't it?"

"It is that," Miss Maddon said happily, forgetting that she had ever been a schoolmistress and slipping easily and comfortably into the speech of her childhood. "I make a right good sponge, too, John William, and I've got a light hand with pastry, if I do say it. Won't it be grand when we have our meals together—just you and me in our own place?"

"Stove doesn't draw as well as it might. I'll speak to the Colonel again. If he's awkward about it, I'll get Joe Peck up an' him an' me will do t'job oursens. I don't want to see thee wrestling with yon smoky beggar, luv. Should you like one of them jellies?"

"I couldn't eat another thing!" Miss Maddon declared. She watched while John William ate two, and thought how lovely it would be to cook for him and watch him eating the results of her cooking.

Her eyes dwelt fondly on him.

He was no beauty, this sudden lover of hers. Skin weathered to the consistency of brown leather. Kind gray eyes set so deep in his head that when he laughed they disappeared altogether. Nose blunt and unremarkable. Thick, grizzled hair, cut so short that he had apparently escaped scalping by a miracle. His adam's apple wobbled up and down when he swallowed. Two side teeth were missing and already it was obvious that he was the kind who needed to shave twice a day.

Plain, rough, hard and male. Male. . . .

Lovely, thought Miss Maddon.

His beard would hurt her, and she would love that. He would sit by the fire in his shirt sleeves and she would not care. His table manners were not blameless, and she would never refer to it, or try to teach him better. She liked him just as he was; plain and rough and male.

I love him, she thought; and knew with astonishment that it was true.

Yesterday she had loved him because he was a man and he wanted her. But now, and in so short a time, already she loved him because he was John William and *she* wanted *him*. . . .

"Doris Maddon's looking right set up with herself," Phoebe remarked, nudging Audrey with her elbow.

Audrey gazed along the table and nodded agreement.

"I've never noticed before how pretty she is!"

"John William seems to think so, an' all," Phoebe chuckled, and turned her eyes to where Mrs. Maddon, enthroned in offended majesty, sternly pursued a meek portion of pink blancmange round her plate with a genteel but totally inadequate fork. "I've got a feeling as there's summat up in yon quarter," she said comfortably. "If so, nobody'd be better pleased than what I should. That girl's never had a chance, with yon owd buzzard allus tacked on. I nivver could abide Agnes Maddon, an' that's the truth."

"Miss Peck seems to be filling the vacant chair," she suggested. "Is there a general revolt of daughters today?"

Phoebe said: "Ah," noncommittally, and drank her tea. However little fondness she might have for Minnie Peck, she had been at school with her mother and she wasn't going to betray any confidences there. The Vicar's wife was a nice little thing, but too young and (in Phoebe's private opinion) too flybeyskybey to understand even the little Phoebe herself understood of the life Addie Peck had lived in the blacksmith's cottage these last forty years. Whose fault it might be was no concern of hers: six of one and half-a-dozen of the other, as like as not. But she and Addie Peck had been girls together, and she wasn't going to gossip about her, and that was flat!

"Daughters have got a way of being awkward," she allowed. "Sons, too. You'll know all about it one of these fine days, luv."

Sons and daughters. . . . Audrey considered this, rather awed by the unfamiliar words. She had never thought of her little brood by such stately names. Much as she loved them, she had never visualized them as anything but hungry, laughing, quarreling, noisy, cuddly creatures whom she was destined to clothe, educate, nurse and watch over for the rest of her life.

Now, at Phoebe's words, she suddenly saw them for what they were: sons who would grow up straight and tall and strong and go flinging off into distant corners of the world, bent on their own business; daughters who would fall in love with men she would probably dislike, or take up careers she didn't approve of, or become so clever she wouldn't be able to understand a word they said. . . . The sons would bring home frightful wives who would be patient and patronizing, and the daughters would laugh at her hats and take her to suitable matinees, and dump their babies on her while they leaped and swooped in Winter Sports or popped over to Paris for the week end . . .

They're *people*, she thought; dismayed, yet not unthrilled by the revelation. Oh, my sweet Allegra, my darling Peter, my tubby little Ruth! . . . And *you*, whoever you are, inside me. You're all *people*. . . . Before I know it you'll all be off on your own affairs, and Andy and I will be left as we started, alone together. . . .

The idea was so disturbing that she felt her eyes fill with easy tears; yet so ridiculous that she had to laugh a little, too. Where's Andy? she thought urgently. I want Andy.

But Andrew was once again caught in the neat toils of Walter Forsythe, who was showing him, with the aid of a knife and fork, two salt cellars and the remains of a blancmange, the general layout of Weston-super-Mare, in which health resort his favorite niece had recently opened a boarding house.

Impelled by a sudden loneliness, Audrey pressed her arms against her body, cradling its precious burden.

You, at least, she thought with sudden fierce love and gratitude, you'll be with me a long time yet. . . .

"Yes, indeed, quite a delightful situation," Walter was saying emphatically. "If ever you spent a holiday at Weston, you might go farther and fare worse than at The Towers. Elsie would make you very comfortable. Mention my name, of course."

His voice trailed off. He knocked one of the salt cellars over and made a great to-do about scraping up the spilled salt. He glanced at his watch, hummed a few bars of an anthem and, pulling himself together with an obvious effort, made three separate guesses at the population of Weston-super-Mare. After that, he gave up all attempts at polite conversation and slumped in his chair, drumming nerveless fingers on the table before him.

It can't be true, he thought miserably. Not Bee. Not yet. . . .

Andrew, who had been mildly irritated, foresaw that unless he took stern measures, he would soon become as knowledgeable about Weston-super-Mare as he now was about the Gregorian Chant, and seized the opportunity of a chat with Minnie Peck, who sat on his other side.

"Well, it has been a lovely day, Miss Peck," he remarked, with that nice suggestion of tottering on the edge of a joke with no real intention of falling over, which is the manner most people demand from clerics on all public occasions of a secular nature.

Minnie Peck stared steadily at her plate.

"Has it?" she answered bleakly.

Oh, dear! thought Andrew. Now what have I let myself in for? Every angle of Minnie's figure was a challenge. Her mouth was pinched up into a tight line. The pallor of her face was accentuated by spots of high color on the cheekbones. Her shoulders dropped and her nose poked. It was obvious that Minnie was cherishing a grievance, but this was scarcely the moment to deal with it.

He determined on a policy of bland obtuseness.

"Yes, indeed," he continued with determination, "I have seldom seen the countryside looking more beautiful. It is quite the best time for the moor, I always think. Such color! And such a splendor of undulating horizon against magnificent stretches of sky! It takes one's breath away." Oh, heavens, he thought, I'm talking like a guide book! But he plunged on, determined not to become embroiled in any of Miss Peck's private feuds, rumors of which he had heard all too often.

Folks said that Minnie Peck hadn't a good word for anybody, man, woman or child. He didn't believe that. There was, of course, good in everyone. There must be something likable in Minnie, even though he had never yet discovered what it was.

Perhaps that was his own fault. No doubt he should have visited at the house more often, instead of smoking a comfortable pipe with Joe in the leaping flame and shadow of the forge. But the sad fact was, he liked Joe and he didn't like Joe's wife and daughter. The phrase "thick as thieves" had always seemed to apply to these women in a marked degree. He thought of them as thieves of Joe's home-life, of his domestic happiness. His sometimes regrettable but always understandable outbursts had been forgiven by Andrew on that account. He had turned a blind eye to them because of Minnie and her mother; a combination that would have sent a saint stumbling from the strait and narrow path—and Joe was no saint.

Nevertheless, Minnie and her mother were his business just as much as Joe, and he would have to do something about it soon, that much was clear. Oh, dear! thought Andrew.

He glanced sideways at Minnie and was horrified to see a tear sliding weakly down her polished, poking nose.

He knew that he must ignore it. It was the only tactful thing to do. A kind inquiry might start an avalanche of such tears, and cause a scene embarrassing to everybody.

It was only now Andrew realized that the woman on the other side of Minnie was not Mrs. Peck, but Mrs. Maddon. Then where, he wondered, astonished, could Mrs. Peck be?

Why, of course, there she was, far down on the other side of the table, sitting next to Joe. He had not readily recognized her. Certainly she appeared oddly different, now he came to look at her. For one thing, she was laughing, and that was a thing he had never seen Mrs. Peck do before. For another, she was not wearing a hat, and it was the first time he had seen Mrs. Peck without a hat. Always the same sort of hat: dreary, and at the same time intimidating. The sort of hat which, in time, established itself as an integral part of the wearer, so that without it there was a suggestion almost of indecency. Mrs. Peck's hair was untidy and her face rather flushed. She presented, indeed, an almost raffish appearance.

But none of these things struck Andrew as being half so significant as the fact that Mrs. Peck was sitting by her husband and not by her daughter. That black and indivisible pair were at last divided. And one, it would appear, was cheerful and the other was not. Dear me!

At any rate, there was only one way of coping with Minnie's tears, and that was to go on talking. Talk about anything. Talk. Jabber. Tell her about getting wet this afternoon and meeting the Raf chap. Probably she wouldn't listen, or care two hoots if she did listen, but it would tide over a situation that threatened to cast a gloom over the Outing and spoil the singing, which wouldn't do at all.

So Andrew passed Minnie's cup to be refilled and almost pushed a large slab of cherry cake onto her plate, and plunged into a lively account of his long walk and his falling asleep on the moor and getting drenched, and his fortunate meeting with Pilot Officer Collinson, and the subsequent changing of clothing and wheel in the barn. He made the account as humorous as he knew how, laughing heartily in case of any possible doubt; and he was gratified to see that Minnie's tears did indeed dry up and that she appeared to be listening, at least.

Listening, but not approving—that much was immediately obvious. She cut her cake like an enemy and her nostrils flared slightly, as if she had detected a bad smell.

"That man!" she exclaimed viciously, as Andrew halted for a drink of tea. "I wonder you could bear to speak to him!"

"I don't understand," he said. "What's wrong with him?"

"What's right, you mean?"

"He was exceedingly kind to me. Not many people would give their clothes to a perfect stranger, as he did."

"I wonder you could bear to wear 'em!"

"I was jolly glad to wear them, I can tell you!" Andrew said stoutly. "I thought him a very likable fellow. And a very courageous one, as you may recall."

"I know all about that." Minnie set down her cup with a bang. "I know more about yon fellow than you do, I shouldn't wonder. This isn't the first time he's stayed in Staving. He was at the hotel a while back—before your time—with a woman."

"His wife, no doubt."

"That's what he called her. She were nowt o' t'sort."

"Oh, come now, Miss Peck, how can you possibly know that!"

"I know it," Minnie said darkly. "I reckon to see as far through a brick wall as most. And a bit further than some," she added, shooting him a glance of bleak disdain.

Conscious of a rising indignation, and equally conscious that he must stifle it, Andrew attacked his cherry cake almost as viciously as Minnie had done.

"Well, well," he remarked, as mildly as he was able, "that's certainly nobody's affair but his own."

"I should have thought it was your affair," Minnie accused him, "you being a parson." *If you can call yourself a parson* her tone indicated. "He drinks too much, an' all."

"He has been through difficult times," Andrew reminded her.

"We've all been through difficult times. But we don't all go getting drunk and breaking the Commandments, do we?"

Controlling himself with difficulty Andrew said: "Perhaps we do not all love our neighbors as ourselves. . . ."

"Meaning me, Mester Stevens?" Minnie asked aggressively.

"And me, Miss Peck. And all of us. And indeed, it is not always easy." He sighed, wishing the meal were over, so he could escape to Audrey.

But Yorkshire appetites take some satisfying. Cups were still plying briskly up and down the table, and Joe was even now helping himself to another slice of pork pie. Mrs. Peck was leaning forward trying to attract Minnie's attention.

"I think your mother wants you," Andrew murmured.

Minnie stared stonily into space.

"Not as much as she's going to want me—not by a long chalk!" she prophesied with ghoulish pleasure.

Andrew turned again to Walter Forsythe.

Walter might be a funny little bore, but he was real, he was human. Let him discourse on the Gregorian Chant if he wished, or list the amenities of Weston-super-Mare *ad nauseum:* Andrew was ready and willing to listen.

Minnie Peck turned Andrew's stomach.

Addie Peck sighed and sat back in her chair.

I shan't try again, she thought. She's seen me all right. She's just paying me back. I don't rightly know what I ought to do, and that's a fact. . . . I reckon she's upset above a bit. And happen I were a bit sharp with her this afternoon, but she's got no call to tek on this way. . . . I reckon I've spoiled our Minnie. I've given up the best years of my life to her—aye, an' the best years of Joe's life, an' all— and this is what I get for me pains.

Passing a hand over her wind-roughened hair, Addie remembered the old hat she had left in the George and Dragon, and the black chip with the high crown, and the two velvet bows that she had intended to buy, and the saucy little forget-me-not hat in which she had looked so daft. . . . Ee, I've made a proper fool of meself today! she thought. If yon lad hadn't thrown cricket ball an' broken me feathers, none o' this would have happened.

"What you eating, missus?" Joe's voice boomed in her ear.

"Nay, Joe, I've done."

[151]

"Done?" Joe's great laugh belled out. "Well, I'm nobbut half done yet. I'm right hungry."

Theirs was the noisy end of the table. There was always noise where Joe was; laughter and shouting; the clang of hammer on metal, the stave of a song roared in his rich bass. . . . Joe laughed and sang, worked and whistled, washed, ate, quarreled and made love more noisily than anyone else. He crashed through life at full blast, with all the stops out and the loud pedal down. Noise was his refuge from the dim unreality of his married life. Noise stopped him from thinking. Almost, but not quite.

Underneath the barrage of noise he now put up, he was thinking. Thoughts milled around in his head; took on life and were gone; showed color and shape and were gone; came and went, but always came back again. . . .

Joe didn't want to think. He'd got out of the way of it.

He didn't want to speculate as to why Addie had followed him into the George and Dragon, why she was sitting beside him now instead of sitting beside Minnie. He couldn't see where it was going to get them.

He was old. Addie was old. Whatever had been between them had died long ago, and its grave had been Minnie's cradle. Now Minnie, too, was old, and it was too late to change. He no longer wished things different.

He couldn't understand it at all. Something had happened to Addie in that hat shop; something he couldn't understand. Her presence at his side embarrassed him. So he laughed the louder, ate and drank the more and told riskier anecdotes than he would otherwise have told, seeing it was Choir Outing, and mixed company. . . .

Rose sat quietly, saying little and eating less. She was not hungry after her lovely tea with Mr. Collinson, and there was nobody really to talk to: Miss Fortune was busy with her tea urn, Jack needed nothing but an occasional smile and nod and, on her other side, Henry Fiddler was too occupied getting his full money's worth to have time for idle chatter.

A queer sort of day it had been, thought Rose. Not at all the sort of day she had hoped for—more, had confidently expected. For a long time now, at the back of her mind had been growing the conviction that this day would see her betrothal to Bob; a conviction based, as she now realized, on nothing more stable than her own romantic fancy and desire.

She stole a look at him now.

He was sitting far down the table, talking to the driver; throwing back his head and laughing, flashing his sound, white teeth. Her heart leaped with love for him. Dear Bob! So kind and dependable and handsome. She was not hurt by his laughter, his apparent enjoyment of the hour. You could laugh, Rose believed, while your heart was breaking in your breast. . . . She didn't want Bob's heart to break; but she would have been more than human had she not hoped that, behind that loud laughter it might be aching just a little. . . .

So you're going to marry a farmer and work hard all your life? Mr. Collinson had said. And she had said: I hope so.

And then he had proposed to her. Well—sort of!

At first she hadn't taken it in—silly goop! . . . All that about pretty clothes and going to foreign parts and that. . . . Whatever must he have thought of her!

It was only now, isolated in the midst of the talk and laughter and cheerful clatter of crockery that Rose fully realized Brian's proposal. She remembered his words with astonishment and pleasure, and blushed warmly at the remembrance.

She gave her imagination full rein.

Suppose she had said yes? . . . Perhaps he would be sitting here now, beside her. There would be small, kindly jokes at their expense, teacups raised in salutation, warm friendliness and excitement. And happen Bob would be laughing the other side of his face, she thought with sharp but evanescent resentment.

And then the drive back; not with the others in the bus, but flashing up hills and swooping down valleys in the blue-and-silver car, leaving all the others far, far behind. Bob and all. . . . Then the interview with her parents. The loving, flustered gratification of Mum; Dad's surliness melting under the bright fire of Mr. Collinson's persuasion.

The brief, exciting courtship, the wedding in the church. Waving good-by to Mum and Dad and young Les. . . . No, that bit wasn't so good: skip it. . . . Flying along the road to London, to Paris, to

Hollywood. . . . The world opening out before her, acknowledging her; yielding up its immense treasure of color and laughter and deep, uncharted experience to her, Rose Batley. Rose Collinson. The wife of a hero. . . .

She drew a deep breath and came to earth. Her eye was caught by the stealthy movement of Jack's hand towards the table leg. Her hand shot out and caught at his wrist, gently guiding the cup back to its saucer. She shook her head at him. That trick of his had always worried Auntie Ag.

"You mustn't do that any more, Jack. Not now, you mustn't."

"Waterfall," Jack explained crossly.

"Aye, but you've got the puppy to think of now. You can't have waterfalls now you've got him. He'd paddle in it and get his little feet wet, and happen to get a chill. You don't want him to get a chill and die, do you?"

Jack clutched the puppy closer, peering at it in alarm.

"Not die," he muttered fiercely. "Jack won't let him die."

"No, I'm sure you won't, Jack. You'll remember that his little feet have to be kept dry, and so you won't pour your tea or your soup or your gravy down the table leg, not ever again, mind! And then he'll grow up to be a big, strong dog, and he'll go everywhere with you. He'll go to the woods and wait while you chop off the branches, and run along by the side of the cart as you haul 'em home, and he'll watch you sawing 'em up. And when you do the shopping for your Auntie Ag, he'll carry the basket in his mouth. Won't that be fun!"

"Fun!" Jack chuckled, listening ecstatically. "Say some more!"

"Well . . . you can teach him all sorts of tricks. To beg, and to shake hands, and fetch sticks when you throw 'em, an' die for the King. And when you want a log for the fire you can teach him to fetch one in his mouth, an' all you'll have to do is pop it on."

"Pop it on!" Jack cried. He began to laugh, rocking from side to side. "Pop it on, pop it on," he repeated, over and over again, till Henry Fiddler ceased his purposeful masticating for a moment, to peer around Rose at old Crackerjack going off the deep end.

"But mind what I say," Rose warned. "No more waterfalls."

"No more waterfalls," Jack promised, dropping from laughter into an immense gravity.

Beatrice Fortune smiled as she busied herself with the tea urn.

Nice child, she thought. Pretty child. . . . Walter and I might have had a darling daughter like Rose, if only I hadn't been so sickeningly noble. If only I hadn't been such a fool. . . . Well, what of it? I should just be leaving her now; just when she needed me most. Poor little Walter, too. I should have made him dreadfully dependent on me. He's feeling it badly enough as it is.

Her eyes dwelt with an ironic tenderness on Walter, who was sunk in his chair crumbling bread on the tablecloth.

He'll get over it soon enough, she thought. Poor little Walter. He's always got his precious choir. "I shall be wanting more hot water very soon, Phyllis," she called, thereby jerking that handmaiden out of a dreamy survey of her crimson nails into the exasperating realities of life again.

"There's a rare crowd of folks waiting in the lane," said Phyllis. "Shall I open t'gates?"

"Not yet," Miss Fortune told her. "Not until I give you the word."

Rose, too, had returned to reality.

Of course, he hadn't meant it. Or only for a minute, anyhow.

And suppose he *were* sitting here beside her, how would he fit in with everybody?

Rose glanced along the table. For a brief, disturbing moment of clarity she saw her companions through Brian's eyes: the weak-witted mouthings of the blond lad on her left. The noisy greed of the dark lad on her right. The shrillness of Pearl and Violet and the unrestrained guffaws of Joe Peck and his neighbors. The drab sanctimoniousness of Minnie Peck. The flamboyant Phoebe. The deflated Walter, shrunk in his starch and glitter. Miss Stacey being strident and Ivy being so dreadfully refined. Young Les and Ronny cuffing each other in animal spirits, with their mouths quite full. Even Bob, dear Bob, in that transient, merciless moment of revelation, looked stiff and awkward in the hot, blue pin-stripe suit and the cheap, open-necked sports shirt, his hair plastered back and his elbows stuck out as he plied knife and fork. . . .

Her glance fell to her own hands clasped upon her knees; rough little hands with stubby fingers and unpolished nails. She had always been ashamed of her hands. . . .

But now, suddenly and quite fiercely she was glad that her hands were rough and square and unlovely, glad that her frock was old

[155]

and her shoes shabby. These were her people, and she was part of them. Her life was bound up in their lives. London, Paris, Hollywood —they were just names; fine clothes and parties, dreams to be dreamed and forgotten, while she got on with the happy business of life. . . .

Rose smiled at her hands; smiled at Miss Fortune who was looking at her so kindly; smiled at Jack and the puppy, and a starling that was striding about the lawn, greedy for crumbs. Her smile traveled down the table, embracing them all. The Vicar and Mr. Forsythe and poor Minnie Peck; Phoebe, sweating from the effects of hot tea, and the valiant Miss Stacey. Ivy and Pearl and Violet and Joe Peck. Miss Maddon and John William Welsh. And Bob; dear, dear Bob, who stopped his laughing with the driver to drink the smile thirstily and ponder the reason for it with his mouth slightly open and his great brown fists planted on either side of his plate. . . .

"Pretty girl, that one in pink," commented the driver. "Smasher, ain't she!"

"Ah," said Bob, trying to catch Rose's eye again, and failing.

"Who is she?" inquired the driver.

Bob turned a baleful eye upon him.

"My fiancée," he said aggressively.

"Okay, chum," said the driver. "Pass us the mustard."

Now what have I said? Bob thought desperately. He passed the mustard; the face of Edie seemed to leer at him out of the little glass.

"Wash that out," he said abruptly. "I'm nuts on her, that's all."

"Okay, chum," said the driver equably. He knew what it was to be nuts on a girl.

He thought about his wife, young Lil. Any minute now, they'd told him. Might be tomorrow, might be a week.

Suppose she went and died. . . . Of course she wouldn't die! A baby born every minute, so they said. And for an instant the whole world seemed filled with the eternal, inescapable anguish of women, so that his body was lacerated by twisting knives. . . .

Young Lil. . . . Danced like an angel. Dance the boots off your feet, she could. . . . Would she ever dance with him again? Yes, of course she would. A baby born every minute. Nothing to get worked up about.

He tried to think of the baby, but his thoughts shied away from it. He could think of nothing but young Lil. . . . The knives twisted in his heart, and he pushed his plate away.

"Eyes bigger than me stomach," he muttered, in sheepish apology for the wasted food.

A black wave of weariness engulfed Miss Fortune. She was suddenly so tired that she swayed on her feet and gripped the edge of the table with panic-stricken hands.

I mustn't die here, she thought dimly. I mustn't spoil everybody's pleasure. "Don't let the pain come now, God," she prayed feverishly. "Not just now. Wait until they've all gone home. . . ."

Somebody pushed a chair against the back of her knees and she collapsed weakly onto it. Somebody poured out a cup of tea and put it into her hands. She sipped at it gratefully, and it restored her.

"Thank you, Rose, my dear," she whispered.

"You've done enough," Rose said firmly. "If anybody has the nerve to send their cup up again, I'll deal with it; but I reckon they've about eaten themselves to a standstill. It's nearly over."

"Yes, it's nearly over," Miss Fortune said dreamily.

"Should you like Miss Maddon to play for the singing?" Rose asked. "I'll nip around and ask her, if you've a mind. She plays very nicely."

"No—oh, no!" Miss Fortune cried in swift alarm. "I'm quite all right, Rose, indeed I am. I just get tired, you know; but give me a cup of tea, and I can go on for hours. It's quite all right."

"Well," said Rose doubtfully.

She had never seen anyone look less capable of going on than Miss Fortune. Her lips were blue, her eyes blank and enormous above chalk-white cheeks and a nose that seemed nothing but bone, the skin dragged away from it, leaving it oddly jutting and bleak.

"It will pass," Miss Fortune urged softly. "Truly, Rose! Don't make a fuss. If you knew how I've looked forward to this day. . . ."

Rose nodded compassionately. She, too, had looked forward to this day for a long, long time. . . . Even if she had been disappointed, that was no reason why she should spoil Miss Fortune's pleasure.

"Well, if you're sure," she said. "I don't think anybody's noticed."

[157]

No, nobody had noticed, thought Miss Fortune.

Her glance wandered round the table, as Rose's glance had wandered a short time before.

And as Rose had viewed the scene through Brian's eyes, so, now, Miss Fortune saw her guests with the clear vision that comes only with bodily weakness and the loosening of earthly ties.

Greed she saw, and envy and bitterness. The white flame of love glowed against the sullen shadow of hate. Fear and resignation jostled ruthless ambition. Weakness sat hand in hand with strength. Kindness and cruelty chattered together. Malice joked with generosity. Hope smiled at despair. . . . Just an ordinary gathering of ordinary, everyday people, she marveled; yet all the human emotions were here, all the attributes of good and evil flamed and seethed under those shy, stolid, shabby, everyday exteriors.

They say it takes all sorts to make a world, she thought, and I see what that means now. This *is* the world—this little group of people in my garden. However far one traveled one would never find anything more exciting, more moving, more in need of help or worthy of praise than these people gathered round my table. . . .

The Vicar was smiling at her, raising his eyebrows. Walter Forsythe, his eyes still downcast, was getting to his feet. Miss Fortune glanced at her wrist watch and nodded. She smiled at Rose and got up briskly.

"I'm fine, now," she said firmly. "A cup of tea—that was all I needed." And turning to the hovering Phyllis she ordered crisply: "Let them in now."

Andrew came striding across the lawn.

"Remember me?" he said hollowly.

"Vaguely," replied his wife, detaching her arm from his grip.

"Where have you been all this time?" he demanded.

"Oh, here and there, you know. Where have you?"

"There. When I wanted to be here," he told her glumly.

"It's been quite a time, hasn't it?" she agreed smoothly. "We shall have such a lot to talk about!"

"Too right. I'm a perfect mine of information on the Gregorian Chant. And I know Weston-super-Mare inside out, forwards and backwards, right, left and center! Remind me to tell you about it, some time."

"Lovely. And I'll tell you about Mrs. Maddon's legs. And the more intimate details of her husband's deathbed."

"Oh, darling," Andrew mourned, "what a lousy day you must have had! Why couldn't we have been together up on the moor? Or fooling about at the Fun Fair? Or swimming?"

"Yes, why couldn't we?" Audrey echoed shortly.

"When I looked around for you, you'd gone."

"You mean," she corrected coldly, "not until I'd gone did you look around for me."

He blinked at her patiently.

"Where did you get to?"

"I went to see Frances."

His face lighted with pleasure.

"Oh, I'm glad. How is she?"

"Very well. Very successful. . . . We had a marvelous tea and a lovely, long, womanly chat. She called me a lump of earth. It was a pity you were not with me." "Shut up, you fool!" she told herself angrily. "Shut up, before you regret it." But something drove her on; something perverse and implacable in her nature that she had never learned to control; a power she hated and despised, yet knew a wry delight in wielding. "I think you'd have enjoyed the visit."

"I'm sure I should," he replied warmly, innocently. "I was always fond of old Frances."

"And she of you." Her eyes, bright and cruel, gazed away over the blue distance, following the soar and dip of a gull. "You should have married Frances, Andrew. She'd have had you into a Bishop's cope before you could say knife."

"I don't want to get into a Bishop's cope."

"Frances would have made you want to."

"Then I'm very glad I didn't marry her."

"So you did consider it!" she pounced.

He stared at her, unhappy and perplexed.

"Audrey," he pleaded, "be nice to me. You were making Happy Faces not long ago." She continued to follow the gull's flight, as if she had heard nothing. "You know how difficult it is," he continued—"We're not here for our own pleasure—"

"—How right you are!" she cut in.

"Yes, well. . . . Be reasonable, darling. You're a parson's wife."

"You're telling me!"

"No," he said, and his tone grew cooler. "I'm merely reminding you."

"Of my duty?" she asked furiously.

"If you like to put it that way. We're both on duty, and you know it."

"Don't let me keep you from yours."

He blew his nose unhappily. The handkerchief was not very white and it had a frayed edge. That, too, was her fault, she supposed. He presented, indeed, rather a crumpled appearance altogether.

"Why are you wearing those extraordinary clothes?" she demanded.

He started to tell her; but two choirboys came paging him with urgent shrieks, and Walter Forsythe could be seen gesticulating on the veranda.

"Tell you on the way home," he whispered. "Sit by me whatever happens. Sorry I was a prig, darling."

"What about our duty?" she inquired caustically.

"Damn duty!" he exploded. "I've done a twelve-hour day already."

He hurried off with the choirboys and Audrey turned away, a smile quivering at the corners of her mouth.

People were drifting through the gate, standing about in little groups along the edges of the lawn, waiting for the singing to begin. They were diffident because it was a free show; appreciative, yet a little patronizing, too. Men jingled the money in their pockets, talking together in self-conscious voices. Women watched Phyllis and her minions clearing the tables, murmuring to each other that girls were not what they used to be; condoled with each other about the impossibility of getting any help in the house and deplored the time wasted in shops. "It's a bit hard!" they exclaimed. And: "I told my fishmonger straight. I said to him . . ."

Audrey wandered to a corner of the garden where an ancient tree threw a patch of shade. Leaning against its rough bole she gazed at the strip of beach below. The tide was running in, making small, sucking noises at the pebbles. A yacht drifted slowly by, red sails flaccid in the evening calm. Someone on board was playing an accordion. The thin sound came sweetly enough across the slowly moving water. "My lady of the lamplight. My own Lili Marlene. . . ." Nostalgic tune, falling on the heart the more peacefully because it stirred memories of war; of incredible horrors now, for the moment, past. . . .

Two choirboys were fighting on the beach. Silently and with enormous concentration they thumped each other, swaying now here, now there.

Feeling suddenly Mrs. Vicarish, Audrey called to them. They ignored her. She shouted again.

"Will! Ronnie! Come up here at once! Mr. Forsythe is waiting for you."

Gasping and crimson, they continued to thump and sway about the slipping shingle. One brought his knee up sharply. The other let out a howl and sank his teeth, apparently, in his opponent's arm.

A figure in worn, elegant tweeds detached itself from a rock and seized a warrior in either hand. Shaking them free of each other, he propelled them before him up the cliff path. Audrey saw that he limped badly.

"Passed to you, please, for action," he grinned.

"Thank you so much." She regarded the blubbering combatants dispassionately. "You two had better go and wash before Mr. Forsythe sees you!" Watching them lumber away she remarked reflectively: "In about twenty minutes they'll be singing *O, Perfect Peace* as if their lives depended on it." She flashed him a smile, adding: "Who'd be a parson's wife?"

So that's who she was. . . .

Brian's glance flicked over her. Good hair, needed grooming. Good eyes. Good legs. Figure going to pot. Dress possibly a bargain about ten years ago. . . . Bit of a looker in her day, probably, but another five years or so, and she'd be a hag. Still, he liked her smile. . . .

He sketched a salute and turned away.

"Oh!" Audrey cried, suddenly recognizing him. "Aren't you Mr.— the R.A.F. officer at the Staving Hotel?"

He bowed. "Late R.A.F."

"And . . . you're in films, aren't you? I mean, I've seen you heaps of times. . . ."

Here we go! he thought wearily. Well, I brought it on myself.

"I warn you," he said with a sour grin, "I don't open bazaars or lay foundation stones. I'm quite poor and not at all famous, and not particularly nice to know. I'm not in films any longer. I'm out of flying. And I left the hotel this morning. So I really don't see . . ."

"Oh," she cut in breathlessly, "but I don't want you to lay anything, or open anything. I only wanted to ask you . . . you see, I've got a little daughter who is perfectly beautiful . . ."

"Lady," he interrupted, "so have a million mothers in Britain."

"But, I mean, she really *is*—not just because I'm her mother! I really do think she'd be marvelous in films, only I don't know how to start. I mean, you have to get introductions and things, I expect, if you want an audition, don't you?"

He pulled out his case, offered her a cigarette which impatiently she refused. When he had lit one and swilled a draught of smoke he said quietly: "Look. For every clever child in films there are a thousand cleverer, more beautiful, who will never see an arc light. There's a dozen on every street in the country. And I tell you this— their mothers ought to thank God fasting for it. If you want your beautiful brat glamorized out of all semblance to nature; if you want her to have contracts for brains and a dollar for a soul; if you want her to grow a hide like a rhinoceros and develop her ego to bursting point, get your ears pinned back and go right ahead. Don't let me stop you. You might make the grade. Some do. But I don't think you do want that. I think—I may be wrong—but I *think* you're too sensible to want it. Don't you?"

"I don't know why I should believe all that," Audrey said.

"There's always the exception, of course." He sighed impatiently, for his leg was aching after the climb, and he was bored with this woman who didn't know when she was well off. "All I know is," he ended rudely, "that I can't help you—and I wouldn't if I could."

With another sketchy salute he turned away.

"Well!" Audrey exploded.

But her anger was short and without real heat. How often she had sat in music-cushioned darkness, watching that figure, debonair, lithe; the eyes, level and candid; the sensitive mouth; the lean, clean line of jaw; that unforgettable turn of the wrist as he flicked the ash off his cigarette. . . . His poor face, so mauled, so marvelously mended, so utterly spoiled; such a grotesque caricature. That dragging foot, the bitter cynicism of eyes and mouth. . . . Out of flying, out of films. Out of everything that would mean the world to a man like that. . . .

"My lady of the lamplight. My own Lili Marlene . . ." came faintly across the water.

"Damn!" Audrey said aloud. "Oh, damn and *damn!*" She felt better for that.

And anyway, she comforted herself as she wandered back across the lawn, he didn't know what he was talking about, because he's never even seen my sweet Allegra.

In a secluded corner of the garden Harry Waterhouse and George Fiddler confronted each other.

"Now then," said Harry with a forbidding glare. "What's all this about a key?"

"I want it back, that's all," replied George.

"Really!" Harry sneered. "Just like that!"

"Aye, just like that," said George, who had had about as much as he could stand in one day. "What's wrong with me wanting me own key?"

"Nothing's wrong with *that*. I can well understand that you *would* want it back with as little fuss as possible. But if you imagine," said Harry, narrowing his eyes and speaking as much like the Senior Partner as possible, "that you can molest innocent young girls with door keys, and then have them handed back to you on a clean plate with parsley around, you are vastly mistaken, my friend. Vastly mistaken! . . . And that is why I propose to hand you, not only your beastly key, but *this!*"

He punched George soundly on the nose, and George sat down on the grass and did a little astronomy.

In a minute he was on his feet again.

Harry was strolling away from the scene of his triumph, elegantly shooting his cuffs.

Unrestrained by any of the nicer points of pugilism, George took a run and kicked him heavily in the pants.

With a yelp Harry turned, and the two closed in deadly combat. Exactly as the choirboys had battled on the beach below, and with as little regard for chivalry, they reeled about the lawn, gasping and grunting; arms flailing, legs twisting and kicking, eyes fairly bolting from their sockets.

It was not an ennobling exhibition; and Pearl and Violet who, with Ivy tagging behind them, came upon the scene at that moment, were not ennobled by it.

But quite certainly they were not repelled.

With whoops of excitement Pearl and Violet entered into the spirit of the thing; Pearl battering her fists on Harry's head, Violet yanking lustily at George's coattails, and both laughing immoderately. Ivy hovered nimbly around them, her damp little fingers clutched together, her nose quivering pinkly beneath its fresh coating of powder.

It was Ivy who heard the whistle, giving notice to all members of the choir that the singing would start in five minutes' time. It was Ivy who shrieked the warning. And it was Ivy's handbag that struck the strategic blow which finally parted the combatants.

"Oh, come *on!*" she piped. "We're going to be late."

"Come on, lads, put a jerk into it!" counseled Pearl.

With hasty hands the two late opponents dusted each other down, pulled each other straight and got their hair into some semblance of order with the same comb.

On George's advice Harry discarded his new tie, which was not innocent of George's blood. On Harry's advice George agreed to have the key put down his own back, in an attempt to staunch his nose bleeding.

And at length, and only half a minute before Mr. Forsythe blew the final blast on his whistle, all five of them went scurrying over the lawn to take up their positions for the singing.

As soon as Miss Fortune's fingers touched the keys a stillness fell upon the garden. Gossiping groups broke up and children were hushed at their play. Phyllis and her helpers ceased their giggling chatter and came hurrying from the kitchen drying steaming hands, patting hair into shape. The dishes could be dealt with afterwards. You could always get dishes to do, but it wasn't every day you could listen to the Staving choir.

A few chords Miss Fortune played, a few rippling arpeggios, a snatch of melody. And then, as Mr. Forsythe's little black baton tapped sharply and lifted she waited, hands ready above the keys, heart beating strongly but quietly, as music always made it beat.

And first they sang an old favorite: *O, Who Will o'er the Downs So Free*. They usually started with that. It limbered them up and got everybody going; an old and tried friend, beloved by choir and audience alike.

And when they had set their true loves free they gasped a little, more from exuberance than lack of breath; turned and smiled at each other and rustled their music sheets and exchanged laughing comments. And then Mr. Forsythe was tapping his baton again, and they began the first soft, slow bars of *O, Perfect Peace*.

The blacksmith's voice was deep and calm, the voices of Pearl and Violet and Ivy rose high and sweet. The choirboys looked and sounded angelic.

"Unfold thy wings," implored Bob and the blacksmith and George Fiddler.

"Thy lovely wings," accorded the tenors in falling diminuendo.

The garden was filled with peace. Her wings fanned weary faces, lustful faces, faces lined with greed and sorrow and fear; folded themselves about warped and aging bodies. Not a heart in that garden but, for one fleeting instant, was touched with tenderness. Miss Fortune smiled as her fingers moved upon the keys, and her lips moved soundlessly. "O, gentle peace; O, long desired peace. . . ."

"Peace," marveled Brian Collinson. "They make it sound like something real and possible. . . ."

He thought of his ruined face, his broken career, his lost love, and he shut his eyes against the sudden shame of tears. But he, too, for that one instant of beauty felt the wings touch him lightly as they passed.

"Ee, that were grand!" sighed a stout, tweed-clad councilor in the audience. He nudged his wife. "When I were in St. Mark's choir I sang in that many's the time, remember?"

They were all remembering.

A daughter's devotion; a friend's quiet courage; the confiding sweetness of a child long since grown up and away; the smell of roses in a garden at night; the morning rapture of a lark heard through an open window after a night of pain; the hallowed stillness of an empty ancient church; the lights of home beckoning down a darkening street; the sudden splendor of a kingfisher by a pool; the poignance of a long-drawn trumpet note. . . .

Just for that little space of time peace touched them with her wings, and each heart knew an instant of beauty.

"By gum," the listeners told each other with stolid faces, "this lot can sing. They can an' all!"

They sang a hunting song in which Joe Peck vastly enjoyed himself with mighty *Tantivvy, Tantivvy!* and Harry Waterhouse caroled *Ta-rah-ta-rah!* in a sweet falsetto, and everybody's feet went tapping at the turf. They glided through a boating song smoothly, tranquilly; and they rapped out a short, merry roundelay. They thundered Joe's storm, sweeping across the bosom of the deep with tremendous gusto.

For all these the applause was terrific; but for the last item on the program there would be no applause. Custom dictated this and Andrew, stepping forward on the veranda, reminded everybody that this was the wish of the conductor and choirmaster, Mr. Walter Forsythe, whose own arrangement of the hymn: *The Day Thou Gavest,* would now be sung. The soloist would be Master Leslie Batley.

"We hope you will all join us in singing the last verse of this beautiful hymn," he added. "Leaflets are now being distributed. We hope you have all enjoyed the singing as much as we have; and I should like to express our deep appreciation of Miss Fortune's kindness in throwing open her gardens once again for our mutual pleasure." (A scatter of applause and a stentorian "Hear, hear!" from the stout councilor.) "As you know," Andrew continued, "no charge is made for this musical treat which the kindness of our hostess makes possible each year. But if any of you feel impelled to record your gratitude in a practical manner, you will find a box at the gate—and nobody is going to hinder you from recording it!" (Polite laughter and another "Hear, hear!" from the councilor, who had put a pound note in the box for more years than he could remember.)

Poppet! thought Audrey. How he does hate having to say his piece every year! She waved to Andrew, who circled round the edge of the crowd and came to stand beside her. She slipped her hand into his and felt it close around her own, hard and tight.

How lucky I am, she thought contentedly.

"Rose! . . . Our Rose!" said a tremulous voice.

Rose looked down into the small, white countenance with sharp misgiving.

"Now what?"

"I can't, Rose. . . . I'm scared."

"Don't be daft!" she hissed fiercely.

"I can't help it. I can't help it, Rose."

"Yes you can. You've got to help it! You just dare let me down, that's all!"

"Rose, I don't want. . . . Ron knows it as well as I do. He can sing it, Rose. I'm that tired . . ."

She knew he was tired. She could see it. Too much excitement, too much food, too much ice cream. Too many goes on the Bump-'ems. Too much of everything and not enough sleep last night. . . . But young Les had got to sing that solo, and sing it well. She'd set her heart on it. She'd practiced it with him over and over again, day after day, week after week. They were all counting on him. He'd got to sing it. . . . But she loved him fiercely, almost maternally. His poor little white wedge of a face, his grubby hands and neck, his crumpled clothing with the lemonade stains down the front, his thin little sticks of legs. . . .

She whipped him with her voice, her eyes.

"You got to sing it—you hear me? Nobody sings it as good as you. Soon as you get going it'll be okay and over before you know where you are. But you've got to sing that solo, or else . . . or else I shan't give you what I was going to give you," she ended weakly.

"What, Rose?" He pulled at her arm, a gleam lighting his heavy eyes. "What're you going to give me, our Rose?"

She thought madly.

"I'll tell you when you've sung your solo."

It was a threat more than a promise, and she had no idea how to carry it out. For she had nothing to give: nothing that would be any inducement to a pleasure-sated child. The words were regretted as soon as spoken, but it was too late to back out now. She'd think of something.

Swiftly she bent and hugged him.

"Go back to your place," she urged softly. "Mr. Forsythe's looking for you. Don't forget what I told you about that slow bit, and watch

Mr. Forsythe all the time. . . . You're going to do fine, luv. You'll have 'em all talking about you until next year's Outing. Go on, now, and sing up for me. Don't let me down!"

"Okay, okay." He pushed her arms away, hoping that Ron hadn't seen. He edged his way back to the front row, wondering whatever it could be that Rose would give him.

Mr. Forsythe tapped his baton and smiled at him, and Les smiled back, his momentary fear forgotten.

The first verse was sung by the whole choir.

They sang it softly, tenderly. They sang it slowly, yet not too slowly. They sang it quite perfectly, thought Walter Forsythe, his heart swelling with pride. Even Phoebe kept her voice down.

> The day Thou gavest, Lord, is ended,
> The darkness falls at Thy behest;
> To thee our morning hymns ascended,
> Thy praise shall sanctify our rest.

Then young Les took one pace forward and sang the second verse alone.

His pure young voice rose high and sweet; a silver chord of sound looping the dying moments of this day, binding them forever to the memory. . . . Unhesitant, faultless, his clear voice soared and fell and soared again in matchless innocence.

Tears started in Rose's eyes and ran unheeded down her cheeks. He'd done it! She might have known he'd do it.

"Ee-e-e!" whispered the councilor, blinking damply and unashamed.

The choir took up the refrain once more, but softly; for now the boy's voice was singing a descant: circling upwards like a lark; dropping gently like a cloud of doves; threading the harmony with an indescribable beauty, pure and passionless.

> The voice of prayer is never silent,
> Nor dies the strain of praise away. . . .

For some the day had been happy, for some it had brought disappointment. But now, at this moment, for each of them there was nothing but the singing, the lovely sounds their massed voices made, circled about and bound together by the silver voice of the boy.

And then Mr. Forsythe's arms spread wide, and with a rustle of leaflets, the audible intake of breath, the whole garden was joining together in the last verse.

> So be it, Lord; Thy throne shall never
> Like earth's proud empires pass away. . . .

This is the last time I shall play for them, thought Beatrice Fortune. After this there will be nothing but the waiting. Ordinary things. Keeping Fred's fingers out of the till. Stopping Phyllis' chatter. Ordering the food. And then one day, the waiting over. . . .

But she was not unhappy.

So be it, Lord, she thought. So be it, Lord . . .

Her fingers stretched for the final chord.

"Amen," she sang. Her fingers touched the keys lightly, surely, and she smiled.

"Amen," the choir sang in gentle unison.

7

THE driver was having trouble with his engine.

He bent over the hood, poking, twisting, peering; he swung the handle and made brief, gloomy excursions to the starter.

Of course, it *would* happen today, of all days, just when he was anxious to get home on time. Hadn't had any bother with the old bus for months; and now, just today, when he wanted to get a move on. . . . Great sufferin' ducks!

Henry Fiddler, who fancied himself with cars, strolled up and offered advice which was sourly received and instantly rejected. "Oh, well, if you *want* to be here all night!" Henry said, nettled. He strolled away, darkly wishing they *might* be stuck here all night, and then they'd see who was right.

"Here all night!" fumed the driver, twiddling and peering. "Young puppy. Who does he think *he* is! Knows all the answers, I shouldn't wonder. Before he gets asked the questions. . . ."

A choirboy, chewing gum as he lolled against the hood, opined to his companion that they always started up better if you turned on the ignition.

"'Op it!" said the driver tersely.

They hopped it, shrieking and jeering. They made rude noises with their mouths. They threw themselves about in exaggerated postures of defiance. "'Op it!" they screamed to each other. "'Op it, 'Op it!" Impossible to associate them in any way with the decorous, silver-tongued songsters of so short a time ago. . . .

Bob Clough strolled up and stood by, hands in pockets, whistling diffidently.

"Give her a swing, chum," said the driver.

Bob gave her a swing. The engine started instantly into warm, purring life.

Bob put his hands back into his pockets and went on whistling, and the driver, rather disgruntled, slammed the hood shut, wiped his hands on an oily rag and climbed into the driving seat. "Engines is like women," he said. "Proper cautions, ain't they?"

He backed the bus slowly, carefully, craning his neck and sounding warning blasts on the horn. He felt suddenly low in his spirits. The day was over. Now he'd got to get all these people safely back to Bishops Staving. Driving bang into the sun the whole blooming way, and that nasty bit across the ridge waiting for him. He hoped the engine wasn't going to play up.

Young Lil would be waiting for him. She always got worried if he ran late, and it wasn't going to help if she started worrying. . . . Good job when the whole thing was over—so long as Lil was okay. Well, of course she'd be okay. One born every minute. . . .

He swore at a prancing choirboy, swung the wheel over and began to maneuver the big bus into position.

He glanced at his watch, frowning. Running late, and no signs of the folks turning up, bar these flaming kids, who were all over the shop: when he'd mown a few of them down, perhaps they'd do as they were told. . . .

He sounded a long, urgent blast on the horn and sat back, waiting; sucking his teeth; worrying about Lil. . . .

Bob jingled his money, going up and down on his toes, watching the driver.

Women and engines. . . . He couldn't imagine any engine that was in the least like Rose. His nerves tingled, remembering the sweet glance she had sent him while young Les was singing his solo. It had turned his bones to water. Darling Rose—oh, sweet, sweet little Rose. . . . What did Edie matter? What did anyone or anything matter so long as he could marry Rose; be near her all day long. All night long. . . . So sweet life would be on the farm he loved, with Rose always near him night and day; with their children playing about the barns and fields: little lads growing up to work on the land, little lasses helping Rose in the dairy and the kitchen. If only Edie weren't in the way. . . .

Rose's voice said: "Bob!" He started violently and his face went the color of beetroot.

She was there, standing beside him. She had tied the pink scarf round her hair again and the little gray coat was buttoned across her round young bosom, ready for the drive home. He looked at her hungrily, dumbly.

"Seen young Les, Bob?" Rose said in a worried voice.

"Les?" he repeated stupidly. Her neck, rising out of the gray coat collar looked so young and tender, so defenseless. Her little nose shone at the tip where the powder had rubbed off. She looked altogether adorable. . . . "Les?" He pulled himself together. "Seen young Les, Ronnie?" he called to a skylarking boy.

"Saw him running off ower yonder," Ronnie shouted back, pointing a hand vaguely up the lane. "He were blubbing," he added, callously continuing his play.

"Nay!" Rose said softly, her face puckered in distress. "I knew there were summat wrong. He didn't want to sing his solo. He was overtired, but I made him sing it. Nay, I blame myself!"

"He'll be none the worse after a night's sleep," Bob comforted her. "All the lads are overtired, only it teks some different from others. He can sleep going home. Come on, Rose, we'll find him."

He held out his hand and she put her hand into it as naturally, trustfully as a child.

It was very quiet in the lane. The sun came low through the trees, lying in thick bars of gold across the narrow track. A rabbit started up, fled before them for a while, its white scut flicking up the barred sunlight and shadow. A hawthorn was murmurous with the sleepy gossip of birds. The distant clank of a pail, the long-drawn-out contentment of a cow, the thin yap of a farm dog merely added to the lovely quietness, the secret enchantment of the place. Instinctively they spoke in lowered voices, fearing to break the spell.

Rose whispered: "A bit higher up there's an old barn. That's where he'll be, I reckon."

That's where he was; a small patch of gray-white in the dimness; a forlorn sniffle, the scuffle of shoes in dust. . . .

Rose put her arms round him, holding his head close against her side. She wiped his cheeks with her small handkerchief that smelt of lavender water, combed the hair out of his eyes and made him blow his nose.

"Now, luv, what's to do?" she said with brisk tenderness.

Les pressed his hot face into her side. The feel of her, the smell of her was comfort. The sound of her voice, kind and soft, yet practical, was full of comfort. Rose was a comfortable person altogether, he dimly felt. He put his arms round her waist and hugged her, since Ronnie was not there to see. He didn't mind about Bob Clough. Bob was different.

"What is it, luv?"

"I'm tired," he mumbled against the gray cloth of her coat.

"That's not all," she guessed shrewdly. "Come on, luv, tell Rose."

It was the puppy, Les was understood to say.

"What puppy's that, luv?"

Bit by bit the whole story came out; bit by bit they pieced it into place, he and Rose and Bob Clough, standing close together in the dimness of the old barn that smelled of dust and damp wood and the droppings of mice and birds.

As soon as it was out he felt better. There was no longer the sense of loneliness, of intolerable loss.

But the grievance remained. He butted his head against Rose's waist, his underlip stuck out babyishly. "It liked owd Crackerjack better'n me!" he kept repeating angrily.

"Well, that just goes to show it warn't your dog," Rose explained reasonably. "It just wasn't meant for you. Anyway, you don't want the sort of puppy that has to be cuddled and nursed and looked after all the while. What you want's a strong, healthy puppy that's going to play games with you and run after you everywhere and not be a nuisance to everybody. . . . Like the puppy I'm going to give you," she added in a rather breathless voice.

Les lifted his head sharply, his grubby hands still holding tightly to her gray coat.

"Oh . . . d'you mean it? Are you really going to give me a puppy, our Rose? *Are* you?"

"I said I'd got something for you, if you sang your solo, didn't I?" she said. Her voice was still queer, breathless; as if she'd been running a long while and couldn't go another step.

"When? When?" he shouted, pulling roughly at her coat. "When can I get the puppy, Rose? Where's it from?"

"Bob's Dinah—the big black-and-tan one—is going to have some pups soon. You can have one of them, can't he, Bob? (Give over pulling my coat, luv, you'll tear it.)"

"Aye, he can," Bob agreed.

"Will it be big, like Dinah? Happen Dad won't let me have a big dog, Rose."

"I'll talk to Dad," Rose promised. "And if he's awkward it can stop up at the farm. . . . An' when me an' Bob's married you can come an' see it as often as you've a mind . . . can't he, Bob?"

There was no reply.

Les gazed up at them, anxious and puzzled. Their faces looked funny; Rose's all hot and red, as if she might blub any minute, and Bob's pale and sort of tight. They just stood staring at each other, not saying a word, not taking any notice of him. "Are you an' Bob gettin' married?" he asked mildly astonished.

"Yes," said Rose in a small, funny voice. "Yes, we are. . . ."

"Yippee!" He tore himself from Rose's arm and went tearing down the lane to tell Ronnie Field about the puppy. A black-and-tan puppy that would grow into a big dog like Dinah, with a long, tapering muzzle and wise brown eyes and a great plumy tail. Ron would be green with envy. Yippee, yippee! . . .

The two in the barn went on staring at each other. Rose's eyes were lifted to Bob's, courage masking a sweet shame. Bob's eyes brooded on her. His breath came as fast as hers. His heart thumped so that it hurt. His mouth was dry, his hands and feet tingled with shock.

"Oh, Rose," he sighed.

He held out his arms and she went into them. He held her in a tense, hurting grip. He stared over her head, shocked with joy, racked with fear and doubt.

From the dim corner of the barn the face of Edie leered at him, the voice of Edie cackled and spat obscenities. He was being a fool, he knew that. Nay, worse than a fool. . . .

But this was the moment he had waited for; the moment he had dreamed of as he plodded behind his plough, cleaned out the cow sheds, drove clanking churns along the rutted track; hoed and raked and planted and reaped and tended the land he loved. . . . This precious seed that had lain hidden in his heart, now, in this moment was bursting into lovely flower. How could he pass it by ungathered?

He cupped her face with his hard, brown hands, kissed the sweet eyes.

"Oh, Rose," he cried, between joy and despair, "I love you so much, so much. How am I going to make you happy?"

"Well, there's a daft thing to say!" she whispered.

Mrs. Maddon fixed her daughter with her own peculiar brand of paralyzing glare.

"Is it permitted," she asked heavily, "to inquire where you have been the whole of this day?"

Doris swallowed two or three times in rapid succession. It was all very well being brave when you'd got John William beside you, solid as granite; but this was the Ladies' Toilet, and she must stand up to it alone. It was all very well reminding yourself that you were thirty-eight and the headmistress of a school when at this moment, you were nothing but your mother's daughter and you felt a rather backward fifteen.

"Well," she replied with a commendable attempt at calmness, "if you remember, the first half of the day I spent with you, Mother. And since then"—she swallowed again—"I have been with—with John William."

"With *whom?*" Mrs. Maddon wanted to know.

"With Mr. Welsh. You know him of course."

"I know *of* him," her mother corrected her coldly. "If," she added, "you are referring to the gardener person employed by Colonel

March." Her eyebrows indicated that she confidently expected to be corrected on this point.

"That's the one," Doris said quietly. She powdered her nose briskly but unsuccessfully, since her eyes were looking through the mirror at her mother rather than her nose.

Mrs. Maddon was fitting her gloves on; smoothing each finger with an exaggerated interest and care that would not have deceived a child; much less her own child. But after all, she *is* my mother, Doris thought desperately. She must love me, want me to be happy. There must be something real there if only I could get at it. Something simple and ordinary and constant. Something that will respond. . . . She put away her compact and turned round, took a hesitating step forward. "Mother . . ." she pleaded. "John William and I . . . we love each other. We . . . we're going to get married."

Mrs. Maddon was not without courage. After one shocked instant of inaction she continued to smooth the gloves onto her plump fingers, even though her heart was beating thickly somewhere up in her throat, and her hands shook, and the floor of the Ladies' Toilet was rocking in a peculiar fashion.

She had no idea what to say; and in any case she could not have said it, for she was quite incapable of speech. The shock, indeed, was so severe that all her senses were affected. Her ears buzzed. Her eyesight appeared dim, so that she must blink rapidly and repeatedly in order to focus correctly. And although her fingers continued their mechanical smoothing and molding and fitting, there was a numbness of touch that she had not experienced before.

I have lost her, she thought. It was like a caption suddenly appearing on a dark screen. She has escaped me. . . .

How could she live without Doris? Who would now fill her hot water bottle, run upstairs for the aspirin or her reading glasses or her library book, pick up her dropped stitches? Who would pop out to the shops when it rained, and do the dishes while *she* popped out when it was warm and sunny? Who would bring her a nice cup of tea in the early morning and a nice cup of Horlick's when she was in bed at night? Who would do the rough digging ready for her to plant and sow? Who would rub her legs? Who would play Sevens night after night and not notice, or not remark upon it (she had never been quite sure which) when she cheated the least little bit? Who would pay for the nice glasses of stout, the sherry and the brandy without which life would be insupportable? Who would pay the rent? . . . *Who would pay the rent!*

The Lomax girls came bursting in, loud with lamentations.

"Hello, Miss Maddon," they chorused. "Hello, Mrs. Maddon."

"Vi's lost her lipstick," Pearl said. "A new one, only bought yesterday. . . . Look in the lav, Vi, it might be there."

"Can't be," Violet said crossly. "I never opened me bag in the lav. Besides, I haven't got a penny."

"Nor me," Pearl said. "Have you got a penny, Miss Maddon? She'd better look, just in case."

Doris produced a penny. Vi operated the lock and looked in, but there was no lipstick.

"Well, don't let's waste the penny, now we're here," Pearl said prudently. They shut the lavatory door. Their muffled voices continued to lament.

Doris stood helplessly, looking at her mother. Mrs. Maddon continued silently to smooth her gloves. Her color was very high: a sort of purplish-red that rose from the neck of the mauve marocain ensemble right up into her forehead. Doris felt a twinge of fear. Was Mother going to be ill—have a stroke, or something? She wished she had not started this. It would have been better to have waited until they were alone in their own house. John William had wanted her to wait. But it was too late, now. Now they'd started they'd have to go on.

How she wished the driver would sound his horn and put a stop to further discussion. Perhaps she could engage Pearl and Violet in conversation, keep them with her until the horn sounded. . . .

"If there's one thing I hate, it's losing anything!" Violet announced, emerging from the lavatory. "I don't mind giving it away, but losing it just makes me see red! A new one, too, in a gilt case. Kiss-proof, an' all. Very dark red. If you should spot it, Miss Maddon, you'll know it's mine."

Pearl gave her a resounding thump.

"You shouldn't tell teacher you use lipstick," she giggled. "She'll mek you stand in t'corner—won't you, Miss Maddon? Do you remember how we was always standing in t'corner when we was in the Juniors? I bet we were a headache, the pair of us!"

Doris looked at the two great grown girls of marriageable age, and her heart was sick with misgiving.

"You were very naughty," she said, smiling with stiff lips.

"I bet!" Pearl agreed.

"I bet I lost it in the Fun Fair," Violet grumbled. "If so, it's a gone-er!"

"Toodle-oo," said Pearl.

They surged out, full of plaintive speculation.

Doris faced her mother again.

Mrs. Maddon's high color had somewhat receded. She still stroked the fingers of her gloves, but her eyes were fixed on Doris. They were bright with malice, hard as polished pebbles. They spoke louder than any words.

"*You* . . ." said Mrs. Maddon's eyes. "You frumpish, faded old maid! Even when those great girls were babies you were old enough to get married and off my hands. Even as long ago as that! . . . And now—look at you now! You're glad to marry anyone—even a gardener! You threw yourself at his head. I'll bet you said yes before he'd fairly got the words out of his mouth! Whoever had asked you, you'd have said yes. . . ."

Mrs. Maddon's lips parted, but still no words issued from them. Only a faint hissing noise that was the noise of Mrs. Maddon laughing. And as Doris watched her, trembling and helpless, the laughing became more violent; the head nodded with it, the eyes screwed up, the thick body jerked about in uncontrollable spasms. And always that hissing noise like an escape of gas. Like an escape of poison gas, filling the bare little room with its deadly fumes; making Doris feel sick and frightened and old, old. Oh, so old and frightened. . . .

"Stop it!" she said hoarsely. "You're horrible. Oh, you're horrible! I hate you!"

Blindly she turned, avoiding the mirror by instinct; tripping absurdly; fumbling at the door latch with clumsy fingers.

Beyond the door there was fresh, sweet air to breathe; there were sunlight and sanity; there was John William waiting, solid as granite, kind as the brown earth, sane as the sunlight, gentle as the flowers his rough hands tended.

"I do love him," she whispered. "I do, I do. . . ."

As the door slammed Mrs. Maddon's eyes fell by accident on the mirror, and she saw a horrid sight. She saw an old woman with a flushed, distorted face, clad in a purple dress. Her hat was askew, her mouth hung open, her thick body leaned at a queer, stiff angle. Her eyes, gleaming between puffed, wrinkled lids, were mad eyes. They were quite mad!

Was it possible that this was herself?

Her limbs began to shake. Her whole body began to shake. Her mouth worked grotesquely and tears ran down the purplish, shaking cheeks.

That wasn't herself, that thing in the mirror! That was something Doris had done to her. Wicked, ungrateful girl!

What had she said? *I hate you. You're horrible.* . . . That—to the mother who bore her! Whom she was casting off like an old shoe, after all these years, just because some man had snapped his fingers at her. . . .

A gardener.

Colonel March's gardener. . . .

Mrs. March bowed to her whenever they met in the village. Once, she had taken tea in the huge, shabby drawing room, and Mrs. March had given her the recipe for a cake.

Doris had put an end to *that* going any further. Wicked, ungrateful girl, sharper than a serpent's tooth. . . .

Mrs. Maddon grasped the edge of the washbasin and leaned her weight on it, screwing up her eyes so that she should not see the thing in the mirror. She began to cry in real earnest.

"Don't leave me," Andrew commanded. "Keep close to me wherever I go. And as soon as the bus pulls around get in and put my coat on the seat beside you. I *will* sit next to my own wife going home."

"Um," Audrey murmured placidly. She drew a long breath of contentment. She felt extraordinarily well. She felt happy. A beatific quiescence enveloped her.

Everything was all right. Everything was lovely. . . .

It was very quiet now, very still. The trees spread motionless arms against a sky of tender, tranquil green. The flowers in Miss Fortune's garden were changing their color to deeper, more vivid hues. Shadows of trees were longer. The tide was at the full. It rocked soundlessly at the foot of the cliffs, as if resting before the long battle with the beach on its outward journey. Gulls, floating on its drowsy surface, were startlingly white against the deep green-blue. The little yacht drifted by once more, tacking so slowly that its motion was barely perceptible. The accordion player had put away his instrument, so that its progress was soundless, too. "A painted sail upon a painted ocean," Audrey thought dreamily. Perhaps we're all caught up in a dream. Andrew and I and the baby; and the singing; and the little boat with the red sails; and the sea, and the gulls floating on the sea. . . .

The silence was shattered by the sudden racing of an engine, the short blast of a horn. The rocking gulls rose in a white cloud and circled the evening sky, startled and clamorous.

"That," said Andrew, "sounds like the Air Force chap. I'd forgotten all about him! I meant to have a word with him before he went."

"I had a word with him," Audrey said. "He's rather disappointing off the screen. I mean, apart from his face, poor darling. His manners are rather awful, and I wouldn't say he was over-burdened with imagination."

"I wonder," Andrew said, "where he's off to now."

"Personally," Audrey murmured, yawning, "I couldn't care less. I didn't take to him."

"I rather liked him," Andrew said thoughtfully. "We were stiff as pokers with each other, but that was my fault, I expect. I wish I'd got to know him earlier. Of course, I ought to have. That's me all over. . . ." He sighed sharply. "Well, good luck to him wherever he's going."

The Pecks were playing a sort of game with each other. Addie and Joe were playing because they must, but Minnie was enjoying herself. Addie wanted to speak to Minnie. She wanted to explain that she hadn't really meant to speak harshly in the hat shop; that she hadn't really wanted to leave her to her own devices for the rest of the day; that she hadn't really taken too much to drink in the George and Dragon.

She knew it was too late to try to explain any of these things to Minnie—oh, years and years too late!—but something compelled her to keep on walking around and around after Minnie, trying to get her alone.

Habit, she supposed. That was it, Minnie was a deep-rooted habit. A bad habit, maybe—today, for the first time, she had seen that clearly—but a habit she was going to find dreadfully difficult to break.

Minnie was perfectly aware that Addie wanted to speak to her; and Addie, who was no fool, knew that she knew.

She followed her about Miss Fortune's garden with the bleak sort of patience that life had taught her, waiting for the chance to get Minnie alone. She wasn't going to call out and risk being snubbed. Sooner or later the chance would come, and she would have it out with Minnie, even if it meant tears and a certain publicity. Better that than have a scene when they got home; all shut in together in the quiet house; boxed up with the hate and bitterness and frustration. . . .

So Addie followed, patiently biding her time, while Minnie darted about from group to group, astonishingly mobile and sociable. As soon as her mother came within speaking distance, off she would go again, her eyes glittering with triumph, her cheekbones splashed with color, her mouth pinched in.

In a blundering and bewildered sort of way Joe was playing the game, too. His object was to dodge both Addie and Minnie until they were safely seated in the bus. If he then made a last-minute rush the odds were he could cram himself in with the choirboys and he wouldn't have to endure the women's company on the way home.

After that it was easy. He'd slip along to The Crown and let the women go in alone—and Bob's your uncle. It would be after hours, but old Alf wouldn't worry about that. You could always walk in the back door of The Crown and be certain of finding old Alf at home.

Come to that, he could stop there all night if he'd a mind. To-morrow would be another day, and more than likely Addie would have got over whatever it was that had made her behave so queer today. They could all get back into the groove; Addie and Min disapproving of him and he not giving a damn. . . . Comfortable, like.

Queer thing, that, Joe reflected, dodging up a side path as the two women came into view. For years he'd thought himself hard done by; thought nobody'd ever had such a raw deal. And now, the last thing he wanted was change. The notion that Addie might suddenly be sorry for the wasted years and want to be a good wife to him, filled him with terror. It was too late. Anyone with any sense would know that. It was a whole lifetime too late.

Seizing a moment when her mother's back was turned Minnie slipped up the side of the Ladies' Toilet, and had the pleasure of watching Addie turn around and around, gaping foolishly, and wander off in the wrong direction. Sniffing with satisfaction she pushed the door open and went in.

Her mouth pinched up tighter as she observed Mrs. Maddon leaning on the washbasin and sobbing convulsively.

Minnie hesitated, uncertain what to do. Mrs. Maddon had not yet seen her and it would be easy enough to escape. On the other hand, Minnie needed to stay, and another opportunity might not present itself. A glance at her watch showed her that the horn might sound for departure any minute; and how foolish she would look if the whole bus was kept waiting; if everyone saw her emerge. . . .

Besides, Mrs. Maddon looked queer, and no mistake. So queer that Minnie involuntarily stepped backwards, her only thought that Doris Maddon ought to be fetched, and that quickly.

But in that instant Mrs. Maddon glanced up. The eyes of the two women met and held.

"Oh," Mrs. Maddon whispered. "It's *you!* I thought. . . . I was afraid . . . it was Doris again."

She held out one hand in a groping, beseeching fashion, and after a moment's hesitation Minnie went forward and took it. The plump, gloved fingers closed round her bony ones with an astonishing strength. She felt herself pulled forward; felt the weight of soft flesh pressing against her shoulders and braced herself to support it; felt the heavy softness sink into her arms. The scent of violets mingled with human warmth and dyed cloth assailed her nostrils. It was not unpleasant. It gave her a rather exciting sense of strength and power.

"What's to do?" she said curtly. "Are you feeling poorly? Shall I fetch your Doris?"

"No—no!" Mrs. Maddon moaned, tightening her clutch on Minnie's hand. "Don't let her come nigh me! Wicked, cruel girl. . . . Oh, the things she's said to me this day—her own mother that bore her! I couldn't repeat them. You wouldn't believe me if I did."

That, thought Minnie shrewdly, was probably true enough. She had known Doris Maddon a long time. They were much of an age—though she was perfectly aware that she looked ten years the older. She didn't particularly care about Doris, but the idea of Doris being cruel to her mother was just daft; she hadn't got the guts, anyhow.

"Happen you'd better tell me," she said after a pause. "I might be able to help you."

Nothing loth, Mrs. Maddon plunged into a repetitive and highly garbled version of the scene between herself and Doris, punctuated by bouts of gusty sobbing on her part and murmured consolation on Minnie's.

"Oh, my poor heart!" cried Mrs. Maddon. "It's thumping away so as I can hardly breathe. Feel how it's thumping." She pressed Minnie's hand against her mauve frontage and held it there; and certainly there did appear to be a disturbance of some sort beneath the quivering upholstery. With a sharp distaste Minnie tried to withdraw her hand, but Mrs. Maddon would not let it go. "My poor heart," she whimpered, clutching grimly at Minnie. "Oh, you feel so strong. I feel so safe with you. . . . Don't leave me, Minnie. Don't leave me alone in the house with Doris tonight. She hates me. She said she hated me—her own mother! She'll do me a mischief, I know she will. Stay with me, Minnie. Why shouldn't you? Your mother and father have got each other, but I've got nobody."

Above Mrs. Maddon's drooping head Minnie's mouth unpinched and widened into the travesty of a smile.

Wasn't it her duty to stay with poor Mrs. Maddon, who was ill and so frightened? Who wanted her, needed her?

Ma and Pa had got each other. Well, hadn't they? . . .

It was at exactly this moment that Addie Peck opened the door and looked inside, searching for Minnie.

Her eyes and Minnie's met above the lolling head of Mrs. Maddon.

Minnie's eyes, coldly triumphant; Minnie's mouth stretched in that venomous smile. . . .

No word was spoken and none was needed.

As silently as she had entered Addie departed, shutting the door behind her with a sense of finality.

The blue-and-silver sports car streaked along the high ridge right into the sun.

Curse this daylight saving! Brain thought, tipping his hat farther over his eyes. He ought to wear sun glasses, of course. He'd got some knocking around somewhere, but they made driving so dim, took the color out of everything.

It was rather lovely, actually, up here. The gorse blazed like fire at this time of day. It must be something when the heather was fully out. He'd like to see it then. He'd like to come here with Beryl. Camp right up here on the edge of the world so that, first thing in the morning, you looked down into a bowl of brightness, with nothing above you but the pale, arching sky. And at night you would lie on the cropped turf and watch the moor and the hills and the sky burn themselves out; and then there would be nothing but you in the darkness. You and your love. . . .

His face twitched grotesquely. He couldn't see Beryl camping out on the edge of the world!

Beryl, he thought. Beryl, Beryl, Beryl. . . . Heartless, worthless. . . . My beautiful, my heart's love. . . .

He glanced at the speedometer. Seventy. She could do eighty-five. . . . How simple to ram your foot down on the accelerator, feel her leap forward; and then, one swing of the wheel, through that gate and over; down. . . . Finish. . . . Better that way, perhaps. For who wanted him, who needed him?

Finish. And then nothing forever and ever. Simple. . . .

But suppose there was something? That parson believed there was something. Rose, too, little Rose. She believed there was something. You could read it in her clear eyes, feel it in the kindness of her arms.

How sweet she had been to him, how gentle. Sweet little Rose, whose arms were made for cradling tired bodies, soothing tired hearts and tortured minds. . . .

Rose needed him, at least! Of course she did! That's why he was turning back on his tracks and driving into the sun. That's why he mustn't swing the wheel over and finish it.

[183]

Only himself or Death could make Rose happy; and Death might tarry for a long, long time, while Rose wasted her sweetness on the desert air, her arms empty, her heart's desire unfulfilled. . . .

He reached the end of the ridge; braked, slowed, stopped.

Now the road fell steadily, winding down the valley and losing itself in greenness that was lightly patched with mist. Far over the valley the spire of Staving church pointed upwards from a clump of elms dark against a smoldering sky.

They would be switching lights on in the hotel. Some folks would still be gossiping over coffee in the lounge, others would be pushing into the hot, crowded bar, loud with good fellowship. Ted would be whisking about in the deserted dining room, flapping at tablecloths, laying breakfast china, joking, grumbling. . . . Ted would be glad to see him back. Surprised, too. Everybody would be surprised. Everybody would come jabbering and exclaiming and prying, making themselves bloody nuisances.

Well, that was just part of it. It couldn't be helped.

He could stay at The Crown, of course. No—why should he?

Let 'em pry and jabber all they wanted; he'd be giving them something to jabber about, soon. . . .

Ivy sidled nearer to Miss Stacey. The tea and the singing had made her feel sentimental. She hoped Miss Stacey would drop something so that she could pick it up for her and break the ice.

One bit of Ivy wanted to ride home with Harry Waterhouse; to creep around the edge of adventure, nibble at the unknown. Another part of her wanted to play safe; to taste once more the remembered delights of holding Miss Stacey's large hand, drooping her head against Miss Stacey's solid shoulder, hearing Miss Stacey lower her loud voice to call her a little silly-billy, and let her cry into one of her crisp white handkerchiefs.

On the other hand, there was Harry Waterhouse. . . .

Ivy didn't like men very much, but you could hardly call Harry a man. Not in *that* sense. Not like George Fiddler who thrust keys down girls' backs and then wanted to go fishing them up again, the nasty common thing!

Ivy had a good mind to tell her mother about the key and get George into trouble; and serve him right, too! But her mother had a disconcerting way of turning around and boxing your ears and saying: "Six of one and half-a-dozen of the other," and things like that, which maddened a girl into protest which, in turn, was called "answering back" and was invariably rewarded by another ringing box on the ears.

No. On the whole, Ivy decided, it would pay her better to keep her mouth shut about the key and hold it over George's head, so that she'd got him just where she wanted him. . . .

Miss Stacey was humming "She'll be coming round the mountain," tapping her foot to the rhythm. Her eyes stared unseeing over Ivy's head and she looked somehow exalted, so that Ivy felt a thin thrust of loneliness and insecurity.

She sidled nearer still. She took a scrap of colored cotton from her pocket and blew her nose squeakily.

Miss Stacey looked down and smiled in a detached sort of way. She stopped humming (though her foot still went on tapping out the rhythm) and asked Ivy quite kindly if she had enjoyed herself today.

"Not much," Ivy complained in a stifled voice. "My nose bled this afternoon," she added reproachfully.

"What's that?" said Sergeant Stacey, instantly alert. "Nose bleed? Stand still while I find my key—that'll stop it."

Ivy let out a faint yelp and leaped backwards.

"Not *now*. I said it *was* bleeding this afternoon. It's given over now."

"Then what are you making all this fuss about!" the Sergeant demanded.

"I'm not making any fuss! Only we were together . . . and then my nose started bleeding . . . and you didn't care. . . ."

"Your nose didn't bleed while you were with me."

"No, because you'd gone off and left me!"

"You just said we were together!"

"No, I didn't," Ivy said desperately. "I mean, I didn't mean it bled while we were together. I mean . . ." She stopped abruptly. For Miss Stacey was humming again and her eyes, bright behind the horn-rimmed glasses, were gazing way over Ivy's head. "You're not listening," she said, dropping her voice sulkily. "You haven't heard a word I've said!"

"Oh, yes," Miss Stacey assured her. "Your nose bled, and I wasn't there. So what? Didn't any other bloke have a door key and a spark of common sense? It's a simple enough thing to drop a door key down a girl's back, I should have thought!"

"It's not that easy getting it up again!"

"Get it up? Get it *up?* . . . My dear girl, why bother about getting it up? Unless you're hermetically sealed, it's a simple enough thing to get it *down!* One good heave and a couple of hops—and Bob's your uncle!" Miss Stacey let out a bellow of good-natured laughter and gave Ivy a slap between the shoulder blades that sent her staggering. "Brace up!" she advised briskly. "What you need is a cold bath and a five-mile route march every day of your life. Do you a world of good. Make a man of you!"

Ivy peered at her malevolently.

"I don't know what's come over you," she mumbled. "You used to be ever so nice to me, and now you're beastly. You've been queer all day. . . . *I* saw you in the swimming pool with Bob Clough! I didn't know where to put me eyes! Carrying on that way. . . . I never thought I'd live to see the day!"

Her little nose quivered pinkly. She dabbed ineffectually at it with the scrap of colored cotton.

Miss Stacey eyed the nose with distaste. Opening her bag she produced a crisp white, man's-sized handkerchief and thrust it into Ivy's hand.

"Blow it!" she ordered. "Blow it hard. Make a proper do of it. And keep the hanky," she added. "I don't think I shall care for it any more."

Turning her back she stalked away from the stricken Ivy, relieved to be finished with the rather furtive little friendship.

Cruel, perhaps; but cruel to be kind.

In any case, absolutely the only possible way of shedding Ivy for good.

The driver sounded a long, despairing blast on the horn. Some folks took their time, and no error! You'd think they hadn't got any homes. . . .

He wanted to get off. The sooner they were over that ridge the better he'd like it. And after he'd dumped this lot in Staving, he'd still got to get the bus back to the depot. And then walk home. But they didn't think about that. *He* didn't matter, of course! *He* was only the poor perishing sucker of a driver!

"Pack that lark up, you lads!" he shouted at two choirboys who were scuffling their shoes against the paint work.

Jack came loping up, carrying his puppy, still wrapped in the blanket. It peered over the edge of the blanket with timid interest and uttered a small, shrill bark.

Jack was delighted. "Wuff!" he said, beaming at the driver.

The driver leaned over and tickled the puppy's ear. "Grand dog you got there, chum," he said tolerantly.

"Grand dog!" Jack boasted. "Jack's dog. Been poorly, but Jack's going to make it better. Be a big dog an' go to the woods with Jack an' fetch logs for the fire. Pop it on!" he chuckled, as memory stirred. "Pop it on, pop it on! . . ."

He's nuts, thought the driver. Wonder what makes kids get born that way? A sudden hollow feeling in his stomach caused him to sound the horn again viciously. Young Lil. . . . She wasn't the sort to get a kid that was nuts. . . . It couldn't ever happen to Lil, could it? Of course not. As bright as they made 'em, young Lil. Bright eyes, bright hair, quick, bright laugh. . . . Cocky little bit of goods he'd thought, first time he'd set eyes on her.

He worried about young Lil. How long now? Tomorrow? Another week? . . . Great sufferin' ducks!

Here they were, straggling up at last. The parson and his missus, the farmer with the girl in the pink scarf, the little choirmaster rounding up the boys, the blacksmith hovering in the background as if he were waiting for something. People hurrying from the Ladies' and the Gents', joining laughing groups, calling to each other, maneuvering to sit next to each other, elbowing each other out of the way. The driver was accustomed to it all, impatient of delay. You'd think nobody'd ever been in a bally bus before!

"Come along now, please!" he called loudly. "Time's getting on."

He walked round the big bus urging people into their seats, giving a hand to those who needed assistance, being politely official with the overexuberant, firm with the irresolute.

"You two Bluebirds perching together?"

"That's right," Pearl and Violet chorused. "But there's room for one inside."

"Name the victim, then," he said with a tolerant wink.

"That's him. The dark one in the mack. Come on, Georgie!" they caroled.

George Fiddler and Harry Waterhouse exchanged glances of resignation. Their furtive, half-hearted plans for ignoring Pearl and Violet and Ivy, and having a bit of peace together on the way home, dissolved in the shrill clamor; and they capitulated without a fight.

"Room for a little 'un?" Joe Peck suggested to Phoebe.

"Sorry, Joe." Phoebe had seized the seat next to the door, had battled valiantly for it.

What with collecting the music and seeing to the lads and all, Walter was always the last to climb into the bus. But the seat by her side was his; it was waiting for him; anybody else took it over her dead body! . . . Happen it would work, and happen it wouldn't. She'd done all she could do, and there it was. . . . "You're crying for the moon," that Madame had said. Well, maybe she was crying for the moon. But anybody who took the seat she'd saved for Walter took it over her dead body. . . .

Miss Fortune came out to the gate and stood smiling and nodding to everybody.

"So long!" they called. "It's been a lovely day." "Wonderful!" "We've had a grand time!"

"Good-by!" said Miss Fortune gaily. "Thank you for coming."

And now here was that Phyllis tearing out of the house with an air of great urgency.

" 'Phone call," she shouted. " 'Phone call for a Mr. Richardson. They're holding the line."

"Mr. Richardson!" bawled the driver. " 'Phone call for . . ." He stopped abruptly and gave a whinnying sound of surprise. " 'Ere— that's me!" he gasped.

He began to run towards the house. His face was chalkwhite. His legs felt like flannel.

Fred Fortune came sauntering to the gate, hands in pockets.

"Think I'll go for a stroll," he said nonchalantly.

Miss Fortune spared him a brief glance. It was weeks since he'd given her any trouble. He was due to kick over the traces any day now.

And why not? What did it matter? Drunk or sober, what, after all, did Fred amount to? Very little.

Let him go down to the local and fill himself up with beer, she thought without bitterness, almost without interest. Let him go. She had finished with Fred even as she had finished with life.

Why, then, must she say: "I shouldn't if I were you. The damp's rising, and you were coughing a little last night."

But she did say it. She thought: I couldn't care less, as they say. But I have to go through the motions. . . .

The scared, resentful look on Fred's face neither amused nor irritated her. She saw his sudden shiver without pity and watched his return to the house as she might have watched the movements of some slightly repellent insect in a glass case.

Walter Forsythe came over and took her hand.

"Bee," he muttered, "I can't go like this. . . . I can't just go off and leave you, knowing . . ."

"Of course you can go, Walter," Miss Fortune said crisply. "I never heard such nonsense! All this fuss about dying. . . . Before long we shall all be dead. Ah, you don't like that! But you know it's true, don't you, Walter?" She patted his hand encouragingly. "You run along and deal with Phoebe's bellowing, my dear. No, not another word! Don't spoil my lovely day. Just go."

He left her then. She watched him climb into the bus and take the seat next to Phoebe. He looked small and insignificant against Phoebe's bulk, less dapper and shining than usual. How could I ever have felt romantic about him! she thought, amused, yet pitiful.

The driver emerged from the house, grinning sheepishly. His face looked like a harvest moon. He held his white cap in one hand and with the other wiped sweat from the roots of his glued-back hair. He jerked his head at Bob, who left the bus and joined him in the lane.

"Whaddyer know!" said the driver, hoarse with happiness and shock. "It's a girl! . . . Yup! Born an hour ago, an' both doin' fine. That was my mother-in-law, that was. . . . Never knew it'd come today. Any day now, they says. Might be tomorrow, might be a week. An' it's all over an' done with, an' it's a girl—whaddyer know about that! Shan't be able to call me soul me own, great sufferin' ducks! . . ."

Bob and the driver smote each other on the back with loud thumps of congratulation and relief. Someone with a long ear passed the word round like lightning. "For he's a jolly good fellow . . ." roared the blacksmith, and in a moment everyone was singing it lustily, to the driver's embarrassment and delight. There was a quick whip around and thirty-two shillings, wrapped in an empty toffee bag, was handed to him by Andrew, for the purchase of a baby's bonnet, and everybody cheered and clapped so that the driver was obliged to blink a good deal, and could hardly see the perishing starter. . . .

And they were really off at last.

"Good-by!" they yelled. "So long, Miss Fortune, see you next year!"

"Good-by," cried Miss Fortune. She smiled and waved her hand. The big bus lumbered away, gathering speed with every yard, and Miss Fortune watched it go, still smiling.

She stood by the gate, alone. The scent of stocks rose strongly all about her, mingled with the smell of trampled grass and fading gasoline fumes and a sharp tang of seaweed newly uncovered by the retreating tide.

The sky was darkening now and a few stars shone palely. The lights of the town were bright. The mechanical music of the Fun Fair came faintly on the stillness.

A bird called harshly from a tree. The muffled chatter of the girls in the kitchen mingled with the thin clash of crockery.

Well, it's over, Miss Fortune thought. "The day Thou gavest, Lord." It's been a lovely day, but it's over. She began to walk towards the house. All this litter! she thought, picking her way. I must get on. I must see to Fred's supper and get him his cough mixture: it'll do him no harm to take a few doses. And all this litter to clear up. Such a lot to be done. . . .

8

BRIAN parked the blue-and-silver sports car on the turf before the hotel and limped up the steps into the lighted lounge.

It was empty. He had been prepared to face a barrage of questions and comments, and to keep up his reputation by dealing with them as rudely as he knew how; but it was a lot less trouble this way. Still, he'd get it tomorrow. You couldn't make people let you alone.

A muffled roar of voices and laughter issued from the half-open door of the bar, but he strode past and through the swing doors of the empty, half-lit dining room.

He pushed a bell. In a minute the service door swung open and Ted came hurrying in. He tried to hide the fact that he was eating.

"Mr. Collinson, sir!" he exclaimed, gulping the mouthful. "This is a surprise!"

"Is my room still vacant, Ted?"

"Why, yes, sir, I believe it is."

"Put my things in it and tell them to make up the bed. And get my car filled up and put a bottle of Scotch in the back. And Ted—"

"Sir?"

"When I come back I shall want a very hot bath, so don't let's have any nonsense about fuel shortage."

"I'll attend to that, sir."

"Good man. Bring me a double Scotch, straight, and twenty Players. And make it snappy, I've got to go out."

His room looked hideously cold and impersonal. He hated it. He threw his things all over it, trying to make it remember him; but still it remained just a room with things thrown over it.

He peered at his face in the mirror and swore softly. It always had done its worst for him, that mirror. Actually, he needed a shave. When he had gulped down his Scotch it didn't seem important any more, but he gave himself a quick lather and scrape—for luck he thought, grinning balefully—and changed his worn tweeds and tie for something smarter. He flicked at his dusty shoes, lit a cigarette and went limping down the stairs.

Old Miss Brent fluttered and squeaked at him from a corner.

"Why, Mr. Collinson! I thought you'd gone and left us all this morning!"

He turned on her, ready to snarl.

But suddenly he saw her for what she was: a lonely, friendless, disappointed fellow creature, whom nobody wanted, nobody needed. Like me, he thought. Worse off than me, because Rose needs me.

"I found I couldn't bring myself to leave you," he said, giving her a small, elegant bow.

"Why, Mr. *Collinson!* Quite a courtier you're becoming!"

Ted had filled her up and was hovering about, hoping for a bit of notice. He didn't want the silver Brian slipped him, but he knew better than to protest.

"How long d'you reckon to be staying, sir?" he said eagerly.

"It rather depends, Ted. A week—a fortnight—might be longer, but I hope not."

"Yes, sir."

For all his hurrying, Brian now seemed reluctant to get away. He drew deeply on his cigarette and his eyes roved over the dusky turf, the scatter of lighted cottages, the broken gleam of a pond, to the dark, solid mass of the church pointing with timeless patience to the stars.

He dropped the cigarette, ground it under his heel.

"You a religious fellow, Ted?"

"Me, sir?" cried Ted, startled. "Well, no, I wouldn't say I was, sir. Not more than most."

"Do you ever think about death, Ted; and what, if anything, comes afterwards?"

Ted shuffled, deeply embarrassed.

"You mean Heaven, an' that, sir?"

"Something of the sort."

"Well. . . . I can't say I go much on Heaven, sir. Harps, an' that. Sounds all right in the hymns, but I don't reckon it's what most folks wants. But I kind of think there's something. . . . Don't seem to make sense otherwise, see what I mean?"

Brian took another cigarette, offered the packet to Ted.

"So you think there's something, do you?"

"That's what I reckon, sir. Course, I don't *know.* Not really in my line, that sort of thing. I just get on with me job and take the rest on trust."

There was silence for a few moments. The cigarettes of the two men glowed and faded in the darkness. Then Brian said casually: "Whatever sort of job it might be?"

"Well, there's all sorts of jobs, sir, good and bad, like. And they've all got to be done."

Brian got into the car and slammed the door. His cigarette described a little arc of light and fell to the turf.

"You ought to have been a parson, Ted," he said. "You'd have made a better job of it than most."

He let in the clutch. Ted saluted smartly, as if he were in uniform, and Brian returned the salute as smartly. He turned the car over the springy turf, ran her into the road and shot away with a roar. His headlights stroked a finger of light over the dark bulk of the church, over the pond and a huddle of sheep cropping the wet grass on its verge. Then he was just a taillight. Then he was gone.

Ted picked up the still smoldering cigarette and took it tidily indoors.

What's bitten *him?* he wondered.

The public bar of The Crown was packed to capacity. A hot smell of sweat and beer and corduroy and shag smote Brian in the face as he slowly pushed his way in. He ordered a pint of mild, took a long pull and set the tankard down on the smeary bar.

His eyes, searching for Edie, roved amongst the crowd. They were mostly decent laboring men with their wives and girls. They all knew him by sight, knew all about him; but apart from a few civil nods, a few excited whispers among the women, nobody took apparent notice of him.

"How far is it to Clough's farm?" Brian asked the landlord.

"Mile. Happen a bit less. Straight down from here, can't miss it."

"I see. . . . I suppose Mr. Clough doesn't happen to be here tonight—or any of the family who could take a message?"

Old Alf poured a Guinness with a nice exactitude.

"Mester Clough's in his bed. Where he's likely to stop until they carry him out feet first."

"Oh. Pity."

"*She's* 'ere, as per usual, if that's any help. Whether she'll be in any state to tek a message by closing time is a different kettle o' fish. . . . If you want to try, that's 'er, ower yonder." He jerked his head towards the far end of the room where a noisy game of darts was in progress.

Brian picked up his tankard and edged through the crowd to watch.

The players were three men and a woman, all unskilled in the game. They threw the darts wildly, shrieking with laughter at each throw, making inaccurate calculations or omitting to add the score at all. They had all had too much to drink.

The men were flashy types with pointed shoes and highly ornamental ties. They called each other "Old Boy" and smacked each other's backs. One sported a tremendous mustache and said "Terrific!" or "Wow!" every few minutes. They were obviously strangers. The laughter of those who stood to watch was directed at them, rather than with them; but there was not much laughter.

The woman was peering into the mirror of her compact, dabbing unsteadily at her mouth with a lipstick. She had a narrow face, heavily made up, and a mass of yellow hair growing out dark at the roots. She wore wine-colored slacks and a satin blouse, the sleeves pushed high up her thin arms. Her toenails showed scarlet and none too clean through the open ends of her sandals.

"Come on, ducks," said the man with the mustache. "Your turn."

"Half a minute," the woman protested. "Can't a girl do her face?" Her intonation was a curious blending of Cockney and broad Yorkshire.

"Why paint the lily?" Mustache said gallantly. "Have another drink, anyway. What's the poison?"

"Ow, I couldn't," said the woman. "Double gin, thanks ever so."

"Last orders, Gents," old Alf called from behind the bar. "Last orders, please!"

"*Good* lord!" Mustache ejaculated. "No idea it was so late. My word, I shall have to push off. You fellows having one for the road? Give it a name, then. Bitter? Bitter?" He thumped on the bar. "Three bitters and a double gin. And have a fill-up yourself."

"I'm not drinkin'," old Alf stated flatly. "An' no more are you."

"I beg *yours!*" Mustache exclaimed in lofty amazement.

"You 'eard." Alf gave a swipe at the messy bar and turned his back.

The man twirled his spreading mustache aggressively and shot a glance at his wrist watch.

"It still wants ten minutes to closing time," he said loudly. "I demand to be served!"

"Demand away," said Alf, rinsing glasses in water of a horrifying scumminess, "only git outa my pub to do it. You've 'ad enough, t'lot on yer, an' yer gittin' no more. I've me license to think of."

"Look here, my good man, are you going to serve me or are you not?"

"Not," Alf said.

"D'you know what I've got more'n half a mind to do?" Mustache inquired impressively, leaning over the bar in a threatening manner. "I've got more'n half a mind—"

"Bert!" called old Alf in a weary voice.

Immediately, through the door at his back entered an enormous young man with a face like a bad-tempered chimpanzee and the muscles of an ox, who leaped the counter with surprising agility, seized Mustache by the shoulders and ran him out into the night.

His companions followed, grinning self-consciously and bearing his hat.

The woman, who had watched this episode in silence, lolling against the wall, arms folded tightly across her narrow chest, now swaggered across the room. She thrust her face over the bar towards old Alf. The harsh light was merciless, showing up the hollows beneath the rouged cheekbones, the smeared mascara, the daubed caricature of a mouth. She was shockingly thin. Her shoulder blades stuck out sharply under the cheap stuff of her blouse. The back of her neck, Brain saw, was not very clean.

"An' what about me?" she shrilled. "What about that double gin my friend ordered for me?"

Old Alf continued to rinse glasses, unmoved.

"Tek my advice, missus, you'll get off 'ome. You know when you've 'ad enough as well as what I do; an' you've a long walk, an' a helpless owd man waitin' to be cared for."

"Mind your own bloody business, will you? I want that double gin as was ordered for me, and I'll thank you to dish it out, fairly sharpish!"

"An' who's going to pay for it?"

"You can chalk it up."

"I'll do nowt o' t'sort. You've got a deal too much chalked up, as

[195]

it is. You tek yourself off 'ome before we 'ave any trouble, my girl."

"You keep a civil tongue in your 'ead! My name's Mrs. Clough, an' I'll thank you to remember it." She scrabbled in her handbag and produced a ten-shilling note. "Here—now give me that double gin, an' make it snappy."

Old Alf hesitated, shrugged and finally pushed the drink over the counter.

She drank clumsily. A trickle of gin ran down her chin and dropped onto the pink satin blouse. Over the rim of her glass her eyes gazed at Brian boldly, professionally. She set down the glass and shrugged, mutely inviting his sympathy.

He nodded, gave a quick, infinitesimal smile. He kept the worse side of his face well in shadow.

"Anything more for you, sir?"

"No, thanks. Good night."

"G'night, sir."

The pub was rapidly emptying. Brian went to the car and started her up; backed and turned so that her nose was pointing down the lane towards Clough's farm. He looked inside the trunk. The bottle of Scotch was there all right. The rug. He fished it out and laid it on the seat. Cigarettes? . . . Plenty.

He began to pace slowly up and down the lane. The car purred in the darkness. The door of the pub swung open and shut; light leaped and vanished. Voices called to each other and laughter rang out, faded and died in the distance. "Time, gentlemen, please!" came the muffled plea. The door swung. Light leaped and laughter spurted.

Brian stared up at the dark, illimitable arch of the sky studded with stars. They were cold, clear and passionless as the voice of the boy singing.

"The day Thou gavest, Lord, is ended. . . ."

He whistled the tune as he paced up and down. He had sung it himself long ago when he, too, had been a choirboy in an old Worcestershire church. With a packet of liquorice all-sorts under his surplice, he remembered, grinning. And the Vicar's son—what was his name, now?—Armstrong. Spud Armstrong. . . . Good lord, he hadn't remembered him for years! They had been at prep school together. . . . Spud always brought *Chums* to church. They passed it stealthily back and forth, stifling giggles with liquorice all-sorts. And Spud had choked one day, and his father had beaten him. . . .

He lit a cigarette. I'm smoking too much, he thought indifferently.

His mind was back in the past.

High jinks at Oxford. Unsavory incidents, too. Things that had thrilled him in the doing; made him feel bold and bad and sophisticated in retrospect—until the war had thrust them back where they belonged: silly, childish indiscretions. . . .

His home, too. His father. The dark, stuffy surgery, the dingy waiting room with its tattered old copies of *Punch* and *The Lady*. The narrow, neglected garden, dark with trees, dank with moss. The slovenly kitchen quarters where Mrs. Truett, the housekeeper, had entertained her cronies with the doctor's whisky, rapping sharply on the window when he peered in at them, fascinated, half scared. The endless procession of sick people, deformed people, scabrous people; the coughings and snufflings and complainings and limpings. . . . The dread of holidays and the wild joy of getting back to school, back to the normal. . . .

What a row when he had wanted to go into films! The breach with his father had never healed properly; never would now, he supposed. His war record hadn't made any difference. No bit of colored ribbon could make Dad forgive his breaking with tradition. For years and years the eldest son had always taken his father's place. Father and son, and his son after him. "It's a fine tradition, my boy, a grand tradition. And you propose to break it—merely to clown in front of a camera!" Poor old Dad. Stiff-necked old idiot. . . .

The fight to get in. The fight to get on. The heady bliss of recognition. Would he ever have become a star? I might have made the grade, he thought. I was no worse than plenty of them. Better than some who landed fat contracts. I was on my way up, all right, if it hadn't been for the war. . . .

He remembered one film in which he had played an amiable drunk at a fair. Staggering towards the leading lady, tipsily gallant. Tipping his hat. "Hullo, Beautiful!"

I've given some fairly ham performances in my time, he thought. This one must be good. This must be strictly box office.

Those war years. . . . They unrolled before him, flickered before his eyes with all their darkness and shine, pleasure and agonizing hurt, valor and dirt and bewilderment.

I'm like the traditional drowning man, he thought, seeing my whole life flash before my eyes. They say it always happens before you die. I don't see how anybody knows: the dead don't tell. . . . He felt himself beginning to tremble, lose control. He stood still. He clutched at the memory of Rose; the warm strength of her arms holding him, the kindness of her innocent eyes. Sweet Rose. . . .

The spasm loosed its grip and left him. He resumed his pacing up and down, up and down. The car purred smoothly. A distant radio blared suddenly and was cut off. A star shot across the sky to some mysterious bourn.

So I'm going to crash again, he thought. I wonder if I shall survive this time? . . . Whatever happens there'll be no medals. Definitely no medals. But little Rose will be happy . . . I'll pin her happiness on my chest. . . . Good out of evil. The parson didn't know. But Ted seemed to think that if you did your job you could take the rest on trust. . . .

"Come along now, *please!*" the landlord's voice was shouting.

Lights went down in the pub. A last trickle of customers emerged, dispersed in the darkness. There was the clink of glasses, the sound of bolts being shot, the drag of chairs over a wooden floor, the whistling of a man doing an accustomed job with cheerfulness and dispatch.

The door swung open for the last time, and Edie came out. It swung to behind her and the bolt shot home.

The bar was plunged into darkness. The whistling receded and a distant door banged. A pail clattered and a dog barked sharply twice. Then there was silence.

Edie began to walk down the lane. She stumbled and whispered a stream of obscenities. When she saw Brian she halted, stood peering doubtfully at him, pulling the edges of a seedy fur coat closer round her body in a pitiful pretense of dignity.

"Well, look who's here!" she experimented.

Brian went towards her, his face twisted in a tight, ludicrous smile. He tipped his hat.

"Hullo, Beautiful!" he said.

9

As THE bus ran along the ridge the driver remembered with a faint surprise how his nerves had played him up on the outward journey. He grinned in the darkness. Good job we don't have a nipper every week! he thought happily.

He supposed it would be too late to see young Lil tonight, but he'd be at the hospital first thing tomorrow morning; visiting day or no visiting day, he was going to see young Lil and the baby.

He wondered what it would look like. He didn't know much about babies, bar the fact that they were red and yelled like the dickens and made a surprising amount of washing.

But it wouldn't always be red and yelling. Before they knew where they were it'd be a little girl, looking like Lil, maybe—or like him. He'd take it for walks and it would hold his hand; and when it got tired he'd carry it, and it would fall asleep in his arms with its face close up against his neck, so he could feel its breath, warm and living and part of him and Lil. . . . He had often felt sorry for fathers thus burdened. Now, suddenly, he knew a sort of ecstasy at the thought of the trustful, limp heaviness that his shoulder would bear, the clutch of small hands on his coat, the warm breath damping his cheek, the dangle of hard little feet against his stomach. . . .

He wondered what they would call her. Young Lil was all for Marlene, but he liked his own mother's name, Ellen. Lil reckoned it was old-fashioned. So it was. He hadn't a doubt it would be Marlene in the end, and that was okay by him. But a kid could have two names, couldn't it? Half-a-dozen if you wanted 'em. Marlene Ellen— what was wrong with that?

He thought of Sunday mornings when he would take the nipper out walking. Lil would dress her up in one of those comic outfits with long pants and a pixie hood; scarlet, perhaps, or bright blue. "Get out o' my way, the two of you!" she'd say; and she'd stand smiling and waving at the gate. "Say bye-bye to Mummy, Marlene." And young Marlene would flap a little paw and say bye-bye over and over again, and him and Lil would laugh to each other over her head, both that proud they could bust.

Then she'd be a schoolgirl with a hockey stick, and a row of film stars pinned over her bed. And then she'd be clattering a typewriter in an office, getting her hair waved, going dancing at the Palais. And then she'd get married and go away, and him and Lil would be left alone, and they'd be old. . . .

Hey, there! the driver thought, braking mentally, give it a breeze, mate!

He whistled a verse of *The Day Thou Gavest,* putting in some nice twiddley bits. He couldn't half sing, that nipper! Young devil he might be, but he couldn't half sing. "The day Thou gavest, Lord, is ended. . . ."

Ah, but for young Marlene the day was only just beginning.

"Make it a lovely day, Lord," he prayed suddenly, feeling rather sheepish in this unaccustomed exercise. . . .

A black sedan overtook and shot past—just as they were coming to the crown of the hill, too!

The driver swore, honking indignantly at it.

All the way from the Good Fortune Tea Rooms they had been singing. As soon as one song died, somebody started another and, voice after voice, they all took it up. If they didn't know the words, they hummed. If they didn't know the tune, they improvised until they picked it up. They had sung anything and everything, from *Bless This House* to *Pack Up Your Troubles, Red Sails in the Sunset,* and *Tea for Two.* Joe Peck had contributed a rather doubtful version of *Clementine,* which they had tactfully allowed as a solo, punctuated by concerted *pom-poms,* and had then broken rather emotionally into *Home, Sweet Home*—and what homing bus could ever ignore *that* tune! They had given it all they'd got. Those who had homes of their own had thought of them nostalgically, and those who hoped for them had warmed sentimentally to the idea.

Jack had rocked the puppy contentedly backwards and forwards, humming his tune to each and every song.

John William gripped Doris' hand very tightly. She was so quiet! He had a notion that something had upset her. That mother of hers, more than likely. The owd bitch. . . . Until today, he had stood in some awe of Mrs. Maddon, having taken her, as so many people took her, on her own valuation. But the bubble of gentility, so carefully blown, so painstakingly preserved by Mrs. Maddon had been pricked, and that by Doris herself. John William no longer felt awe, but plain contempt for her. Not because she had been brought down to his level, but because she had ever pretended to be above it. The poor, silly owd bitch, with her Rolls-Royces and her genteel flummery! Well, he wasn't going to stand any nonsense when they were married. So long as she behaved herself she'd be welcome to visit the lodge. Let her start any of her tantrums, and he'd see to it she never came no more. He wasn't going to have Doris upset this way!

He wondered whether to talk to Doris, or to let her alone and just keep on holding her hand tightly.

Because silence always came more easily than speech to John William, he remained silent, except when he was singing with the others; and Doris Maddon blessed him for it. She didn't want to talk. She had received a double shock today. Her mother had shocked her, and she had shocked herself.

All her known world had quaked and shivered with the shock. Memories had perished, ties had snapped asunder, loyalty had disintegrated; all swept out on the sour tide of realism that had rushed over the barren, wasted land.

In all that desolation only one thing stood steadfast, immovable as a rock. John William.

John William. . . .

His solid body crushed against her; one arm circled her waist, hard and possessive; one hand gripped her hands with a grip that hurt, that comforted and blessed, that made her long never to be free of that reassuring pain. We'll be married right away, she thought feverishly. We'll get a special license, or whatever it is. If he can't afford it, I can. . . . I shall have to go back with her to-night. I shall have to. . . . I don't know how long it takes to get a special license. I'll find out. People will talk but I don't care, I don't care! . . . She'll say awful things about me, turn people against me. I don't care. I shall have John William. I shall have a man, a home of my own. I shall be loved. . . . Oh, God—she thought confusedly

—how good You are to let me be loved at last, when I so little deserve it!

Tears chased each other rapidly down her cheeks, and she let them flow unchecked. John William saw them but he made no comment. Only he tightened his arm until one big, blunt-fingered hand cupped gently round her breast, so that an arrow of pure joy sped through her body, and her breath came quick and uneven.

They were coming up onto the ridge.

From the shelter of Rose's arm young Les gazed dreamily, half asleep.

The sun had long since dropped behind the hills; the flaming banners of the west had been hauled down. Night waited in the sky; not fallen yet but ready to fall when you were not looking, when you least expected it. One minute you'd be looking at the lights pricking out in the valley, at the spire of Staving church away over yonder in its dark clump of trees, at the fearsome rocks snarling like bared teeth on the land that fell so precipitously away from your wheels; the next—it would be night. The bus would be alone with the stars.

Les did not wonder what would happen if the bus crashed through the stonewall into the valley below. He knew.

He knew that he would float somewhere between the earth and the stars, and he would sing as he floated. He would sing his descant. The tune would rise and fall and circle, till it wound about him a buoyant cocoon of softness and safety. . . . He tried to imagine the puppy inside the cocoon with him; but he couldn't imagine it. Because the puppy didn't like him, it liked Jack. Old Crackerjack. It lay in Jack's arms quite happy and content, and Jack was going to have it for *his* puppy. . . .

He tried to cry about that, but he couldn't squeeze a tear. Anyhow, he wasn't going to cry about any silly old puppy that liked silly old Crackerjack better than him! Anyhow, he didn't *want* the puppy. Because Rose and Bob were going to give him one of the collie pups from the farm, and it would not only behave like Lassie, it would look like her, too! And be just as clever.

He'd get Bob to give him a bitch, and then it would have lots of puppies of its own, and he'd sell them and make heaps of money, and Mum could get a servant to help in the house. He might let Ronnie have one cheap. . . .

So who wanted a silly old puppy that had to be carried about in a blanket! . . .

Les leaned against Rose and shut his eyes. He didn't care if Ronnie Field saw and called him a sissy; he was too tired to care about anything. He was glad Rose was going to marry Bob. It wouldn't be so nice at home without her, but she wouldn't be very far away. There would always be the farm to go to when Dad got the rats. And as soon as he left school he could work on the farm with Bob. He'd go clumping across the wet fields every morning, very early, before the village was awake, and Lassie would go with him, leaping ahead and running back and doing every single thing he told her to. He'd wear his cap on one side of his head, with the peak slanting over his ear, because it looked tough. He wanted to look tough. . . .

And at night they would come home together and Lassie would sleep close by his bed. He would hear her breathing. If he put out his hand in the night he would feel her long, warm body, her feather-soft ears. She would push an icy nose against his hand, loving him, loving him. . . .

"He's dropped off," Rose said quietly. She shifted him more comfortably against her shoulder, smiling down at the tousled head, the limp, grubby hands, the socks wrinkled round spindly ankles. "He sang fine, didn't he, Bob?"

"He did an' all!"

She laughed tenderly.

"He got the jitters. He wanted Ronnie Field to sing, 'stead of him. I had a job with him! . . . But he was fine; I knew he would be."

"That's how she'll hold our children some day," Bob told himself, his throat swelling at the thought.

The narrow, painted face of Edie leered at him through the dusk. He pushed at the face, pushed it violently out of sight.

Get out, *you!* he thought bitterly. Get out! . . . Lay one finger on Rose, or open your filthy mouth to her, and I'll kill you. . . .

His heart thumped heavily as hatred of Edie poured through him in a slow, black tide. I could kill her, he thought. Easy. . . . I could push her down the stairs when she's sozzled. They're dark enough in all conscience, an' she's bin warned a hundred times: there'd be plenty of witnesses to that. . . . Or I could tek her rabbitting with me an' have an accident wi' t'gun. That'd be easy, an' all. Everybody knows what she is; it'd be easy as falling off a log.

He thought of the shotgun hanging on the kitchen wall. He thought about it with sudden, fierce pleasure. His hands curved to hold it, his arms braced to take its weight.

So easy. So quickly over. So soon hushed up and forgotten. . . . He could do it all right.

He'd always thought of himself as a peaceable sort of chap, but they'd learned him different in the army. Taken him on battle courses and made him scream and yell and work himself up until he really saw red, jabbed away at them dummies like one o'clock. They had complimented him on his ferocity. Him! He'd never been so ashamed in all his life. . . .

But it had come in useful in the jungle. He'd let those little yellow bastards have it good and proper. He'd felt no pity. He didn't remember feeling anything at all except a sort of surprise that he wasn't feeling anything. And them Nips, bad as they were, at least were fighting for something they believed in. Edie didn't believe in anything, not even in herself. . . .

He felt Rose's head against his shoulder; and in a sudden surging of love he cupped her round, warm cheek, pressing it closer against him, feeling its soft bloom under his calloused fingers. Little Rose. Sweet little Rose. . . . His bones melted with love for her.

"Ee, I do love you, Bob!" he heard her whisper. "You're so strong. And yet you're so kind an' gentle with it—that's what I love about you. . . ."

His happiness was shot through with despair.

For of course he knew that he could never kill Edie, not even for Rose. Not even for little Rose. . . .

As they left the ridge and began the long descent into the valley, darkness fell upon them; and with the dark came quietness, and the knowledge that at last the day was done.

There was no more singing. Laughter was not so loud. Conversation was carried on in murmurs, in the significant touch of an elbow, a foot, a knee pressing against a knee, a hand tightening its clasp on a hand.

In the kind darkness Audrey relinquished all pretense of being Mrs. Vicarish and leaned her head, as Rose in front was doing, against the shoulder of the man she loved.

"We're not on duty any more, are we?" She yawned and wriggled a little closer. Andrew rested his cheek on the top of her head, feeling the soft hair flutter with his breathing. He yawned, too, and gave a long, tired sniff. "Don't do that in my ear!" Audrey complained sleepily. "Darling, are you very tired? I'm *dead!*"

"The thought of bed," he murmured, "is almost unbearably attractive!"

"I didn't have time to make it this morning," she remembered guiltily. "Everything was such a rush."

"It won't take a minute. You do the bed and I'll make the coffee. We'll lie between lovely cool sheets and drink it in peace. We haven't got the children to worry about."

"I've done nothing else all day," she complained. "I had Peter drowned in the pond inside the first hour, and since then I've buried all three of them."

They giggled drowsily together.

"Andy, I've had the most marvelous brain wave about Auntie Ag and Jack coming to live with us."

"Be your age, darling," he muttered into her hair.

"I'm all that, and more! And I mean it. All those great rooms eating their heads off, and poor old Auntie Ag scared stiff of being turned out of her cottage. The woman who owns it has a daughter with a quiverful of kids, and she's always nattering at the poor old thing. Oh, don't you *see!* Jack would do the garden and Auntie Ag would cook; and we shouldn't have to pay them such an awful lot, because they'd be living rent free. It's a wonderful idea!"

"It would be even more wonderful if we knew we could pay them anything at all," he said mildly. "We shall be having school fees to reckon with soon, don't forget."

Audrey wriggled excitedly.

"I'm not forgetting. That's the whole point, Andy. There won't *be* any school fees, not for several years, anyway, because I'm going to start a school. No, wait a minute! Don't you see, I shall be filling a long-felt need. I know of a dozen kids I could get right away, to say nothing of our own three. And they'll be coming along all the time."

"Under this new educational scheme," Andrew began gloomily; but Audrey disposed of the government with a snort.

"The village school is quite full and the next nearest means a long bus ride in all weathers. I tell you, there'll be private kindergartens flourishing for years yet. Got to be! I'm fully trained and qualified, and quite capable of dealing with at least twenty children up to the age of eight. There'll be a bit of outlay, but I shall soon be raking in the shekels. And Auntie Ag will do the house and Jack will be endlessly useful . . ." She drew a long breath and squinted up at her spouse, excited and expectant.

"And do you imagine Jack will go down well with the parents?" was all his response.

"Why not!" she exclaimed impatiently. "There's nothing wrong with Jack. He's just simple. He's not repulsive to look at. He's kind and clean and hard-working and obedient—what more do you want? Have you seen him with that puppy? He's marvelous with it! So gentle and understanding. That's how he'd be with the children."

Andrew said doubtfully:

"Last week I saw him giving young Field the hiding of his life for chucking stones at a chicken."

"And serve the little beast right!" Audrey said fiercely.

"Yes, but would the parents care about that sort of thing? You've got to look at it from all angles."

"Our children wouldn't chuck stones at chickens."

"I trust not. But others might."

"Oh, darling, don't be so pernickety and obstructive!"

"I know. I'm sorry, my sweet. . . . Look, let's sleep on it, shall we? I think you may have something, but we must proceed with caution. There are all sorts of snags. The Bishop—"

"To hell with the Bishop!" Audrey cut in blithely.

"I couldn't agree more. But need you declaim it quite so resonantly?" He grinned into her hair and hugged her with sudden boyish fervor; albeit discreetly, for it was surprising what some folks could see, however dark it might be. "Kiss me," he demanded.

"You know you'd be horrified if I did!"

Now, she thought. Now is the moment to tell him. She shut her eyes, tightened her clasp of his hand. Now. Tell him now. . . . Why did she suddenly feel shy? It was ridiculous. I'm like one of those awful females in Victorian novels, she thought, flapping a knitted bootee at her husband and simpering about little strangers. What on earth's come over me!

"Oh, my sweet, I do love you!" Andrew was whispering. He was breathing rather quickly. Really, it was very gratifying, she decided, that he could behave like this on a bus, after all these years of being married to her. . . .

All she had to say was: "I'm going to have another baby."

Six words. The most miraculous, and at the same time the most matter-of-fact words in the whole language.

"Andy—" she began.

No use. She couldn't tell him here and now.

"What is it, sweet?"

"Nothing. . . ."

She picked up his hand and rubbed her cheek against it. Dear hand. Much too thin. Rather impractical. . . . Not a money-maker's hand: anything like that would have to be *her* pigeon. She didn't mind in the least. She had married Andy for love, not for money. When you fell in love, you didn't worry how you were going to live, you just knew that you couldn't live at all if you couldn't have that one person. . . . And how stark and practical Frances would be about that!

She hadn't always remembered it herself. One didn't. It was the sort of truth that got fairly frayed at the edges when doctors' bills came in, or boots disintegrated, or the shed roof clattered off in the night. Or when one longed quite desperately for a holiday without the faintest hope of being able to afford one.

I mustn't forget how utterly unimportant money seemed, so short a time ago, she thought soberly. Even if I make oodles of money with the school, I mustn't forget that in the long run it's our love that really matters.

She pulled his arm across her body so that it sheltered her and the child within her. Relaxed, she lay against him in the purring, hurrying bus. And quite suddenly she fell asleep.

Andrew held her carefully.

I'm fairly sure she's going to have another baby, he thought remorsefully. Poor darling. I must remember to be astonished and delighted when she tells me. I expect we shall manage somehow. . . . What am I to do about this school business? I'm not at all sure it would work, but she seems to have made up her mind. . . . The money would be useful. I could put Peter down for a good school. We could have holidays, new clothes. . . . I wish I'd taken a stronger line with that R.A.F. chap. I've thought of a dozen things I could have said that might have helped, and now it's too late. . . . Can good come out of evil? How do I know? How does anyone know? . . . I'm a rotten parson.

He thought with sudden nostalgia of the dark peace of his church, in which he could forget earthly claims, earthly problems; lay his burden on the steps of the altar and escape to God in that strange, white ecstasy of solitude. . . .

No, I've done too much of that, he thought contritely. I won't go tomorrow morning. Nor tonight. Tomorrow I'll take her breakfast up to bed, and she must rest while I go and fetch the children home. Even if I'm a rotten parson, he thought, I can be a good husband and father, I should hope.

"How are you feeling now, luv?" Minnie inquired.

"Middling," Mrs. Maddon admitted grudgingly. "But not at all the thing. Sort of sickish and sinking. If only I could get a drop of brandy. I've got some at home: Doctor told me never to be without. I shall be better when I've had a drop of brandy."

"As soon as we get in," Minnie encouraged her, "you get straight to your bed, and I'll bring you some brandy. I'll look after you. I'll stop all night if you've a mind. But you must mek it right with Doris. I don't want," she added austerely, "to come between Mother and Daughter."

"Daughter!" Mrs. Maddon exclaimed violently. "She's no daughter of mine! The things she's said this day! . . . And she's going to marry yon clodhopping gardener of Colonel March's. She's going off with him, leaving me alone after all these years. . . . How I shall manage, I do not know, me alone in yon house, in my state of health. Downright heartless, I call it! . . . But she can go—and good joy go with her! I hope she fancies herself as the gardener's wife, curtsying and bobbing to the Colonel and grubbing about in her dark little lodge. I hope she'll be satisfied. . . . Only she needn't come whining back to me, that's all. As she makes her bed, so she'll lie on it, and not a penny-piece will she get from me. Not a penny-piece. . . ." Caution pinched up her mouth. "Not that I've anything to leave," she added. "There's enough for me to live comfortably . . . and anyone living with me, of course." Her eyes slid round to Minnie. But Minnie was gazing straight ahead, almost as if she had not heard. "Well, I don't say there mightn't be a little *something*, if I went careful. But not for Doris. Not for anyone who could go off and leave me, like she's doing, without a word of warning or a thought of all I've done for her. No, thank you! . . . But anyone who was prepared to stay with me and take Doris' place, well, I don't say there mightn't be a little something. . . ." She sighed gustily. "But who would want to come and live with me now? Nobody wants you when you get old." She snuffled a little. "And of course, I can't live like I did when my husband was alive. No maids or motorcars now! . . . I don't suppose I shall get anyone to stay. I'm just a lonely, unwanted old woman. . . ." She whimpered into silence.

Minnie gazed stonily ahead; she was occupied with her own thoughts.

She wasn't interested in anybody's money. She had her own money, that her Auntie Maud had left her, to say nothing of what would come to her later on: bound to, because there was nobody else for them to leave it to, even if they wanted. She wasn't interested in Mrs. Maddon's poor heart, which was, in all probability, more stomach than heart, or in Doris' defection, or her silly love affair.

All that concerned Minnie was getting her own back on Ma. . . .

She knew when she wasn't wanted, thank you! And if Ma was going to start them silly capers, running after Pa, drinking with him in pubs and mekkin' herself a byword, well, she washed her hands of her, that's all! If Ma could do without her, after all these years, she could do without Ma.

Something had happened to Ma in yon hat shop. Just what, she couldn't imagine, but there was *something*. She couldn't sum it up. What was more, she shrank from trying. There was something revolting in the thought of Ma and Pa behaving like ordinary married couples behaved. She wriggled her shoulders in distaste.

"Are you cold, Minnie?" Mrs. Maddon asked. "I wish I'd brought a rug; the nights are getting chilly now. Sit closer to me."

"I'm not cold," Minnie said briefly.

She had never cared much for Pa, not even as a child. She remembered how he had bawled at her, poked her in the ribs, tossed her sickeningly up to the ceiling, pricked her with his coarse, unshaven cheeks.

She had never had any power over Pa.

But Ma had been different. She had held Ma in the hollow of her hand. She looked back down the years, remembering how she had first come to realize her power.

Lying awake in her small, dark bedroom, she had listened to the whisperings, the smothered laughter, the creakings in the adjoining room, until rage and jealousy had made her cry. That had brought Ma at a run, thinking she was frightened of the dark. . . .

"Should you like a night light, lovey?"

"No. Stay with me. Stay with me, Ma!"

It had taken a bit of time and a rare lot of shouting and crying and argument. But before long Ma had moved in permanently with Minnie, and after that it had been easy. . . .

All these years. And half an hour in a hat shop had undone them. . . . She couldn't sum it up.

She felt Mrs. Maddon draw a long, quivering breath. She reached out and took the woman's plump hand between her own hands, long and bony in their black cotton gloves.

"I'll look after you," she said dryly.

Ma had been easy, but Mrs. Maddon would be even easier. Doris had been frightened of her; but Doris was a rabbit, anyone could frighten her! In six months she'd have Mrs. Maddon exactly where she wanted her. She'd put a stop to all this port and brandy business. And if Mrs. M. thought Minnie was going to be a dope and do all the housework, she'd got another guess coming. She does too little and eats too much, she thought. I'll put the stopper on that. She'll be all the healthier for it.

Power welled up in her, flowed down her arms into the hands gripping Mrs. Maddon's plump fingers.

Perhaps Mrs. Maddon felt it, for she made a feeble effort to pull her hand away; but Minnie held it the more tightly.

"I'll look after you, you don't want to worry."

Her nose poked and gleamed in the shifting light, and the black shoulders were bent. . . .

Across the aisle, Ma and Pa were sitting together silently.

Ma kept her face rigidly away from Minnie, but Minnie knew she wasn't missing much. She would know that Minnie was holding Mrs. Maddon's hand.

She would see them walk away together, up the lane towards Mrs. Maddon's house on the crest of the hill. Minnie didn't think she would attempt to stop them: if she did, Minnie knew just what to say, and how to say it. More likely, she'd make no sign.

Ma hadn't lived with Minnie for the best part of forty years without knowing when she was beaten. . . .

Addie Peck sat silently by Joe's side. She kept her face turned rigidly away from Minnie, but she wasn't missing anything. She knew Minnie was holding Mrs. Maddon's hand. . . .

She knew that she had lost Minnie, just as she had lost Joe, but she didn't care much.

It was going to feel strange at first, and of course, folks would have a lot to say, but that couldn't be helped.

It wasn't losing Minnie that mattered.

It was the girl with the brown hair and the dimples—the girl who had suddenly stared back at her from the mirror in the hat shop—that she mourned. Addie Simmonds that was. . . .

She had been such a happy girl, such a gay, pretty girl! She should have lived a full, strenuous life filled with noise and laughter, even with honest sorrow; bearing children and seeing them grow up strong and lusty about her. Strapping sons working in the smithy; tramping away to the war and coming back again, or lying in some foreign field, making her sad and proud; going courting and bringing their girls to Sunday tea. Pretty daughters filling the house with bright clothes; singing and quarreling and laughing; with lads whistling for them at the gate; running in and out with husbands and babies, with worries for her to share, problems for her to solve. . . .

Addie Simmonds that was. Such a gay, pretty girl—the prettiest girl in the village, forty years ago. She had worn a forget-me-not hat, and Joe had whispered daft things to her. She had been avid for life and love. . . .

[211]

She would have grown old, of course, as all must grow old. She would have lost her teeth, her figure, her bright brown curls. That was normal. She wouldn't have minded that. Life, taking from her, would have given back generously, in full measure; memories, shared laughter and tears, children, grandchildren. . . . However old she became, she still would have remained the girl in the forget-me-not hat.

Instead, she had died very young, and no one had remembered her, not even herself, until today.

Nay! she thought bleakly; and wished for the benison of tears, but none came.

Addie Simmonds could have cried, and been comforted; but Addie Peck did not know how to cry.

Joe sat stolidly beside Addie, his head sunk on his great chest. His eyes were shut but he was not asleep.

He had drunk a great deal, but he was quite sober. He'd put that right, he promised himself, as soon as the bus stopped at Platt's Corner. He would nip straight over to The Crown and the wordless welcome of old Alf. They'd make a night of it. And tomorrow he'd work it off on the forge. Tomorrow would be another day.

> As o'er each continent and island
> the dawn leads on another day . . .

Aye, that's how it went. Morning and night and morning, an' then night once again; an' so you got through life somehow. What with choir and work, and evenings at The Crown, it wasn't too bad. . . . Not what he'd hoped for when he started out, happen, but not too bad, either. . . . Anyhow, he didn't want it changed now. It was too late. . . .

Addie was quiet, and he was thankful for that. He'd got nowt to say to Addie. Least said, soonest mended.

It looked as if Addie and Min had had words. He couldn't help that. Min was no concern of his, and never had been from the time she could walk and talk. They'd gone their own way, had Addie and Min, and there was no turning back now.

When Addie had followed him into the George and Dragon he'd been too flabbergasted to protest. Drinking her port and lemon. Sit-

ting perched up on her stool, with yon paper hat on her head. . . .
In retrospect, it was unbelievable. At the time, of course, he'd had
a proper owd skinful, or he'd never have let her do it.

It wouldn't happen again. If Addie had any idea of making up for
past neglect by becoming his boon companion now, the sooner she
forgot it, the better. Nothing doing.

It was too late. It was a whole lifetime too late. . . .

Walter Forsythe was glad when the singing died and the day
could fairly be called finished. He did not feel like singing, or listening to other people singing any more.

Red Sails in the Sunset, indeed! . . . When had the cloying
pathos of a music-hall ballad ever before brought tears smarting to
his eyes? I'm over-tired, he thought. That's what's the matter with
me. I'm played out. It has been a long, hot, difficult day, and I'm
not so young as I used to be.

One leg in the grave. . . .

That, of course, had referred to Booker, honeymooning, rather absurdly, in Bettws-y-coed. But Booker was two years younger than
himself, which threw rather a sinister light on the subject.

One leg in the grave. What a horrible—what a really revolting
thing for anyone to say! The sort of thing nobody ever would say,
if they had any imagination at all. . . .

By his side the massive figure of Phoebe sat silently. Her hands
were clasped in her lap, quiet and unfidgeting. Her bosom rose and
fell in slow majesty. She exhaled serenity, security, dependableness.
She looked as if nothing had ever worried her, nor ever would. She
looked immortal. . . .

He had to have a little talk with Phoebe: he mustn't forget that.

Phoebe really must resign from the choir soon. It was a sad, an
inevitable, but not a terrible thing to contemplate. Everything came
to an end. Some time—though not for a long time yet!—he himself
would have to give the choir into the hands of a younger man. That
was life. That was how it went. . . .

He tried out one or two approaches:

"I wasn't altogether pleased with that slow passage in the boating song, Phoebe. It should have been kept strictly *piano*. . . ."

"You know, Phoebe, my dear, you really must remember. . . ."

"You must get the *feeling* of the thing, Phoebe. You must have a sense of *fitness*. . . . Your voice is strong, and must be kept down. . . ."

The thought of her red, astonished countenance daunted him.

"You will have to be quite ruthless, of course," Bee had said. And of course, that was what he would have to be. Quite ruthless. It was the kindest in the long run; but it was a wretched thing to have to do. . . .

He drew his legs together, held them together by pressing his hands on either side of his knees. He looked at his hands with distaste. They were not very clean; the nails needed attention; he had broken one of them, playing cricket. He felt dusty, scruffy. There was dust on his coat sleeves, sand in the turn-ups of his trousers. His tie was askew, his shirt cuffs creased. His skin felt sore with sun and his lips tasted salt.

He longed for a bath, the moral support of clean clothing. To-morrow he would get his hair cut, have his beard trimmed. He'd go into town and buy himself some new shirts, maybe a hat. . . .

Might as well let the doctor go over him. That pain in his knee. It was nothing, of course—a touch of rheumatism—still, might as well get rid of it. He got a bit of headache now and again. More than likely he needed his glasses changed. New glasses often gave you a new lease on life. So they said. . . .

The idea of a holiday occurred to him. Weston-super-Mare. Very nice at this time of the year. Elsie would make him very comfortable. Nothing like a change of air and scene for setting you up. He might drop a line to Elsie tomorrow. Yes, he'd do that. . . .

His fingers beat a staccato tune on his small, bony knees. He felt old and ill, dusty and crumpled and frightened.

What's the matter with me? he thought. I didn't feel like this this morning. I felt fine this morning. . . . I've aged ten years in a day. What's the matter with me!

He knew what was the matter with him. It was Bee. Bee, who was going to die. He couldn't bear it. Suddenly he felt that he hated Bee for dying.

"I can't bear it," he whispered to himself, panic-stricken. "I can't bear it. . . ."

"What's that, luv?" Phoebe had turned her head, was bending to catch his words.

He smelled the warmth of living flesh, the cleanness of eau de Cologne, the tang of leather, the faint austerity of cloth that has been laid away in camphor. Good, reassuring smells, strong, earthy, robust smells; smells that might wrinkle your nose, but had nothing to do with frailty, with mortality. . . .

"I—I've been wanting a word with you all day, Phoebe," he got out.

Phoebe laid a large, strong hand on his knee.

"Nay, Walter, what's to do? You're shekkin' like a leaf!"

He seized her hand with both his own, gripping the hot, shiny kid with all his strength, so that she gave a small whinny of alarm.

"Phoebe. . . . I've been thinking . . . for a long time I've been thinking . . . how stupid we are to go on living in those two houses, when . . . when we don't need more than the one. Why don't we get married, Phoebe? Why don't we? We've known each other a long time, we suit each other. . . . We could let my house—or yours, if you'd prefer that—and live in the other. Or we could knock down the party wall and make a good-sized place of it. Do you think you could bring yourself to do it, Phoebe? I'm not too old, am I? I'm not really old at all, am I? I mean . . . well, what I mean is . . ."

He knew he was babbling, but he couldn't stop. He was so afraid that if he stopped talking for one instant Phoebe would say "No," and he knew that she must not say "No." If she did he would die, like poor Louise had died, and Phoebe's husband. Like Bee was going to die. . . .

". . . party wall . . ." he heard himself jabbering. ". . . herbaceous borders . . . musical evenings . . . Weston-super-Mare . . . in my left knee. . . ."

And abruptly Phoebe's laugh broke across his fervored jabbering; that good, rich laugh of Phoebe's that he had often frowned on as being too loud; had mentally dubbed "common."

"Give over, do!" said Phoebe, pulling her hand away by main force and inserting her elbow in his ribs. "Do you want everyone to hear you!" And she laughed again, not ill-pleased at his agitation. Indeed, richly gratified by it. For whoever would have thought Walter had felt that way about her all these years! And never breathed a word—the daft thing.

Her face glistened with heat and happiness. Her dreams had come true beyond her wildest hopes.

A husband, a home, companionship—these she had dared to dream of. But a lover—a breathless, trembling lover incoherent with desire —this had been beyond even prayer. . . .

Nay! she thought, bewitched and bewildered. Happen it's a bit daft, our time o' life. I don't know as I really wanted that. It weren't what I'd thought on. . . . Ee, well, I don't know!

Walter's hand was thrusting through the crook of her arm, clinging to it with a surprising tenacity.

"You don't think I'm too old, do you, Phoebe?" he was insisting.

Fishing for compliments, eh? As if he didn't know she herself was only a year the younger!

"You've got a good twenty years yet, luv," she said robustly. "More than that, happen, with me to look after you. An' you can give yon slut of a lass her notice as soon as you've a mind." Ee, my word, she thought, practical still, for all her joy, I've wanted to get at them shirts of Walter's a rare long time! I'll have him looking a fair treat!

And the faint distress his outburst had caused her began to subside before the rich promise of Walter's shirts blowing in a white curve across the sizable garden there would be, when both gardens were made into one.

Crying for the moon, was I! she thought. A fat lot that Madame knew about it! I'd best have kept me money in me pocket. . . . Or got meself some nylons, she thought surprisingly.

In the very back seat of all sat Ivy and Harry Waterhouse, Pearl and George and Violet, in that order.

This wasn't George's own idea. Anything but.

George had planned to sit next to Harry Waterhouse, safely barricaded against all females, and get a bit of shut-eye. He had to be up early in the morning, and this day—he admitted it frankly—had taken it out of him above a bit.

George was, in fact, at a very low ebb. His arms, burdened, as they were, by blossoming young womanhood, were assailed by pins

[216]

and needles. His neck and jaws were alternately tickled and scratched by the permanent waves, and the bobby pins and pins that assisted those waves of the Lomax girls. His eardrums were deafened by song and laughter. His shins and ribs were sore from girlish feet and elbows emphasizing the points of innumerable, if obscure jokes.

Adding to his miseries—indeed, predominating over them and rendering them well-nigh insupportable—was the key.

They had thrust it down his back in order to check the flow of blood caused by the impact of Harry's fist upon his nose. It had achieved its purpose and had remained, forgotten, somewhere in the uncharted regions between his collar stud and the leather belt supporting his flannel trousers.

Owing to the bouncing movements of the bus, the wriggling and nudging of Pearl and Violet and his own futile attempts to relieve the pins and needles in his arms, the key had now assumed a position of such acute discomfort that his eyes watered with pain and vexation.

It should, of course, have been a simple enough matter for George to heave up the reclining bodies of Pearl and Violet and deal with the situation in a swift and common-sense manner. A few hours previously George would so have dealt with it, and no nonsense.

But George was a changed man, a far more cautious, more danger-conscious man than he had been a few hours ago. He no longer entertained complacent notions of choosing either Pearl or Violet to be the instrument which should consolidate his position. The events of this day had proved conclusively that you did not "choose" either Violet or Pearl. They chose you. Or not, as the case might be.

He realized, also, that this process, if ever it materialized, would, in all probability, take a considerable time, coupled with the greater part, if not the whole of his savings.

It was going to be a long, arduous and damnably expensive business. Feeling as he did now, George was not at all sure he wanted to go on with it. Either one or t'other on 'em, he thought despairingly, but not both. There's no future in it.

As for his immediate sufferings, he was determined that, though the key should pierce his very spine—which apparently it was already doing—he would never, by word or sign, reveal his agony to the Lomax girls.

Shuddering, he knew that they would have his mack off before you could say knife; have his jacket off; think nothing of ripping out his shirt and releasing the key with loud shrieks of pleasure and excitement which would expose him to the hearty attentions, the spicy badinage of the whole bus.

Since the sudden truce between Harry Waterhouse and himself, George had learned, with nausea and foreboding, of the disgraceful scene on the Lower Front in which Harry, a hapless victim, had been involved—and that before the very eyes of his superior. . . .

And so, as the huge bus bounced and rocked along roads that were fair and roads that were none too good and roads that were a downright disgrace to the councils concerned, George Fiddler joined that vast company of martyrs who are never eulogized in song or pictured on canvas or immortalized in sculptured stone; suffering stoically while his neck was scratched and his arms nearly fell off and his spine was punctured, bored and lacerated. And only the knowledge that his soul was still his own brought him the smallest consolation.

"Cheer up, Georgy-Porgy," Pearl advised. "You'll soon be dead!"

And how true that was, George reflected hollowly, they little knew!

"I believe he's dead now," Violet suggested. "Dead, but he won't lie down."

They choked with laughter at this sally, scraping their bobby pins against George's cheeks and causing his arms such exquisite agony that he was obliged to grit his teeth lest he should cry out.

"He's dead but he won't lie down," Pearl sang; and Vi joined in with rich harmony; "Dead, but he won't lie down. . . ."

"Wouldn't you like to lie down, Georgy-Porgy?" They peered at him, bright-eyed, boiling over with animal spirits. "Wasums tired, den?" Pearl inquired, poking a playful fingernail at his shrinking eyelids. "Diddums want to go bye-byes, den? . . . Hey, Vi, what say we put old Georgy-Porgy to bye-byes on the seat? We can sit on top of him, then, an' get a grand view!"

"Yippee!" was Violet's instant reaction to this proposal. "Come on, Georgie!"

Cascades of girlish giggles rippled out on the night air. They began to manhandle him with the greatest possible gusto. They punched and pinched and elbowed. They tickled him under the ribs. They hauled at his numbed arms, trampled his toes, yanked and heaved at him, bore down upon him violently, shoved him and shrieked their discordant enjoyment in his ears.

Harry Waterhouse, much incommoded by the schemozzle, uttered a faint, protesting: "I say—!" but thought better of it when Violet turned a bright, interested glance in his direction.

"Let 'em be!" Ivy whispered urgently. "You can't do nothing with 'em when they get like this. We don't want to get mixed up in it."

"Steady on, You Boys!" the voice of Sergeant Stacey came crisply through the night. But neither Lomax heeded her.

The Vicar shook his head at them, unnoticed. Mr. Forsythe frowned and John William Welsh muttered a tolerant: "Now then!"

But on the whole nobody really paid much attention to the goings on in the back row. They were used to it. At every Outing the back was the recognized home of high spirits and a certain amount of skylarking. After all, you were only young once. . . .

"Go to bye-byes like a good boy, George."

"Give over, will you!" George snarled. "Pack that lark up!"

"Oo, temper! . . . Swing his legs round, Pearl."

"Yippee! You're going to lie down, Georgie, and like it!"

They were strong, the Lomax girls, and they were ruthless; but they were off their guard.

They grabbed at George's legs. The key bit savagely into his flesh and slipped downwards, releasing him.

The pain, and the abrupt relief from pain, were too much for George's equilibrium. With a strength of mind and limb that secretly astonished and delighted him, he grasped a frizzy permanent in either hand, swung them round and brought them together with a resounding crack. And the noise of their coming together was music in George's ears. . . .

"Now happen you'll give over," he said.

The eyes of Harry Waterhouse regarded him with apprehension deeply tinged with respect, and Ivy's little nose quivered in anticipation.

But for once in his life George had done the one thing needful; and peace—a shocked, resentful, but most blessed peace—fell upon the back row of the bus.

10

THE village slid into view like a half-remembered dream.

Lighted cottages keeping vigil among dark shapes of trees. Blaze from the hotel at the far end of The Green, and the church spire dark and slender above star-studded elms. Faint strains of dance music from some distant radio. The closed secrecy of The Crown guarded by the bark, the rattle of chain from an invisible watchdog.

Platt's Corner, and the big bus sliding to a standstill.

Weary stretchings of limbs and stiff descendings. Undisguised yawns and subdued laughter and the flexing of cramped muscles. The sudden clamor of resuscitated choirboys; scuffle and shrill argument and inevitable, tolerant head-slappings; tears and jeers and scuttling disappearances across The Green.

"Good-by. So long. Good neet all! . . ."

"We've had a lovely day. Grand! Wonderful! . . ."

"See you tomorrow. Back on t'job. . . ."

Bob and the driver slapping each other's shoulders in farewell. The bus revving up, moving onwards, outwards, away into the darkness and the last lap home to the depot.

Small groups forming and wheeling and reforming in gradual dispersion. Voices calling through the darkness and hidden voices answering. A few whistles and catcalls and a girl's shrill laugh.

Cottage doors opening; framing in light the dark forms of homecomers; touching to momentary life the welcome of a white apron, the gleam of a fireguard, the corner of a picture, the polished bars of a chair.

"Ee, it's been a lovely day! See you tomorrow. Good neet all. . . ."

Doors shutting all round The Green. Voices fading down dark, twisting lanes. The radio suddenly cut off in mid-rhythm. The dog's bark grumbling into silence, its chain rattling along stone. . . .

Houses that were dark before now show a transient life.

Walter Forsythe is neatly stacking away his music sheets, humming the descant which young Les so satisfactorily sang today. The pain in his knee has gone. Now and then he eyes the party wall which is so soon to come down.

Phoebe Braithwaite is rubbing glycerin and rose water into her hands. For even if you *are* getting on, and a bit on the stout side, and no oil painting, that is no reason why you should not make the best of yourself. Especially now. . . .

The two cottages are lavish of light, making a sturdy stand against the encroaching dark. That is how the place will look when the party wall is down; no longer two houses but one home, strong and indivisible.

In the old-fashioned, bitterly clean house beside the blacksmith forge the light in the kitchen goes out, reappearing in a moment in an upstairs room.

One light. Only one. And soon that, too, goes out. For there is no one to keep it burning for, and no excuse for waste.

The back door of The Crown shows a crack of light. A figure passes in and the crack is closed. The dog does not even trouble to raise its head. A tail thumps in the kennel, acknowledging a friend, but that is all.

Up the steep lane to the house on the hill's crest the figures of two women slowly climb. They walk close together, one leaning on the other. Their voices are ghost voices, scarcely disturbing the immense silence. Their shadows lie behind them, long and black, intermingled; almost like one shadow.

John William holds Miss Maddon in a comforting clasp. "It'll none be long, luv," he murmurs; and Miss Maddon, clutching what courage she can summon, knows that it cannot be too soon.

There is a light in the Vicarage kitchen where the Vicar is preparing coffee, setting a tray with cups and saucers, peering disconsolately into tins where biscuits ought to be and are not. But there is no light in the big, bare bedroom, for none is needed. The open windows are filled with stars and in the mirror the hotel lights are caught and thrown back into the shadowy room, and it is enough. In any case, there is no oil in the Aladdin lamp, for nobody ever remembers to fill it.

The Vicar's wife lies in the old-fashioned double bed, cherishing her lovely secret. She hears her husband's footsteps in the hall below, hears his accustomed stumble on the loose stair rod and the mild, patient oath which it calls forth, and she smiles in deep content.

Now, she is determined. I will tell him now. . . .

Miss Stacey sings as she plods her manly way. She sings a martial ditty, all ten verses of it, even the most indelicate ones. Especially the most indelicate ones. For Miss Stacey fears her years on Civvy Street have made her slightly sissy, and the sooner she gets back into the old, tough ways, the better.

And if the thought of Ivy creeps into her mind she banishes it immediately, with immense resolution. For soon Miss Stacey will be with The Boys once more, and the memory of Ivy Carter's slight form encircled by the arm of Harry Waterhouse will cease to have the slightest significance.

Miss Stacey is not the only one who sings; for Jack sings to his puppy as he lopes happily across The Green which is barred with beam and shadow, and down the dark, twisting lane home to Auntie Ag, who is sure to be keeping something hot for him on the back of the stove. "*Bring* back, *bring* back . . ." he croons, taking great care lest he should trip and the puppy fall from his arms. He is so eager to show the puppy to Auntie Ag, because she will love it as he does.

Yet Jack is a little worried because he keeps forgetting something important. Something Rose told him he must be sure to remember, and which keeps slipping out of his mind and slipping in again and then out, just like the tadpoles in the pond at the edge of the wood.

Something about the table leg. . . .

That was it! He must never, never pour his tea or his gravy or his porridge milk down the leg of the table. Not even the last, tiny drop of it. Because the puppy might get its little feet wet and die!

No more waterfalls. . . . Now he remembers perfectly.

He repeats the warning out loud, three times, and the puppy peers trustfully from its blanket, yawning pinkly.

Rose pulls the too-tight frock over her head and draws a deep breath, stretching round white arms, glad to be free of the constriction.

She is so tired she can scarcely stand, but there are still things to be done; she must wash, brush her hair and teeth, say her prayers. . . . She is aware that young Les, already asleep in his slip of a room, has evaded all these duties, and she smiles tolerantly, for Les is just a bairn.

But Rose is grown-up, she takes life seriously. Soon she will be a married woman, full of duties and responsibilities. There will be joys, too: fun with Bob; wind-blown and fire-warmed happiness with Bob; lapses into childishness and laughter; deep unimagined mysteries which her body whispers to her heart and her heart accepts but does not understand. . . .

But, strangely, it is the responsibilities, the cares, the shared work and problems, the ordinariness of marriage that now fills her with deep and sober happiness. These her heart understands as well as her body.

She thinks of Edie; meets the thought with courage and is unafraid. Somehow it will all come right. She knows it.

Trustfully she kneels and whispers her childish list of petitions, not forgetting poor Mr. Collinson: from this day he takes a permanent place in her prayers. And she rises secure in the knowledge that it will all come right. . . .

The church clock strikes with slow solemnity. Rose winds the alarm clock, sets it, gives it a little shake for luck and stands it on the floor beside her bed.

She opens the window and the cool night air flows through her thin nightgown and over her body like water. Leaning out, she can just see the dark mass of Clough's farm with its back humped against the east.

Bob should be home by now, for he has taken the short cut across the fields. She imagines him undressing in the dark bedroom, careful not to waken Hugh; eating, perhaps, something he has grabbed in passing from the pantry; winding his alarm clock as she has wound hers; thinking of her as she thinks of him. Her heart yearns over him. Dear Bob, it will all come right. I don't know how—I just know it. . . .

A thin pencil of light touches the dark farm, swings over and runs up the lane towards the village. The light from a car. Not often there are visitors at Clough's so late!

The light reminds Rose of the searchlights that used to fan across the sky—how long ago it seems already!—seeking out the enemy. She had always found them very comforting. *Don't you worry, Rose, they had seemed to say. We'll see to this for you.* . . .

The light runs up the lane to the village, and vanishes, and Rose climbs into bed and gives a long sigh of content.

It has been a lovely day. Tomorrow she will have to work twice as hard to make up for it; but this day is hers forever and ever.

The clock's tick threads the silence with a shallow diligence. The window is dark behind its flowered curtains. The clock face, the mirror, the blue-and-white china jug on the washstand are blurred points of light in the dimness. The skylight frames a star.

And Rose lies quietly, her bland, white brow untroubled, firm lips folded, brown lashes fanned on fresh, sweet cheeks; so young, so touching in the oblivion of sleep.

All life lies before her, all eternity. . . .